A Practical Potions Mystery

Practical Potions
and
Professional Courtesy

Wren Jones

WOOPS!

PRACTICAL POTIONS AND PROFESSIONAL COURTESY

Cover Illustration by Esther Bellefontaine
https://estherb.myportfolio.com/

Typography by Amphi Studio
https://www.amphi.studio.com/

ISBN 979-8-9890410-3-9 (*print edition*)

ISBN 979-8-9890410-2-2 (*ebook*)

1 2 3 4 5 6 7 8 9 10

www.wrenjones.net

To those in the arena who get back up after
every fall.

May we inspire the spectators to join us
every time we rise.

ONE

The Haunting of the Apartment with the Emerald Door

"I won't stand for it!" the voice cracked like a burst of thunder.

The little gold bell above the shop door chimed loudly, though the door itself remained closed. From behind the counter, Sella, the kitchen witch, watched a shimmering mist materialize into the form of a young human woman.

The ghost huffed loudly. Her long auburn hair floated around her as though she was underwater, a clear sign that she was in some kind of distress. Whenever the wind around her picked up, Sella knew things were seriously wrong.

A deep crease formed between Sella's brows as she stepped quickly out from behind the long counter and onto the shop floor. Behind her, the bubbling of a metal coffee pot quieted. "Cali? What's the matter?" Sella asked the ghost, concern thick in her tone. She held her hands out to Cali but she sidestepped Sella's open arms, dodging her entirely.

Cali plopped herself onto a stool at the counter and her head hit the wood, making no sound.

Sella's outstretched hands clenched to fists. The rejection of her comfort stung. She felt stupid for making the wrong choice and providing nothing but an obstacle for Cali to move around. She took a deep breath in. She tried not to take it personally and instead, went back behind the counter and crouched below to look over her ingredients and potions. Something calming to add to their morning coffee.

Cali couldn't drink it, that was beyond the limit of what she was able to do in death. But she always enjoyed smelling it. And Sella's brews seemed to have at least some effect on the ghost, even if it was all in Sella's presentation.

She grabbed "Don't Strangle People", a caramel hinted powder infused with patience.

When she rose again, Cali was quick to grab her arm. It was a cold, fog-like feeling that sent chills down Sella's back, and yet, flared heat in her stomach. Sella looked down at Cali's hand and tried to rein in her racing thoughts.

"I'm sorry," Cali said quickly. Her green eyes shifted over Sella's expression carefully. She looked at the witch from the tips of her horns, to the creases in her forehead, and down to the thin line of her clenched jaw. "I'm sorry… It's just…"

Sella pulled away gently. She relaxed the muscles in her face, trying her best to look peaceful. "Just what?" she asked as she added the patience blend to the coffee grounds. She closed her eyes and the fire beneath the pot grew larger. She set her intention, *everything will turn out alright.* Her fingers warmed.

"A couple has moved into my flat," Cali said. "They moved all my things and put their own in. They're sleeping in my bed!"

Sella opened one eye, hands still gently holding the pot. "A couple? Moved here?"

Cali nodded. Her hair blew more violently, then, just as suddenly, stilled. She sniffed the air, her head rising a little to catch all the subtle notes. "Good blend," she said quietly. But her expression quickly shifted to annoyance as she continued, "Yes. They've moved my things and put away my wyvern tea towels. They've kept the window shut all morning and it's raining outside. You know how I love to hear it."

Sella hummed. Marra, their tiny town by the sea, didn't get many people moving in. Or, anyone moving in, really. It was always just a point on the map to somewhere else. People sailed into the little port, stayed a night or two in the hotel, and moved on. She wondered who it could be. "Humans?" the witch asked.

"Hmm. Humans," another voice spat the word.

Sella glanced behind her to see her familiar, a gray tabby cat, descending the stairs. His tail was up, a little curve in the tip as he reached the bottom of the steps. He jumped up to the counter and sat between them. "What is this about humans?"

"Hello to you, Beejee," Cali said. She was human and blissfully never offended that the people here seemed to find that odd or worthy of putting down.

"We're past pleasantries," Beejee said with a wave of his paw. "So these newcomers, humans or…" He looked at Sella's horns. "Orakan folks?"

"Orakan," Cali wasted no time getting back to her complaints. She was usually much more chipper than this. Sella made a mental note to dive deeper, ask more questions, when Beejee wasn't around to tease her. "A full set of antlers on the both of them. And Sella! They're moving my stuff!"

"Go to the rooms next door," Beejee said. "Half those homes are empty."

"I don't want the one next door. I want mine."

"You're spoiled," Beejee hissed.

"I'm dead."

"You can't keep saying 'I'm dead' to win every disagreement. It's getting old."

"Beejee!" Sella flicked the cat's ear.

He pawed her away with claws slightly extended. "Whaaaat?"

The witch cast a narrowed glance at him. "Watch it," she warned.

Cali crossed her arms, but her expression was gentle nonetheless. She leaned forward and grinned brightly, her typical demeanor returning despite her momentary outburst. "I'm tired of no one being able to hear or see me. I'll have to resort to the sheet."

Sella smiled despite herself. Ah, yes. The sheet.

When she first met Cali, the ghost had appeared in the corner of her room with a sheet over her head and glasses on, asking for help to solve her own murder. Apparently, it had taken her all night to summon the strength to manipulate her environment enough to get the sheet and glasses over her head and Sella had blissfully slept through the whole thing. The memory of that night still made Sella feel an odd mix of silliness and a little pain.

Witches could see ghosts and the sheet only made an appearance now when Cali wanted others to see her, or at least, her outline. Though, because Cali was human, or for some other reason still unknown to either of them, this ghost was different from any other Sella had encountered in her travels. She was vibrant. Powerful. Aware of her own death and her place in the world of the living.

"I'll talk to Ovina," Sella said. "See if she can move the new tenets to another place."

"Thank you," Cali said. She closed her eyes with another large inhale as Sella passed her favorite mug closer to her for her to breathe in the steam.

"I've been looking," Sella said quietly. She rested her forearms on the counter, her own mug held tightly in her hands. Though the steam rose from the dark liquid, the heat didn't bother her hands at all. She tapped the handle of the mug with her finger. "For a spell. So you can talk to everyone."

"I know," Cali sighed. "I guess I just thought that since Beejee's spell was easy—"

Sella raised a brow.

"Relatively easy," Cali corrected. "That this would be too."

"Maybe across the sea. Where there more than just… kitchen witches," Sella said. She rose up again, pulling the ceramic mug close to her as she did. "Maybe they have the spell for something like this. We could travel."

"Finally!" Beejee yowled. "This stupid town is too small for us. Our brilliance is wasted on these people."

The bell above the door was barely audible above the sound of the door swinging wildly open and smacking the wall near the bay window with a thud.

"Opora!" Lohrna screeched as she burst through the door.

Sella flinched at the sudden sound. She set her mug down and, wide-eyed, watched as her best friend shook herself off in the doorway. Droplets scattered across the dark wood floor as Lohrna threw her coat to the far wall, missing the long, empty shelf. Despite the weather, Lohrna's hair, curly, and tangled up in her thin antlers, lost none of its bounce as she skipped into the room.

Sella raised a brow. She glanced at Cali quickly and whispered under her breath, "Don't worry. I'll talk to Ovina and get this sorted." She turned to her friend. "Cali's on the second stool," she said as she crossed the shop to retrieve Lohrna's coat from the floor.

Lohrna was shaking out her long skirt as she came into the shop. She kicked the door shut with her heel behind her.

"Did you say, 'Opora'?" Beejee asked. "What about it?"

Lohrna wasted no time sitting at the stool beside the ghost. She looked in Cali's direction, though she always seemed to look just a little too high up. Cali adjusted herself to catch Lohrna's gaze even though the other woman couldn't see her. "Hey Cali," Lohrna shouted. She turned to Beejee and Sella, who had already made it back across the counter. "Opora. Opora is coming to town. To Marra. In two days!"

"What?" Sella shook her head, trying to make sense of what she had just said. "But, why?"

"Wait, who's Opora?" Cali chimed in. She inched closer to Lohrna.

Lohrna shivered at the closeness she didn't know was

there. She looked back to the space where Cali was, then to Sella, awaiting translation.

"Opora." Sella said to Cali. "It's a traveling festival that happens every year in autumn. It's kind of a big deal to a lot of Orakan folks. Mostly to the… previous generation. Marra hasn't hosted in—"

"In over *one hundred* years!" Lohrna jumped in. "But listen to this. Horta—" She turned back to Cali, realizing the name was most likely contextless to her, "—the big city south of here—" She looked back to Sella, and went on, "There's a plague sweeping through. Can you believe it? A plague! Everyone in town is getting this wild sneezing fit. I heard people have had to board up their windows to avoid it. So, they're relocating the festival!"

"Sounds serious," Sella said.

Lohrna shrugged. "Sneezing fit isn't the worst thing. But, it's enough that no one wants to chance going there and catching it. Imagine the rib pain…" Lohrna trailed off, massaging her own rib with her hand as if she felt it too.

Sella's brows rose at the news. She sipped her coffee and looked past them to the window. It was the usual quiet time on their dead end street. It wouldn't pick up until the tavern opened and people flocked to Hazen's for their usual drinks and usual company.

The bell dinged again, and a woman who looked much like Lohrna but smaller and with mostly gray hair entered. Still, she was no less enthusiastic in her entrance. "Get ready to make a signature blend, Sella!"

When she stepped in further, Sella flicked her wrist so the little floating fires overhead grew brighter and ambient music, a spell of her own creation, played.

"Oh, Lohrna. Good, you're here," Aadel said kindly. She approached the bar, and Cali quickly hopped off her stool so the older woman could sit. "Did Lohr tell you about the Opora?"

"She did," Beejee grumbled. He scampered away to the bench at the bay window and curled up into a little ball on the yellow pillow so he could see out into the street but keep his distance from the group. "I do like the idea of a signature blend to commemorate it though."

"Yes! To sell to the folks who are coming in from out of town!" Lohrna said. "Ooo! I'll bet they'll bring in a ton of money for the shop!"

"None of them know about… *The Incidents*," Aadel said. "It should be great for business."

Sella sighed as she prepared Aadel's usual drink, a coffee with calming properties to keep her mind clear but her jitters down.

Yes, *The Incidents*. The first 'incident' was a spell gone wrong when she was little. A harmless spell that backfired and gave everyone temporary, and otherwise harmless, spots. No one ever let her forget it. Most were a little more than cautious when she came back to town with new recipes and remedies. Nobody wanted another… 'incident'.

Of course, the townsfolk of Marra had recently, and dramatically, added the 's' after the situation with Cali. It didn't seem to matter to most of the town that she and Lohrna were innocent of any misdeed at all. It only mattered that they had been *accused* of the murder.

It also didn't seem to matter that they had taken over as detective consultants after Marra's ancient resident detective finally retired. Her reputation was cleared, but *The Incidents* were still very much the talk of the town a whole year later. She heard whispers of it when people came to buy her potions or honey and every time, it made her feel like she was some kind of monster.

Marra was so small. A place where everyone knew everyone. It seemed to affect their sense of tact. In all of Sella's travels across their continent, people in the bigger cities were at least less obvious about their distrust of magic.

"Has Hazen heard yet?" Sella finally asked after she had scooped a generous spoonful of 'Comfy Cozy' into Aadel's mug. She stirred it up and slid the mug to Aadel.

"I went to his tavern before I came here," Aadel said, taking the steaming mug in her hands. "But Cirian had already told him the news."

"Cirian found out something before you? Shocking," Beejee commented. His eyes were closed as if thoroughly bored with the conversation.

Cali twisted to look at him. "Beejee. You know people can hear you now," she whispered, as if anyone else could hear her. Even dead, Cali had more politeness than most in this town.

Beejee opened one eye and looked at her like he hadn't considered it. He closed it and the tip of his tail flicked. He didn't care.

Aadel simply chuckled in response. "I will take my gathering of knowledge as a compliment." She sipped her mug and said, "Well, Cirian knows people too. And at the hotel, Penya is also in a fit about it."

Of course she had stopped at the hotel too. Aadel knew everything and everyone in this town. How she managed to travel from one end to the other and gather all the latest gossip all while making whoever she was talking to feel like they were the most important person in the world, was a trick Sella had long given up on learning.

It happened, it seemed, by magic.

"I don't know what she's so stressed about. Penya's often booked up." Lohrna waved her hand. "It'll be fine."

"I suggested the empty flats," Aadel said, to her daughter, mostly. "Have travelers stay there, help Ovina make extra coin."

Cali huffed and an ember overhead snuffed out.

Only Sella seemed to notice. She snapped her fingers and two more took its place. She did her best to not look at Cali directly. Instead, she focused on occupying her hands at the coffee station, polishing the same spot over again.

"So all those rooms there will be taken too?" Sella asked for Cali.

Aadel nodded. She downed the rest of her coffee in a final, large gulp. "Alright my little honey bees," she said, "I'm off to the market. I want to get supplies before everyone floods into town soon. Do think about making a signature cuppa, though. It'll be good for business, and I know Beejee's been worried."

The corners of Sella's eyes crinkled warmly. Aadel was ever the mother to her when her own was long gone. "I'll think about it," she said.

Aadel rose from her seat. She raised a finger, stressing her words, as she said, "Something to really cure headaches in the morning, if you know what I mean." She shrugged her coat back over her shoulders. "Opora was a little wild last time it was in town. That was before Hazen's tavern even opened. I better warn him, too."

Cali tilted her head. "Lohrna said Opora hasn't been here in a hundred years… How old *is* Aadel?"

The bell chimed, and Aadel made her way out into the misty rain.

Sella glanced at Lohrna. "Wyldes live longer than humans."

Lohrna raised a single brow. She turned to the empty stool, her expression difficult to read. "How old are folks on your side of the sea?"

Sella's heart sank. Cali was too young to die, by human standards. Even younger for most in Orakan. It wasn't fair, and she suspected Lohrna was thinking the same thing.

Cali shrugged, not letting the question bother her. "Not over a hundred."

Sella glanced at Beejee, then to Lohrna. She cleared her throat. Lohrna's question would have to go without an answer for now. She didn't want to linger on talk of life and death. "So. Opora. You both want to help me make a signature drink?"

Lohrna sat up straighter and tapped the counter with both hands. "Do waves make rocks sand?"

"Yes. Count me in!" Cali said.

TWO

The Golden Ladle Doesn't Matter

OUTSIDE, it was dark. Rain pattered lightly on the large circle window above a cluttered writing desk. In the one room home above the shop, a warm, bright fire was burning brightly in the fireplace. Beejee, lean and gray, curled up near a much larger, very fluffy orange cat on pillows piled by the hearth.

Cali beamed at them warmly and rested her head in her hand. "I'm glad Koukie is happy here." Her voice was listless, as if she hadn't meant to say it at all.

"She's a good cat. I'm proud to take care of her," Sella said. She was mashing herbs in a stone mortar, trying to get the proportions right for an anti-headache, anti-nausea addition to her usual coffee.

From what she had experienced at Opora in the past, the people would need it.

Lohrna had volunteered to brave the market, but wouldn't be back until the following day. Far too much to do, she had said, but did not elaborate as to what exactly that meant. With Lohrna, it really could be anything.

Chances were equally good she was gathering rocks to sell to the tourists, or inventing her own language for them to speak in code at the festival, or even something Sella couldn't begin to guess.

In the meantime, Sella had to work with what she had available. It wouldn't be perfect tonight, but it was a start, and she didn't have much time to prepare. She figured she'd play with the other ingredients when they arrived later. Right now, she had to get her mind working.

"I think Beejee is glad to have her, too," Sella continued. "I think he gets a little lonely."

Koukie had shown up at her window one evening a year before to tell Beejee that her owner had died. Beejee had called her a liar and threatened to kick her out. Later that night, Cali, with a sheet over her head, had confirmed the story was indeed true. Beejee had not relented in his disdain or distrust of the other cat. But, very slowly, they had formed a close bond, even if he'd never admit it.

As if sensing her thoughts, her familiar's ear twitched and he opened his eyes to look at her with a bored expression. He yawned, then closed his eyes as if it wasn't worth arguing with her.

"Sella," Cali said, breaking the witch's thoughts again. "I know it's a little unreasonable, but I want to have my space back."

"I know you do," Sella said with a heavy sigh.

"It's not looking good with Opora in town, is it? All the rooms will be booked, it sounds like?"

Sella paused her recipe. She looked at Cali for a long moment, trying to read her expression.

All she got from the ghost's face was sadness, and... a

little hope. Her lips were still slightly upturned despite her pleading eyes.

"I'll still talk to Ovina and see what she can do," Sella said at last. "You could always... stay here... At least while the festival is going on?"

Cali face reddened slightly.

Could ghosts blush? Sella was still discovering new things about the human ghost a year later. She blinked, and the warmth in Cali's cheeks was gone.

"I like my wyvern towels," Cali finally fumbled out her words.

"Ah yes," Beejee grumbled, eyes still shut. "If Sella's anything, it's anti-wyvern decor." Sarcasm laced his tone and Koukie, still laying beside him, took in a large breath as if to hush him.

Cali's lips pressed into a thin line. "Ha, ha," she said dryly.

"I know what you mean. You want your space to be just yours," Sella cut in before it escalated any further or she could dwell on the sting of Cali rejecting her offer. "I'll talk to Ovina, and I'll keep looking for a spell to help you communicate. I promise, Cali. It's out there somewhere, and I'll find it." But her words felt dry, like ash coating her tongue. She wasn't totally sure there was a spell that could help Cali like that.

But she knew she would keep trying.

Cali shook her body as if releasing pent up anxiety. She stood tall at last, and stepped lightly over to the other side of the counter. "Anyway," she said, chipper again. "Can you tell me more about this Opora? What's the big deal?"

"It's a yearly event, and it travels all over Orakan. I

haven't been to one in a long while…" Sella drifted off, remembering vividly being at her last Opora where another witch spotted her using magic without her wand. The other witch had a fit about it, calling her out in front of a crowd. She looked down at the herbs in her bowl and continued to mash at them, drowning out the echo of it in her mind. No love for elemental witches here. Especially wandless ones. "There's a variety of contests. There's some formula for figuring out the winner of the whole thing. But the biggest and last competition is the cooking contest, and the winner of the whole thing wins a Golden Ladle." Sella paused. "Well, they kind of win it. It goes back to next year's festival."

"A Golden Ladle?"

"It's impossible to explain why people care so much about it, to be honest," Sella said with a shrug. "There's other competitions. Feats of strength and endurance, things like that. But the Golden Ladle is the prize."

Cali hummed.

"I think it started to celebrate the Glimmergill migration, when they all come close to shore. Or something like that," Sella said with a shrug. "It's been a while since I thought about the history of it."

"Glimmergill?"

"They're fewer now than they were a long, long time ago. But the festival remains," Sella said. "I don't think they've been spotted for as long as any of us can remember."

"Wyldes live longer than humans, but as a ghost, maybe I'll have you all beat."

The tips of Sella's pointed ears burned. She wasn't quite

sure how to take that, was Cali joking or serious? Either way, she was quick to change the subject.

"I think your signature blend should also include some self-love," the ghost said. "Does that mess up your recipe?"

Sella looked up. "No, I like that."

"Because if it's all about competition," Cali continued, "then people might need a little extra dose of compassion for themselves, don't you think?"

Sella nodded. She felt horribly lost, yet profoundly lucky. The feeling started in her chest and radiated out to her limbs. A heavy weight in her arms and a lightness in her fingertips.

Cali had a way of making her feel both at once. She was starlight. A point of light to look to in the darkness. She shined brightest when things seemed their most bleak. And always pointed Sella in the right direction.

Sella focused her fingers on the herbs and breathed in deeply. Compassion. Love. Kindness... all things Cali was. She felt it flow through her fingertips as they warmed the stone.

Infusing her blends with self-compassion was going to be a steep challenge. But she felt up to the task.

THREE

That Grackle

THE DAY AFTER, Sella, with Lohrna a good distance away on the other side of the room, had been tinkering with the latest potion for several hours. Beejee forbade Lohrna from coming anywhere near the active ingredients.

"She'll contaminate it like last time!" Beejee had yowled at them.

Sella's eyes flicked to Beejee to tell him to be quiet, but she said nothing.

It was true, when they were children, Lohrna had 'helped' with a recipe. It promptly exploded and made them smell rotten for longer than either of them cared to remember. No amount of washing rid them of the smell and Sella's mother had refused to create a counterspell, insisting that this be their lesson.

Sella's nostrils flared. She could still smell it now, if she thought too much about it.

She got back to work, adding a small amount of heat to the pot as she channeled her fire into just the tips of her fingers. She breathed deeply. *Self love*, she thought to herself. *Come on…* But the feeling didn't come. Her jaw tightened.

"What's the matter?" Lohrna asked, clearly noticing her friend's expression no matter how Sella tried to hide it.

Beejee's tail thumped harshly on the wood counter. He was annoyed.

Sella's eyes opened. "Cali thought it would be good to add some self-compassion to the blend," she said. She wanted the conversation to end there. But she knew it wouldn't.

Lohrna leaned back on her heels. She was perched next to the fireplace, petting Koukie gently. Her mouth drew into a line but she kept scratching the orange cat's ears. "That's not a bad idea," she said at last. "From what my mom says, folks will need it the morning after some of these competitions."

Sella felt like a stone was sinking in her stomach. She had felt heavy all day and now she felt a little nauseous. "I'm looking forward to it," she said as she stretched, trying to alleviate some of the weight from her core. It wasn't a lie. She was, at least a little, excited for the challenge. The idea of meeting new people and trying new recipes was stressful, but stress could be good, she reminded herself. "Hazen's been like a storm since the news broke, though. I haven't seen him except when I spot him rushing through the window." She paused, her eyes drifted back to the ingredients on the counter. "Have you checked in with Penya at the hotel?"

Lohrna nodded. "Penya's ancient, I could hardly get much out of her. All the rooms are booked, I think that's all that matters to her. Oh, and she's charging for those books stacked all over the lobby now. You have to rent them or purchase them. And she's charging way too much, you would not believe it."

"The 'free to go home' books?"

"Yep!" Lohrna shifted closer to Koukie. She leaned in until their noses touched before she smiled and pulled away. "Gotta make that coin somehow, right?"

"The booked hotel isn't enough?" Sella asked.

Beejee bared his teeth. "Please."

"You know those pixies come out in full force on the new moon," Lohrna said, finally rising from the floor. "I'll bet Penya doesn't know how much they steal from her but it's got to cut into profits."

Sella shrugged. That could be true. Penya was old. She was old when Sella was young. At least, it had seemed that way at the time. She wondered for a moment how long Penya had been running the hotel. How long she had been ignoring her pixie problem. It was a known infestation from all the way back when she was little.

Sella poured the coffee into a green ceramic mug as she mumbled to herself about how maybe her own coin might be stolen by the infestation next door.

"Doubt it," Beejee said. "I'd spot them before they got through the door. You're just bad at business. Always giving away freebies and making bad trades."

Sella had to admit, he was right. Besides, her mother had enchanted the shop. Pixies couldn't enter and both she and Beejee knew it.

She slid the mug across the counter, ignoring him for now.

Lohrna hopped over the velvet loveseat between them

with ease and drank the entire cup, though it was still steaming. She had already had several that morning and her mood had shifted with each drink, depending on what Sella had put in it. She didn't even seem to taste it anymore, just waited for the effects to kick in.

Sella stared at her friend's face, eyes analyzing every microexpression.

"I do feel something…" Lohrna said. "Caffeinated."

Sella's shoulders slumped.

Lohrna's body did the same. After a long moment, she sat up a little straighter. Her fingers tapped the mug as the caffeine settled into her muscles, making them twitch. "Maybe give it a bit more time for the self-love to kick in?"

The witch rolled her shoulders. "No," she said, defeated. "I'm done for now."

"Maybe I just can't love myself," Lohrna suggested.

Sella looked up, she watched her friend carefully. Was it a joke? It didn't sound like it.

"Kidding," Lohrna said.

"Did it at least taste good?"

Lohrna laughed, a booming sound. She was back to her old self quickly, or the combination of potion infused coffee was proving too much for her. "Sella, I am going to vibrate out of this place. I have no idea how it tasted. Maybe there was some nutmeg in there?"

"Yeah, there's nutmeg…"

"Well, there you go! This tongue knows!"

Sella rolled her eyes and beside her, Beejee's tail flicked again.

Lohrna set the mug on the counter, hard. She flinched at the sound. "Speaking of self-compassion… Maybe I could get that suppressant this month? What with Opora and all…"

"Of course!" Sella moved from around the counter. She held her friend's hand gently. "I can do that for you anytime you want it."

"But we will charge you," Beejee said. He leaped from the counter to the floor soundlessly and walked past them to the desk in front of the large circle window. He pressed his nose against the glass, smudging a little wet spot where he looked.

Sella let Lohrna's hand go. The corners of her mouth twitched upward gently, then turned to Beejee, her expression shifting to worry.

"What's going on?" Lohrna asked. She went to the window and stood beside the gray familiar. Her eyes narrowed, trying to see into the fog and light drizzle.

Beejee turned behind him to Sella. "Something's coming…" he whispered.

"What—?" Sella was cut off when a flutter of black wings and sharp talons scraped across the glass.

The bird squawked, then flew back into the rain.

"Majla! That *grackle*!" Beejee spat. He pressed both front paws into the glass and bared his teeth.

Sella felt her stomach twist into sudden knots. "Sediri's here..?"

"Who's Sediri?" Lohrna asked, backing away from the window at last.

Beejee, still glaring into the rain, spoke for Sella. "Another witch," he spat.

"I gathered that much," Lohrna said with a light, nervous laugh. "What's her deal? Why the creepy check in with her familiar?"

Sella slumped onto the couch. "Sediri works for Kepilla," she said.

Lohrna raised a brow at her.

Of course, no one in town would know that name. In general, Orakan didn't hold too much love for witches, even the kitchen kind. This far south, the distrust was even more prominent. Her mother had worked for years to build up trust and goodwill with the town. Sella had managed to burn it up at almost every turn until she left town.

And, of course, when she came back, she had been wrapped up in a murder.

Sella suppressed memories of her fire flickering into the front of her mind. She rubbed her eyes with the palms of her hands and went on, "Kepilla. It's a series of shops in the north. They sell really tried and true blends of teas and pastries. At least, they call them tried and true."

"Like a coven but of stores?"

"Yeah," Sella sat up at last. "You *have* to get certified through them, that's where we got our credentials. But, then most witches who want to make a living off their magic end up working in their shops. They can't deviate from the recipes—"

"Which are ineffective," Beejee cut in.

"Less creative," Sella said. But she knew he was right.

Lohrna dragged her hand against the window, clearing the condensation from the glass. She looked back out onto the road below. "And Sediri? An ex?"

Sella's laugh was dry, it escaped her throat before she could catch it.

"Don't insult her," Beejee scolded. "Sella would never.

Besides, Sediri is obsessed with her boyfriend in Tollintal—last I checked."

"A human?" Lohrna pressed for more.

Sella waved her hand. "Anyway," she said, "Beejee and I couldn't take it anymore. Working for them was awful. We started traveling, and did okay for ourselves despite them."

"Until we ran out of money," Beejee said.

Sella ignored him. "But Sediri… her whole wing of the company is shutting down local kitchen witches in whatever town she goes to. Replacing them with a Kepilla."

"Rude," Lohrna said. She sat beside Sella. "Maybe it's just a pop up for Opora and she won't stay? Lots of vendors come in for the celebrations and leave when it's done, right?"

Sella sighed. "Yeah," she said at last. "Maybe."

"Majla seems like kind of a jerk though," Lohrna laughed. "He scuffed up your window."

"You don't even know," Beejee said.

"I'll get to making that suppressant," Sella said, changing the subject. She rose from the couch before Lohrna could stop her. "Don't want you buying it from the competitor."

"As if Sediri were capable of making anything more complicated than a cup of focus," Beejee scoffed.

FOUR

The Mild and Mannerly Brotherhood of Shifters, Sisters Accepted

SELLA HAD IMAGINED that the travelers for the event would trickle in slowly, like the quiet rising of the tide. Instead, it was like a tidal wave. One moment, her quiet street was empty. And the next, it was a flurry of activity as Marrans rushed about, decorating the brick buildings and setting out even more potted plants and warm colored gourds along the sidewalks.

Faces she didn't recognize quickly mingled with ones she did. People passing by were busy talking and laughing, pointing out various things that were so familiar to her but were clearly novel to travelers. They pointed at her shop, the vines creeping up the walls, and gawked as if they'd never seen such a thing. They shouted to a friend that the tavern was just a quick walk away.

She envied them. It must have been interesting to see their small town through new eyes.

The bell chimed and Hazen, the tavern owner next door, ducked in to accommodate his large ram horns.

"Good news!" he said, jovial and spry despite his deepening wrinkles on his face. "Branzo has chosen the tavern to host the Golden Ladle!"

"Branzo?" Sella asked.

"The mayor of Horta." Hazen shook his head as if he was a little disappointed that she didn't know the local leadership.

So, the mayor of the town with a plague was still making decisions here in Marra. She felt herself bristle a little.

"Congratulations," Sella said with what she hoped sounded like sincerity. It was great that his place was chosen to host. But he was also the only large gathering place in town, except the market square. And the only tavern.

Hazen set two brass coins down on the counter and sniffed the air. "Blueberry today?"

"Blueberry scones. Extra motivation baked in."

"Just coffee for me, then," Hazen said. "I have enough motivation." He patted his stomach beneath his tunic gently.

Sella got to work preparing Hazen's usual. She added coffee grounds to the pot and a spoonful of 'Don't Strangle People', a blend with warm caramel notes at the finish. She focused her fingertips at the kettle and warmed it with affection and care. She smiled despite everything worrying her mind. She wanted his drink to have the same warmth and kindness he had always shown her.

The coffee began to bubble, the sweet scent of caramel filled the air.

"I'm excited for you, Hazen," she said when she opened her eyes. "That's a big honor. So the mayor of Horta is in town? What about the sneezing illness that was plaguing the city?"

Hazen shrugged. "I guess it skipped him."

Sella slid the coffee across the counter slowly. "You're sure no scones? You may not need the motivation, but you do need sustenance. Other than caffeine."

"I have plenty at home," he said. He took a sip and closed his eyes to savor it for a moment. "Cirian keeps me stocked."

Sella nodded. "Of course." She paused, her hands hovering above the counter as if they were already lit with flames and she was afraid to burn the wood.

She flicked her wrist and the heat from her nails transferred to the floating flames overhead. The little shop grew a bit brighter and Hazen lifted his eyelids slightly. A vine in Sella's stomach began to take root in her. It twisted her up until she felt like she was going to burn it all down. She blurted out before she could stop herself, "Have you heard of a new kitchen witch in town?"

Hazen took another long drink before he answered. "Aadel tell you?" he asked.

Sella shook her head. "It's just, with Opora, I thought maybe some other witches might be in town."

Hazen looked at her intensely over the rim of his mug. He set it down. The steam rose between them like silver fingers reaching to pull the tension from the air. They failed. "I've heard of another kitchen witch in town. She set up a place almost overnight."

"I think *actually* overnight," Sella grumbled. She bent down to the small shelves behind the counter, looking for something to brighten her mood. "What's the feeling among the Marran folks about her?" Her head poked out from the top to gauge his expression.

He was hard to read. His face remained neutral. He simply shrugged. "What's life without a little competition?" he said at last. "I heard she set up in one of the vacant shop fronts on the other side of town. At least it's far from us."

"Nothing's far in this town," Sella murmured to herself. It sounded like Beejee's words. His recent bad mood seemed to be rubbing off on her.

Sella frowned and ducked back down. The idea that competition was a good thing sounded like it was easy for him to say. He was the only tavern in their small town and had made a name for himself immediately.

If anyone wanted a drink or a good, warm meal, Hazen's was the only place to go.

But, she reminded herself, she didn't know anything about him from before he came to Marra. He had *seemed* as though he was already established when she was little. Maybe it had been difficult for him and she had simply never realized it. She closed her eyes and grabbed a glass potion at random before she rose, eager to finally ask him about his life before.

But Hazen had set his empty mug down and was already rising from the counter. He tapped the coins on the wood and slid them closer. "The Golden Ladle calls," he said and turned to the door without another word.

Sella watched him leave, his large form moving past her bay window and down the street back to his tavern. She found herself looking around the shop with a worry filling her core. She wanted Cali there, more than anything. To ask her what she felt about all this. She wondered how she was doing in her old place, with new people there. Their little town was suddenly full. And she had no one to talk to. Her heart ached as though it was pumping slower. Working harder.

She looked down at the potion in her hand.

Sella felt herself scoff. It was a jar of plain, lavender honey from the hives at her mother's old home. It was misplaced, apparently. Just like her.

A little sound from the stairs behind her alerted her to Beejee's presence. He reached the last step, then looked from her hand to her face. He scoffed as though he could read her thoughts. "Sediri and *that grackle* can set up wherever they want," he said, in spite of Sella's bad mood. As he passed by her, he headbutted her calf with his soft face and the rest of his body slinked along the hem of her long dark skirt until just his tail was wrapped around her leg. "I, for one, am ready for those two. Our products are better."

Sella picked him up, but her familiar didn't protest as he usually would. He purred into her embrace before pushing gently at her chest with his two front paws.

"What's this?" he asked, landing on the counter before her.

Sella bit her lip. "I just feel like we were finally getting things under control here. And now…"

"It's not too late to sail away," Beejee said.

He had always wanted to go across the sea. She had never been brave enough, and now… Now he never let her forget it.

Sella felt her breath catch in her chest. "Yes, maybe someday. With enough money."

"Let's steal the Golden Ladle," he said.

It was a joke, or at least, Sella thought it was. She gave his head a quick pat. "It does feel like everything is moving so quickly all of the sudden," she said. "It's been a quiet time for a bit. I think I was getting used to it."

The bell above the door chimed.

Sella plastered a customer service grin on her face and straightened her back as a group of impeccably dressed Orakanians entered. But, as they came in, silent, and rigid, she noticed that each of their horns were cut at the tips. Spiraling antlers, or large looping horns, it didn't matter. Each one had a piece of the tip missing.

She felt her fingers warm, ready. But for what, she wasn't sure. She did her best to push the feeling of unease aside, and she shook her hands to free the fire contained within. Small sparks flung from her fingertips, hidden, she hoped, behind the counter. "Good morning," she said. "How can I help you folks today?"

A few of them spread out, looking at her potions and various nicknacks in the floor to ceiling cubbies. One sat down at the open table by the window, another looked outside as if to check if they were being watched.

The tallest among them, broad, and dark curls threading through his thin horns at his forehead approached her with confident steps. He looked down at her with gray eyes. His hands rested behind his back as if he was trying, but failing miserably, to be casual.

"You are the local kitchen witch?" he asked.

"I am. This was my mother's shop, so it's a legacy. I've

been back about two years now." Sella's grin grew. "Specializing in coffee blends, honey, and remedies."

"I saw the consulting sign outside as well." He turned part way to the door, but then Sella noticed his eyes were locked on one in his group who was holding a jar of lavender honey and showing it to another.

Sella moved her body to make eye contact with the two who were looking the container over as if they had never seen such a thing. "Happy bees make happy honey," she said. "Lavender is a special blend. It calms."

"Put that down," the man ordered, ignoring Sella.

She felt Beejee suddenly beside her. "It's alright," she said. To her familiar, and the two who were sheepishly putting the honey away.

"No, it isn't," the man said. "We don't touch others' things without express permission."

Beejee looked up at Sella. He was pretending he couldn't speak, and for that, she was grateful. This interaction was awkward enough.

"It really is fine. It's a shop, you can browse," Sella said. She caught his eyes again, watched them turn from hard and cold to warm and friendly so swiftly that she was worried she imagined it. She went on, "And yes, we do detective consulting. Our local detective retired last year." She paused, trying to decipher his every expression. "Are you… in need of a detective?"

"No," he said. "It's just interesting. We haven't met kitchen witches who dally in other professions."

"I'm one of a kind," Sella said with a shrug.

Beejee's paw landed harshly on her foot. He stalked off

to the bay window as if he hadn't meant to step on her at all. But he was trying to get her to focus.

It was true, Sella knew. The less she said, the less others could use against her.

But the silence went on too long. Sella kept glancing at the others in the group. They were all… immaculate. Not a hair or thread out of place. It made her uneasy. "Then… you're looking for potions?" she prompted.

"Suppressants, yes," he said, standing a little taller. "And to announce ourselves to local establishments, as is our custom. We are the Mild and Mannerly Brotherhood of Shifters, Sisters Accepted. MAM-BOS-SA for short, if it pleases you. You may have heard of us."

Sella blinked, unsure of what to make of any of what he had just said, least of all the ridiculous name.

From across the shop, Beejee narrowed his eyes.

"I've been all over Orakan… and I have to say, I'm sorry. I have not heard of… Mimosa," she did her best to pronounce the acronym. "You're shifters? All of you?"

"MAMBOSSA," he corrected gently. "Indeed. And it is our intention to participate in the Opora. Do you sell suppressant potions?" He cut back to the heart of it.

Sella nodded. "I do. I was actually just making a fresh batch. Can you come back in after sundown?"

"Twilight is better, if possible," he said.

"I will do my best."

"Thank you." He held out his hand and Sella grabbed it before they both gave a quick and awkward shake. It was a Tollintal tradition, one she hadn't used since trying to solve Cali's murder. Back when she had last interacted with humans. She wondered where he had learned it. But he broke her thoughts. "I am Mims. Leader of this chapter."

"Sella," she said, pulling her hand away.

Cali had taught her that about two shakes was the agreed upon standard. Mims had held her hand for far too long, shaking it far too many times. Sella knew that the custom must have seemed so foreign, even elegant, to most in Orakan. She could understand why Mims adopted to do it, if they were openly shifters.

Their mere presence must put a lot of people they meet at unease. She didn't want them to feel that here. "Can I offer you all a cup of coffee? As a welcome to Marra. On the house."

Beejee shot her a stare. One that said silently, 'I will kill you'.

Mims and the others all stopped still. All eyes were on her. Sella squared her shoulders. Any apprehension she felt earlier was beginning to dissipate. She thought she saw gratitude reflected back at her in each of their faces.

One of the members approached, stood at Mims's side and looked up at him with a hopeful gaze. Mims looked down at him, then nodded once.

"That is an incredibly generous offer, Sella," Mims said. "Of course, we insist on payment."

Sella busied herself behind the counter. "Payment when you come back for the potions. For now, just enjoy a cup and be glad you're out of the rain." She reached for her blend of 'It's All Good', a light and easy drinking flavor profile that she was sure would brighten their day. She began to brew and hints of orange blossom filled the air.

She focused her mind on peace and warmth as the water

came to a quick boil. She looked up at the group and found relief on their faces. She could only hope that wherever Lohrna traveled, if she ever decided to, she would find this kind of feeling too. She felt the corners of her mouth tilt up in an easy smile. The past few days had been chaotic but she was able to do one thing right: make a delicious brew and cheer up a group of misfits.

FIVE

Free Coffee Pays

TWILIGHT LIT the streets in a pink and orange glow though the sunset was hardly visible behind the layer of clouds.

Sella had been working through the day as customers from out of town trickled in at a slower pace than she, and especially Beejee, would have liked. She told him that it was because people were still arriving but they both knew she was lying.

Still, Sella hadn't minded the slower pace much. It gave her more time to work on the potions for the society of shifters. She put each one in its own separate little glass jar with a tag labeled 'Full Moon, Full Heart' and placed them gently into the woven seagrass basket along with a large jar of 'Thimble Fix', her headache reliever.

She wasn't sure if they would get headaches after the full moon like Lohrna did even if they didn't shift into their other forms. It was possible that the ill consequences Lohrna suffered the next day were only a side effect of the change. Either way, she figured it couldn't hurt to be a little extra courteous and kind. She was certain they didn't get that kind of treatment in most Orakan towns.

Mims arrived just as she secured the instructions with a little twine around the handle. He strode across the shop floor with confidence, not sparing even a glance at anything but her.

Sella looked up from her work. Her eyes quickly darted about his tall frame. Though the day had been long, there was still nothing out of place about him. Even his shoes were spotless. "How did today go? Are you enjoying Marra?" she asked, her voice warm.

His body seemed stiff, like when he first arrived at the shop. He took in a big breath, then sighed it out though his form was still rigid. "This is a lovely town. The hotel is generous with their room sizes."

Sella laughed.

Outside, the sky grew darker.

"Well, if that's impressive, then the real place you need to see is Hazen's tavern, at the end of the road," she said. "That's a spacious place with a lot going on."

"We introduced ourselves, as is custom," he said simply. He stepped closer to the counter and Sella felt a little shiver prickle at the base of her neck.

She shrugged it away, Mims watched her shoulders roll.

"Thank you for the rush order. Some of us are a little more nervous than others about the approaching full moon."

"It was no trouble."

The bell chimed and Lohrna, bright smile already on her face, bounded up to the empty stool next to Mims. "Just who I wanted to see!" she beamed up at him.

Sella glanced at her friend, then pushed the basket closer to Mims. "I also threw in some Thimble Fix. It'll relieve headaches. Instructions are inside, but please just be sure to reiterate to the others to only take just a very small amount."

"Otherwise, you'll end up numb all over, take it from me!" Lohnra patted his arm.

Mims withdrew immediately. He looked at his arm like her hands were made of slugs and left a slime all over him.

Lohrna looked at him with a puzzled tilt of her head. "Well, let's leave the kitchen witch to her work," she said, folding her arm across her body. "You all are the Mimosas?"

"Mild and Mannerly Brotherhood of Shifters, Sisters Accepted, actually—"

Lohrna cut him off. "Excellent! My mom heard all about you. Let's drop these off for you all. You and I need to have a chat." She scooped the basket in the crook of her elbow and was halfway to the door before Mims seemed like he even heard what she said.

He cast a look at Sella, one brow raised slightly.

"Welcome to Marra," she said with a chuckle.

A shimmer glistened in the corner of the shop and the shape of Cali, long waves of auburn hair, and bright smile, appeared. "Are you seeing all these people?" she asked. As she approached the counter, her form took on a more physical look, transforming from transparent to, gradually, more solid. She huffed as she boosted herself onto the stool and rested her head in one hand. She outstretched the other hand, palm up on the counter.

Sella felt warmth spread through her face and up to her ears. She reached out and rested her hand on Cali's for just a moment, afraid her hand would pass right through. She turned away before her expression could give away any hint of negativity. "Coffee?" she asked.

Cali sighed. "No, I'm okay for now. Have you been busy today?"

"Not particularly. More than usual, I suppose. The town is quite busy, though," Sella said. She turned back around once she was sure her body language would look effortless. "Have you heard of the Shifter Society going around introducing themselves?"

"Shifter Society?" Cali asked. Her back straightened, intrigued. "No, somehow I missed that! Does Lohrna know?"

"Seems to. I guess Aadel told her," Sella said. She leaned on the counter, mirroring Cali's previous pose. "You just missed her escorting their leader out of here. I suspect we'll hear all about it tomorrow."

"I hope so! This is exciting for her."

Sella smiled. "Yeah, it really is."

They looked at each other from across the counter. Each with an easy and happy expression. For a moment, Sella felt the disappointment of the day fade away. As long as she got to be quiet for a moment with Cali at the end, it was a good day. She reached out again for Cali's hand and the ghost tapped her open palm, lightly tracing the lines.

Their peace didn't last long.

The door burst open. The loud flapping of bird wings filled the room.

Sella was up on her feet, fire flickering in the palm of her hand, ready.

Filling most of the doorframe, a tall figure loomed in all black. A graceful, long nailed hand pulled back the hood of the cloak to reveal two large, curled dark horns decorating the top of the woman's head. They made her look all the more intimidating and imposing.

A black grackle flew back from within the shop to perch on her shoulder. She tossed a shining lock of deep red hair that fell around her slim figure and she strode into the shop with long, confident steps. Her full lips drew up into a half smile but her eyes locked on Sella with a frightening intensity. When she was halfway into the shop, her expression changed to a deep grimace. "You," she pointed at Sella.

Sella's hand clenched into a fist to stifle the fire. She stuffed her hand into the pocket of her skirt.

Cali's eyes followed her motion and she nodded carefully, inching away slowly from the two of them.

"*You* stole my business today," the other witch said, adding extra disdain this time as if not saying Sella's name was an additional insult. As if she couldn't be bothered to remember.

"Hello, Sediri," Sella said. She did her best to sound confident but her arms started to prickle as worry crept up from her fingertips to her spine. "Welcome to Marra."

"Don't you dare pretend you don't know what you're doing to me." Sediri's voice was a low growl. She hadn't blinked once. She stared at Sella like a wolf stares at a rabbit. Hungry. Determined. Vicious.

Sella squared her shoulders. "I didn't steal anything."

"You knew I was setting up a Kepilla here," Sediri said. "The MAMBOSSA was going to purchase their potions from me before they stopped into your dreary little shop. You swooped in and took my business."

"Well," Sella said, "did you offer them free coffee?"

Sediri scoffed. The bird on her shoulder, her familiar, flapped his wings in annoyance.

"There you go," Sella said with what she hoped was a casual shrug. "Try offering free drinks next time. Or, is that against policy?"

Beejee, so fast he seemed to materialize, leaped onto the counter and sat at Sella's side. He hissed at the bird and then looked up at Sella with adoration. Sella was certain later he would praise her free coffee choice. She wouldn't remind him that just earlier he had been raging about it. She smiled back at him.

Sediri looked from Sella to the cat, then back. "Hm. Free coffee. We'll see how long that lasts you. We'll see who's still standing at the end of Opora."

From the corner of Sella's view, Cali materialized and slid a stick near to her hand on the shelf below the counter. She waved, then pointed to it.

Sella almost laughed. The stick was just a piece of wood snapped from what looked like the bush outside of a neighboring shop. But, it would do. It looked enough like a wand and she definitely didn't want Sediri knowing she could use magic without one. Cali was quick to remember.

Sediri's eyes narrowed at Sella. Then, they shifted to the ghost.

Sella's gaze followed and her eyes grew wide at Cali with the sudden realization that Sediri could also see her.

"A ghost!" Sediri drew back. She drew her wand from beneath her cloak.

Sella quickly moved her body so it obscured Cali. She grabbed the fake wand from beneath the counter and pointed it at Sediri. With the other, she pushed Cali further back gently. "The ghost is with me," she said, her tone suddenly firm.

Majla squawked, neck out like he was about to attack them.

"Best not try anything," Beejee hissed, batting his clawed paw.

Sediri blinked a few times as if she was certain her eyes were playing tricks on her. She shook her head a little, then took another step back. But she regained her composure quickly. She straightened and gave the bird a little scratch under his beak. "You're keeping ghosts for company now?" she asked, sounding uninterested in the answer, as if she had not just been completely caught off guard. She turned to Beejee. "And your familiar speaks?"

"A lot's changed," Sella said.

"It seems we have a lot of catching up to do. Perhaps once the spirit of competition has lessened."

Sella let out a breath, she lowered the stick in her hand. "Sediri, you need to know that this town isn't always friendly to witches."

Sediri cast another lock of hair behind her free shoulder, a clear sign she was still collecting herself from the moment before. She brushed the front of her black dress, wand still held loosely in her grip. "Many aren't," she said. "But Kepilla always gains their trust in the end." She looked around the potion shop, eyes lingering on the little cubbies, then to the fires overhead that floated about the ceiling. "So this is your mother's shop..?" she whispered. Then, she scoffed, a light and wicked laugh. "Make arrangements. Kepilla will have this place closed before the end of the festival."

She turned on her heel and cast one last look at Cali who was peeking out from behind Sella's shoulder. "I look forward to talking with you, little human ghost."

Sella locked the door as soon as it shut with a flick of her hand. She dimmed the fires and the faint music that had filled the air extinguished. She turned to Cali and bent her head a little to catch her eyes.

"I'm sorry," Cali said. Her image flickered. "It's been so long... I... forgot witches could see me."

Sella held Cali's face with her free hand. She dropped the stick and smiled gently. "Don't apologize."

"If anyone should apologize for anything, it's the *grackle*," Beejee motioned with his paw to a feather that had fallen onto the hardwood floor. "Disgusting beast." He descended the counter and was already halfway up the stairs to the flat above the store when he called, "Come on, then. We need to strategize."

Cali laughed. But it sounded forced.

Sella felt herself cringe a little. "You heard him," she said, trying again to lighten the mood. "Let's go and we can talk about this where we're comfortable."

THE AIR WAS warm and dry despite the rain outside. Sella pulled a large ceramic dish from the fire oven and the smell of rich garlic and bright lemon filled the room. She set aside a dish of chicken for the cats and brought her own plate to the table. Cali sat at the chair with a cup of tea in front of her. She was hovering over it with hunched shoulders, breathing in the calming steam. "What've you got there?" she asked when Sella sat beside her.

"Roasted vegetables," Sella said. She slid the plate closer to Cali so she could take a look and smell. "Nothing fancy tonight."

"Good thing too," Cali said. "I can't handle watching you eat something fancy after the scare we just had."

Sella's heart tightened in her chest, as though it couldn't beat strong enough to keep her up. She bit the inside of her cheek and then pulled the plate back. She scarfed it down before she could even taste it. She was certain she looked ridiculous, with a mouthful of food, not chewing properly, but she didn't care. She was hungry, and she didn't want Cali to have to watch her savor her meal.

Cali eyed the empty plate. She looked at Sella at last. "You didn't need to do that."

"Don't worry about it," Sella said, swallowing her last mouthful of carrot. "But, thank you for bringing me a fake wand. That was quick thinking. I really had a bad time last a witch found out I could use magic without one."

"Quick in one way, stupid in another." Cali shook her head.

Sella rose from the table with her plate. She wanted to give Cali the space to express herself without her intense stare. She knew she had a way of analyzing Cali when she got like this. The ghost was usually chipper, optimistic. Until she was incredibly hard on herself. And when she got like that, Sella would catch herself staring like a hawk. She kept her back turned as she made herself her own cup of tea.

As Sella suspected, Cali went on at last, "I knew she was the other kitchen witch everyone's been talking about. I should have expected she'd be in and brought you a fake wand sooner." She sighed, sinking into the steam once again. "I feel so foolish for showing up like that."

Sella stared at her cup for a moment. When Cali stayed quiet, she turned and walked back to the table with her tea. "It's alright, Cali. Really," she said. "And it's not on you to bring me things. I should have done that myself, a long time ago."

"Do you think she'll try to banish me?" Cali asked, shuddering a little at the thought.

Sella felt her stomach turn. The last run in with a witch a year ago was painful to even think about. Images of Cali hanging in the air, her flickering in and out of sight while she screamed in pain flooded Sella's memory. It was one of the most horrible things she had ever seen. She never wanted Cali to have that kind of pain or fear again.

"No," Sella said. "She won't. I'm not going to let anything like that happen to you again."

"Sediri talks a big game," Beejee said, still licking his lips from his own dinner. "But she's no match for our magic."

Koukie was still eating her share beside him.

Beejee looked at the other cat like she was a monster for taking her time. He went on, "Although, we may need to worry about her taking over the shop. She's not wrong. Kepilla does usually end up establishing itself and running smaller kitchen witches out. Even in places like Marra."

Sella rubbed her temples with two fingers. "That's true…" She wanted to just tackle one thing at a time, but already, things were getting ahead of her.

"Do you really think she'll be able to shut you down?" Cali asked. "I mean, people in town are starting to trust you again."

"They never really trusted me in the first place... I don't know," Sella said honestly. "It's basically all Kepilla does."

"They should try starting a shop in Tollintal. They'd be the ones run out. The witches there don't take that kind of intimidation or let anyone push them around."

Sella lowered her hands. She set them in her lap carefully. "I'd like to see that," she said, her voice light, like it was a joke. But really, she did want to see Cali's homeland. The sun burning brightly, those plants she spoke of that stung you when you got too close. Where witches and shifters were able to practice as they pleased. Although, she looked at Cali from the corner of her eye, remembering that witches in her home had put a Witch's Mark on her face simply for associating with the wrong person. Maybe it wasn't such a bad thing that witches weren't emboldened to do whatever they wanted in Orakan. She closed her hands into fists.

"Hey," Cali said, placing a gentle, solid, hand on Sella's shoulder. "We won't let her take this shop from you, right? Beejee and Koukie and Lohrna and I. Hazen and Aadel too. We got you." She gave the witch a small squeeze, then stood, smiling suddenly. "Anyway, I want to tell you how my haunting is going! I think I'm starting to make some scares!"

Tomorrow, the start of the festival, and all its chaos could wait. Sella and Cali stayed up most of the night talking, laughing, and baking, pretending the outside didn't exist.

Socks, Spoons, and Spells

THE NEXT MORNING CAME QUICKLY. Sella locked the store door and joined Cali in the street to make their way to Hazen's for breakfast. And to, begrudgingly, see the famous Golden Ladle.

"I, for one, am excited to see it," Cali said as they made the short walk down the gray cobblestone street. "A trophy that spans back generations? I mean, that sounds pretty interesting."

Sella side eyed her. "It's a golden spoon," she said dryly.

When they entered the tavern, they were immediately thrown into a scene beyond Sella's expectations. The usually lively space was now packed with mostly out of towners, faces she didn't recognize. Some were human, some were not, and it was hard to tell with so many in the space which horns were connected to which heads.

It was loud. Sella and Cali looked at each other briefly and shrugged. There'd be no talking here unless they yelled at each other.

People crowding around the few high tables and at the

bar seemed all to be fighting for a space to sit while most just stood with plates in their hands looking quietly resigned to their standing fate.

Sella looked up. The usual brass chandeliers had been cleaned of their dripping wax, replaced with new, clean, white candles. The huge, round pillars that held up the rafters were freshly waxed, shining brightly in the candle-light. The beams above them were free of dust and cobwebs.

Sella grimaced. She wished that Hazen had asked her for help with all this cleaning. He was too proud, of course. But it must have been an incredibly taxing and time consuming feat to accomplish for him, and, she had to assume, Cirian.

Above the din of the crowd, Lohrna raised her hand at the bar and called as loud as she could, "SELLAAA!"

Sella stood on her toes to see her friend waving her down. She smiled at Cali and inched to reach for her hand but pulled away before she could touch her. There was no guiding the ghost through this crowd.

Cali giggled and faded from view.

She was getting better at this.

Sella wormed her way through the crowd, bumping several less than happy folks along the way. She didn't stop to say sorry, though. She was on a mission to get to her friend and relay the previous night's events.

When she had nearly reached the bar, a large hand grabbed her wrist.

Fire ignited in her fingers and she spun to face the very large Cirian, who was already holding his hands, a cup of mead in each, aloft. "Don't burn the messenger!" he cried, joking. He held out a glass of mead to her, the other he took a long sip from. "Already got you one. You're late, you know. Hazen's been waiting."

"Late?" Sella asked. She couldn't tell if he had heard her. She was about to try again, louder, when Lohrna called again.

"Sella! Cirian! This way!"

The large man tilted his head to Lohrna. Graying curls caught in his ram horns as he did. "You heard her. Let's get a move on."

The three of them huddled together and Cirian, the local eccentric, was already scolding Lohrna in a way Sella thought only siblings could. Except, despite their familial banter, they weren't related or had even known each other longer than a few years. Cirian had only blown into town somewhat recently, despite what his familiarity with everyone would suggest. No matter how Sella tried to pry at his backstory, or where he got all his money that he spent freely and previously, she never got it.

Finally, Cirian looked past Sella's shoulder. "So, Cali," he said, pointing with one finger as he held his cup up. "I was thinking maybe you could give me an education on human culture. I'm making a fool of myself with all these newcomers. Someone held their hand out to me when they said their name. So I kissed it. What else am I supposed to do with it? It was very uncomfortable for both of us."

Sella glanced behind her. "She's not here yet," she said with a light laugh. She sipped her mead and asked, "Anyway, what are we late for, then?"

Cali appeared at the other side of the counter where Hazen was busy working. She beamed at Sella and waved.

"Cali's there," Sella gestured to the ghost.

"CAL!" Lohrna said. She leaned across the counter. "Ignore Cirian and his oddity. He kissed a human he shouldn't have and is making it everyone else's problem. But listen! I have incredible news!"

"But first," Cirian said, pointing to Hazen who stood beside Cali now.

Cali looked up at her former boss with a gleeful grin and joyful eyes. Before she died, he was one of the few in town who truly cared for her. She still did little things from time to time to make his life just a bit easier, like stack his paperwork and give people the chills when it was past closing time.

Hazen winked at Sella and then called over the crowd noise, "Welcome! To the Annual Opora! We are so grateful that it is hosted in Marra this year! Marra may be a small town but what we lack in size, we make up for with personality! There's a lot of things to see and do here, and we hope you all have an incredible experience! And with that, we have: THE GOLDEN LADLE!"

Sella's eyes widened. She had never seen Hazen so preformative. She took another sip of her drink and wondered if he really was so enamored with a gold spoon.

Hazen held the large ladle over his head carefully and the crowd cheered.

Yep. It was a big gold spoon alright.

Beside her, Cirian hollered. Lohrna banged on the countertop with her hands.

Cali and Sella locked eyes. Cali shrugged with a half smile.

Hazen set The Golden Ladle down on a shelf behind the bar with reverence. "Today, we begin the first challenge!

A Glimmergill catching contest! All sailors and fisherfolk competing, please report to the docks!"

The crowd cheered again and began to file out.

Sella peered over the heads in the crowd and spotted a few locals. Arda and Yorro, with their cracked horns and sea-weathered faces pushed through together. Sella snorted a little. She had to sell Arda's wife and son seasick remedies somewhat regularly after they had left town for a while during Cali's murder investigation. She must have endeared herself, because they kept coming back whenever Arda brought them out to sea.

It was a good memory. Wrapped in horror.

After many of the visitors had cleared the hall, Sella turned to Cirian. "Alright, move one stool down?" she asked.

Cirian laughed. "Oh, yes, Beejee's special spot." He moved down a seat. "Of course, the cat comes first."

Hazen leaned his forearms on the bar. "That went well, I think?"

Sella held his hand and gave it a small squeeze. "It went great. You held up the ladle and everyone cheered." There was no sarcasm in her tone, no malice. But she cringed a little. She didn't understand the whole thing and it was clear in her tone.

Hazen laughed a little. "This must seem silly to you youngsters," he said.

"Hey now!" Cirian protested.

"I wasn't talking to you," Hazen narrowed his eyes, but the playful sparkle remained. He turned back to Lohrna and Sella. "The Golden Ladle is a tradition, one that spans back generations. But Marra is something of a nothing town. A pass through for folks off to other, bigger places. To have the Opora here is… Well, it's a big boost for this town."

"How's Branzo handling it?" Lohrna asked. "Wasn't his town supposed to host? Before they caught the sneezing sickness?"

Hazen waved his hand.

"He's basically our mayor, too, right?" Cirian cut in.

Lohrna leaned in to make eye contact with him. "We don't have a mayor."

"Yeah, so the neighboring town is kind of the mayor."

"Says who?"

"Benka?"

Lohrna slapped the counter. "The *retired* detective? Ridiculous."

"That is NOT how we behave." The voice was stern, low, and threatening.

At Sella's side, Cali appeared. She ducked behind her a little on the empty stool as Mims approached.

"What? I…" Lohrna stuttered for a moment. But then she sat upright, held her hands steady on the counter. "No, you're right."

Sella felt the hair on her neck bristle as he approached with the group of shifters she had seen the night before. She steadied herself on the stool, ready to defend her friend, but Lohrna smiled. She didn't look intimidated, but rather, relieved..? Sella took in a long, deep breath until her lungs began to sting.

Lohrna shook her arm. "This is Mims! You sold him the suppressant potions yesterday."

Sella nodded. "Yes, I remember." She turned to Cali at the empty stool for a brief moment.

Cali was watching the interaction intently.

She turned back to face the shifters. "Mims, what do you mean 'we don't behave that way'?"

Mims stood taller, behind him, the rest did the same. "We at the MAMBOSSA do not engage in any behavior that may appear threatening. That includes, but is not limited to, slapping objects, banging items, closing doors too harshly, throwing—"

"I see," Sella cut him off.

"We also do not drink honey liquor."

Lohrna looked down at her mug and then pushed it away.

"But, happy bees!" Cali said from her stool.

Mims turned away, unaware of Cali's protest, or Cirian's cold stare. "Well, I will be viewing the fishing contest today. We have a champion in our ranks who we must support. Good day."

Sella's brows furrowed as she watched half of his crew walk away. A few stayed behind. One, waited by Lohrna's stool.

"Sorry," the other shifter said kindly. "We don't drink because it could lower inhibitions and inhibitions are what separate us from animals."

Sella's muscles tightened. But he didn't seem to notice.

Lohrna pushed her drink further away. Her face was bright. "Sella, Cirian, this is Tazel," she said. She turned back to the other shifter. "I said that right?"

"Tazel, yes," he said. He smiled warmly at the others but Sella got the feeling that he was anxious. He looked a little strained. Something in his body language felt off. "Lohrna sounds very lucky to have friends like you here.

Many of us don't find this kind of friendship outside of MAMBOSSA."

Cirian downed the rest of his drink in one big gulp. He stood from his stool and slapped Sella on the back, making her cough. "That's it for me then," he said. "I'm going to go help Hazen out."

Sella's gaze tracked Hazen to the other side of the tavern, speaking to a group of newcomers with broad gestures. He pointed to the Golden Ladle with pride.

"Alright," Sella said. But Cirian was already out of earshot. She bit her lip briefly before she looked back at Tazel and Lohrna.

Cali, her figure semi-transparent, was standing extremely close to Tazel. If she could manifest herself, he would probably faint at the sudden appearance of a woman an inch from his own face. She was studying him closely, but careful not to touch him, even if he couldn't feel it. "Well, he is certainly well dressed and clean," she said to Sella, stepping back at last. "He seems alright."

Sella's mouth tightened to a thin line. She did her best to play off the budding feeling of thick roots taking hold in her stomach. "So, Tazel," she said, "can you tell me more about the MAMBOSSA?"

Tazel's smile widened. He was handsome, Sella noticed, in a way that was unassuming at first. It probably helped him when they moved from town to town. "We're the only recognized society of shifters by the King," he said proudly. "We do our best to benefit any place we go. We do service projects and try to leave the places better than we found it, in any way we can. But it can be lonely to be nomadic," the last part of his words drifted off, as if he hadn't actually said it.

"Lonely?" Cali wondered aloud. "Seemed like most of them stayed close together."

Sella nodded at her and Tazel's eyes followed to the empty space where Cali stood. He brushed it off and another in the group stepped closer and whispered something in his ear.

Lohrna leaned in. Obviously, trying to overhear.

"Well," he said quickly, "I suppose we'll be off for now. It is almost time to press our socks."

Sella frowned.

"Press your socks?" Lohrna said what Sella and, from Cali's puzzled expression, were wondering.

"Yes," he said, matter of factly. As if that answer should suffice.

"Is that a euphemism?" Cali asked.

When he was met with only blank stares, he went on. "The pixies in the hotel are relentless. They keep taking our socks and crumbling them. One must not have wrinkled socks. They are the barrier between the foot and the shoe, and the shoe is what separates us from the animals."

Sella felt her frown deepen. She couldn't help it. All this talk of animals... That wasn't what her friend was, and pressed socks didn't make a difference. Tides knew, in all her travels, she had met true animals. And they seemed like anyone else until you got to know them.

"Good day," Tazel made a quick bow of his head and then left the tavern with the remaining group.

Sella felt herself deflate when the doors shut. "Okay, tell me you're not getting involved—"

But Lohrna turned to her with a wide grin. She cut her off as if she hadn't heard her at all. "Sella! This Opora is amazing. Can you believe the festival had to change cities so quickly, *and* they came to Marra? A plague is the best thing to happen to me!"

"Are you talking about the Opora or MAMBOSSA?" Sella raised a brow. She took a sip of her mead and watched Lohrna's eyes dart to her own glass.

"MAMBOSSA," Lohrna said. She looked a little sheepish about admitting it.

Sella had never known her friend to be embarrassed about anything. She always held her head high, and said what she meant to anyone. Suddenly, the honey in her mouth tasted sour.

"Aren't they great?" Lohrna continued. "They've agreed to have me in their ranks as a mentee."

"What does that entail?" Cali asked.

Sella repeated her words for the both of them.

Lohrna leaned in. "Well, it's all very official. I have to be a mentee for three cycles, then, I can enter *The Society* as their member. Lowest ranking, but still. It's very exciting."

"Is it? You can't drink what you want and you have to press your socks?" Sella spit out before she could think of a kinder way to put it.

Lohrna shrugged. "I heard we can't eat meat either."

"You love cured meat—"

"I do, but it's fine. I can give it up."

Sella shook her head. She was trying to wrap her mind around it all. "Wait, three cycles before you can officially join? Are they staying that long?"

Lohrna looked down. Her leg began to bounce, her

booted foot tapped the stool leg quickly. "You went away for years too, you know," she said at last.

Sella felt the tips of her pointed ears flush red. Her face stung as if she had been slapped. Lohrna was right, of course. She had left her all alone for so long. "I'm…" but no words found their way. Sorry? She was. But it didn't seem like enough. Not sorry? She wasn't, in some ways. It was what she needed to do. At least, it had felt that way at the time.

Lohrna smiled, but it looked like it hurt her to do so. The corners of her eyes remained wide, the happiness didn't reach any other part of her face. "We don't have to worry about that at this moment, right?" She got off the stool and gave Sella's shoulder a quick squeeze. "I'm going to go check in with my mom. See if she needs anything before tonight's big winner is announced."

Sella hung her head lower. Of course. The big event. The first of many. She was already exhausted just imagining it.

A voice in her mind, long forgotten, whispered to her. It's not the wind and waves that takes down the mighty ship. It's the little cracks where the water gets in.

Sella couldn't remember when her mother had said it to her. But she wished she could forget it.

SEVEN

Marra Signature Blend

"I CAN'T GET the proportions right." Sella grimaced at the coffee.

Cali sat across from her at the wood island in the loft above the shop. They still had an hour before they had to be down at the tavern to witness the festivities and see the winner of the first challenge.

Outside, it was clear. A welcome surprise of stars dotted the night sky. Though from their seats in the little home, all they could see was their own reflections in the large round window as little flames passed by.

"Maybe it's because you're making that face at it?" Cali's laugh was light and sweet.

Sella snorted. She pressed a finger between her brows as if she could magically remove the crease there by doing so. "Yeah, maybe you're right. I really need a good signature blend to keep up with Sediri, though… Something to get the town talking about *Practical Potions*, not Kepilla."

Cali hummed. "Maybe we're going about it the wrong

way? Instead of worrying about making competing coffee, maybe we should focus on the honey sales?"

"Ah yes, the retirement honey," Beejee said. His eyes were still closed, but his ears moved forward. He was curled up at the red brick fireplace. Light from the flickering flames danced off his gray fur with every breath he took. "It's our bestseller, don't you know?"

Cali crossed her arms, playfully angry. "I think it'll take you decades to remember that everyone can hear you. Good thing you live so long."

Beejee opened one eye at her. He yawned, as if unfazed and said, "Speaking of cats who won't if they keep making stupid choices. Where's your mangy cat?"

Cali and Sella both looked about the room, but Koukie was nowhere to be seen. Sella crossed the room and crouched down to look under the bed. She was met with only a few clumps of dust and cat fur. She recoiled at the sight and threw the sheet back down before Cali could come inspect the mess.

"Beejee?" Sella prompted, groaning a little as she lifted herself from the floor.

Her familiar simply thumped his tail in response.

"She goes out more than you'd think," he said when Sella had made her way back to the counter. "Try adding more cinnamon. People love cinnamon."

Sella looked down at the pot of coffee. She pinched a bit of cinnamon from a bowl beside her and flicked it into the ceramic pot while she wished: *Safety.*

Cali leaned in as Sella's hands wrapped around the pot and grew warm. "I like the smell of this…" she said, dreamily, as if she was at ease.

Sella's fingers clenched. She wanted Koukie to be safe out there. She wanted Cali to feel safe. To feel at home. She was already displaced by people in her space, now Sediri made her feel as though she was going to be banished. She couldn't abide by that.

Cali had decided she wanted to stay in the realm of the living. It was Sella's job to protect that wish. Against any witch. Against any law of nature. She didn't care. She had to keep Cali safe.

The stool scraped hollowly against the wood floor as Sella rose quickly. "I'll be back," she said quickly.

"Inspiration strike?" Cali asked.

"Something like that," Sella said as she flung her coat over her shoulders. "I won't be long."

Beejee trotted over to her. "I'm coming too," he said sternly.

"We'll be back soon," Sella said with a, hopefully not too fake, smile.

It was only when they made it out into the quiet street that Beejee looked up and said, "Can I at least knock the bird around a bit?"

Sella shook her head. "No, we just need to talk some of this out with Sediri. She can have her shop. And we can have a stupid competition for our sales. But she has to leave Cali alone."

"I feel like the message would be more impactful if I knocked the bird around a little."

They turned the corner quickly to a row of shops. Outside of the little circle where Hazen's, Penya's, and Sella's misfit buildings with overgrown plants creeping up the walls, the town was largely uniform. Identical brick buildings with well manicured potted plants lined the road. Most were decorated for Opora with gourds and pumpkins, beautiful colors of red and orange and muted yellow.

Above them, strings of triangle banners hung, sweeping between the buildings and zigzagging across the street. They moved in unison as a small breeze blew in from the sea. It would be lovely, Sella thought, if she had the time to linger in the empty space and watch them wave gently. If she had time to participate in the festival. If she was able to summon the excitement about the spoon, and the decorations. If she could just talk to new people instead of trying to prove herself or make a sale.

Beejee dodged a puddle where the stone in the road had worn down as they turned another corner, finally, at the other witch's new shop.

Her torch lights were low, casting a warm yet ominous glow from the large window. Gold lettering on the glass read 'Kepilla Coffees, Teas, and Remedies: All Your Needs in Friendly Recipes'. Sella wanted to gag. The stupid motto brought back a flood of bad memories. She pushed them away and looked down at Beejee. "No violence, right?"

"None for *you*, we don't want to burn the place down… Yet."

Sella moved to nudge him with her boot.

He evaded with ease. But then he stopped suddenly, his ears swiveled forward and he hurried into the shadows just outside the window's glow.

Sella followed him. "Wha—"

Beejee swatted at her, a warning to be quiet. He peeked his head up to the corner of the window. "Someone's in there," he whispered. "Something's not right…"

Sella pulled her hood up and leaned over Beejee to look inside the shop. In the faint light, she saw a man, someone she did not know, and Sediri behind the counter. He slid a box to her and was tapping his finger against the top. "I did my part," his muffled, angry voice carried. "You fix this *now!*"

Sediri took the box quickly from under his hand. She said something back to him that Sella couldn't catch.

Sella looked down at Beejee whose eyes were still fixed on the scene.

"Fix this or I will have this place closed before you can make another ridiculous potion!" the man shouted, his voice got louder as he made his way to the front of the shop.

"Go! Go!" Beejee hissed and darted for the alley.

Sella followed, squeezing her way into the darker shadows just as the door opened. The two watched as the man strutted down the street, completely unaware of them and, seemingly, unfazed by the interaction.

Sella and Beejee looked at one another. They waited a while until the lights of the shop went out, then they both dashed out of the alley and down the street.

"What do you think that was about?" Beejee asked in a hushed tone.

For a moment, Sella wished he couldn't be understood by everyone. The street was starting to fill up as people wandered from the hotel, the various shops, and homes, to Hazen's for the opening ceremony. She scooped him up quickly, and though he stiffened, she knew he understood she needed to be quiet and this was the best way. Sella whispered quietly, "We'll talk about it in a moment. Let's get home first."

"We can't be late for the night's festivities, or it'll look suspicious. We can't afford to miss out on business because out of towners hear about *The Incidents* or because people think you're involved in Sediri's sinister dealings."

"I know, I know," Sella said, squeezing Beejee tighter to her chest. She quickened her pace, maneuvering through the crowd carefully.

They made it to their shop and the street was already busy. Sella and Beejee slipped inside and raced up the steps to the loft.

"That didn't take long," Cali said once they closed the door. She looked up from the writing desk. She had been reading something, but Sella was too flustered to ask.

"I didn't end up getting what I needed," she said. It was a half truth. She had gone to tell Sediri to back off, to not come near Cali again. But left without saying a word. She thought back to the conversation she overheard. What did the man mean by 'fix this'? And what was in the box?

She'd have to determine that another time. For now, she did her best to smile and smooth out her dress. She went to the counter and poured herself a cup of the blend she had been working on earlier. Safety.

She was safe. They were safe.

For now.

THE CROWD WAS GATHERED in Hazen's tavern and some even spilled out into the cobblestone street. It was noisy, but in a warm and friendly way. Despite the day she had, Sella found herself swept up in the joy of those around her. She was grateful that her signature blend, while not what she had anticipated at first, was finally finished. After her own cup, she had begun to feel much better.

Self compassion was difficult, especially when she felt like she was failing at everything, but feeling safe? That was something everyone needed. That, she could provide.

She looked around the room for Lohrna but couldn't find her among the heads and horns around her. She did catch Sediri, her grackle perched upon her shoulder, near the front of the room. Sella was grateful that Cali had elected to stay behind and move some items around her old place, even if she didn't really agree that haunting the new tenets was necessarily the right thing to do.

Her eyes narrowed in on the witch and Majla She wanted to march across the room and demand to know what nefarious business they had been up to. To tell them that the ghost was off limits. That their coffee was terrible and they may as well just leave now.

She also wanted to sink into the cracks in the floor like rainwater and never resurface.

She breathed a sigh out and held the blue ceramic travel cup of coffee closer to her chest just as a man stood on a table at the center of the room. Sella leaned forward a bit, he looked so familiar.

"Well, well, well!" he said, starting on the least interesting phrase possible. Still, the room quieted, mostly, to listen. His presence was captivating, but in a way Sella couldn't quite discern. He stood tall, wore an outfit that looked mostly velvet with sleeves down to his wrists though he was already glistening a bit with sweat at his brow. He was missing a horn. Only one, straight and pointed, reached toward the ceiling. She couldn't tell if the other one had ever been there at all, or was shaved down after it broke. Judging by his immaculate appearance, she assumed he was born with only one. He didn't look like the kind to get into trouble. Not physically, at least.

Sella tilted her head a little to make out more of his expression. She pulled back when she recognized him at last. The man from Sediri's shop just earlier that evening. She bit her cheek, wondering if she had been wrong about his propensity for trouble.

He went on loudly, "Marra is quite the little port town! But I have to say, the fishing is excellent! We had many contestants today and picking the winner was difficult!"

Beside her, Cirian wedged his way between the next person and her, bumping both of their shoulders as he did with his wide frame. "Hello, kitchen witch," he whispered to her, his tone playful.

One corner of Sella's mouth lifted. She side-eyed him. "Who's this?" She motioned with a tilt of her head at the man on the table.

"Branzo. Horta's mayor."

Sella hummed. "Quite the character."

"Aren't we all?"

Sella shrugged, she supposed he was right.

Branzo waved his arms as he went over the criteria for judging the best catch. There was the size of the fish to consider, the color quality of the scales, and the number of teeth, which Sella found odd. "And it was a close one!" Branzo concluded.

"Have you talked to him at all?" Sella asked.

A person beside her turned to her with a glare and shushed her loudly.

She held up a hand in surrender. "Sorry," she mouthed.

"And the winner is: one of Marra's own, Arda Stormstone!" Branzo announced. His arms swept from side to side as if trying to conjure Arda from the air. "Arda!"

Arda, one arm in the air to indicate he was on his way, approached the table as the crowd, mostly Marrans from the looks of it, erupted into cheers. The rest of them politely tapped their hands together, but there were many disappointed faces in the crowd.

"Good for Arda," Cirian said as he joined in the applause.

Sella raised a brow. Arda had been on her short list of people she'd gladly send out to sea since Cali's death. He had been callous about it, until his wife and children convinced him to go away to seek shelter. She knew, logically, that she couldn't blame him for any of his responses. But, emotionally? She was still holding a grudge.

Beejee would be proud.

She looked up to Cirian but he was already making his way to the bar counter. She crossed her arms and watched as Branzo gave Arda a little bow and bestowed a slip of paper, and a small bag of coins.

She shifted uncomfortably as she felt eyes on her. She found Sediri in the crowd, glaring at her. She did her best to shrug it off. A glare was good.

It meant Sella was a threat.

A Soup-er Serious Crime

SELLA AWOKE WITH A STARTLE. Cali was sitting at the edge of her bed doing her best to shake the sheets.

Sella scrambled awake, clutching her heart. "What are you doing?" she gasped, sleep still lingered in her body and made her voice hoarse.

"Jahra's outside looking really concerned," the ghost shimmered slightly.

Jahra?

Jahra was the assistant to the former detective in town. A tall, willowy young man who smiled nervously at everything. He was much more confident behind a desk, doing paperwork and minding his own business. Especially since Benka left town. Despite their consulting business, they hardly ever saw him. Nothing ever really happened in Marra and he was very happy to stay hidden until he was needed.

The ghost leaned over Sella urgently. "Come on. He won't pound on the door, I think he's nervous."

Sella rolled her neck, rubbing her eyes with tight fists. "He's nervous about everything. All the time."

Cali pressed into Sella's shins. "I'm serious," she said.

Sella sat up straighter. "Right. Sorry." She cleared her throat as Cali rose.

Sella threw on a new black dress and slipped into her boots. "Hair check," she said, turning to the ghost as her hand was on the knob of the door.

"Beautiful bedhead," Cali giggled.

Sella's cheeks burned. She ran a few fingers through her dark hair, mindful not to tangle any in her horns, before she descended the stairs like the ghost was chasing her.

Beejee was already at the door, staring up at it. "Jahra's here," he said.

Sella gestured at her outfit and boots. "I know, thank you." She opened the door just as his curled fingers were about to rap on the door.

He looked surprised, but stepped past her and Beejee quickly. He turned to shut the door behind him and locked it. He bent his body to look out the bay window, then his eyes caught the stairs.

"Everything–?"

Jahra cut her off. "I am certain this is entirely improper, but can we *please* go upstairs?"

Sella looked down at Beejee. He silently led the way through the shop and up the steps with a tail raised in a little question mark.

When they were all in the loft, Sella's magic filled the space. Little flames in the rafters illuminated brightly, banishing shadows. The bright fireplace roared to life. Her eyes scanned the space. Koukie was home, sleeping soundly on her desk. Sella smiled gently, grateful she was home. Then, she turned to Jahra. "What's going on?" she asked.

Jahra's hands wrung in worry. He crossed the room to look out the large circle window. Koukie stirred slightly, her tail thumped in annoyance. "The Golden Ladle's been stolen," he said quietly, quickly, as though he hadn't meant to say it at all.

Cali gasped, clutched her hands to her mouth. "The Golden Ladle?"

Sella's brows came together, her jaw twitched.

"What?" Cali said, smiling brightly despite her initial shocked response. "Come on, this is exciting"

Sella sighed. "It's missing?" She prompted Jahra to go.

When he didn't, but simply stood there looking at her, she tried again. "On a scale of one to—"

"Very bad," he interrupted her again.

This was deeply unlike him. Sella felt her scalp begin to itch a little.

He went on, "Hazen will be ruined. Marra will be ruined. This Ladle. It's *everything* right now."

Sella pulled out a little stool at her counter. She motioned for him to sit. She may not care about some gold spoon, but Hazen? That was something to take very seriously.

Jahra sat. He hung his head in his hands. "This is bad. This is really bad."

"He's acting more distraught than when I was murdered," Cali said with a little chuckle. Her voice sounded more humored than spiteful. Sella had no idea where she got her kindness, or her ability to simply brush off major horrors like her own death. At least, most of the time she seemed to.

Sella narrowed her eyes a little. Cali was right, and it

made her heart hurt. She got to work on making a pot of coffee. It was so early morning, it was basically still night. They'd need the caffeine and the extra ingredients of her spellwork. She added a spoonful of Clarity, a sweet, mild flavor that would not only offset the strong coffee beans, but hopefully provide a little direction for them.

Jahra's eyes were far away the whole time. He kept leaning back in his seat to catch glimpses of the window, as if they were being watched from the second story.

Sella handed him a cup once the brew was done. "Drink up. It's Clarity. And we'll need all we can get. Tell me what you know."

Jahra's hands were shaking. He held the cup to his lips and blew gently. He sipped at last, eyes closed.

"It's just clarity," she reassured him. "Nothing scary." She drank her own cup quickly, as if to show him it wasn't poisoned. He had been too young to remember *The Incident*, but she was sure he had heard about it.

Jahra watched her drink her own and then took a long sip of his with a nervous smile. "Thank you," he said at last.

For the cup, for her help, or for understanding that he might be hesitant to try her magic, she wasn't sure. She also wasn't sure she cared. She simply caught Cali's glance and her face softened.

Jahra set down his cup once it was mostly finished. "Hazen alerted me as soon as he found it missing," he said. "He said he didn't want to come here in the middle of the night and have folks notice him knocking."

"So he knocked on your door instead?" Beejee jumped up to the counter to look at him.

"Yes," Jahra said. "He did and he wasn't alone. Cirian

and Aadel were there too. They all made a bit of a fuss about it. He said he wanted to go through the proper bureaucracy. But also didn't want to look suspicious himself. He was also a little rude about it… He doesn't want anyone thinking it's him."

Sella and Beejee locked eyes.

That was plausible. Anyone who knew Hazen would know he would never do anything to hurt Marra's reputation or jeopardize his tavern. But that didn't mean the out of towners, or Branzo, would agree.

"I told him to keep it quiet," Jahra said.

"But Aadel knows," Beejee scoffed.

Jahra took another shaking sip of his coffee. "Trust me," he said. "The elders here are not going to gossip about this one. It will ruin us."

"So you said."

"Beejee!" Sella swatted at the cat. "We have to help Hazen."

Cali moved in closer. "Ask him what Hazen remembers about the scene of the crime."

Sella nodded. "Can you tell me about what Hazen could recall?"

Jahra's eyes grew wide. "That's the thing," he said. "There were no signs of force at the door. Nothing else was missing. It was like it had vanished from its place."

"Well, then, that solves it. Sediri did it. She used magic," Beejee said.

"Come on, Beejee," Cali said. "You wouldn't want someone saying that about Sella just because she's a witch."

Jahra looked at the cat, his expression was still surprised whenever Beejee spoke no matter how often heard it. It was relatively recent, but Sella thought someone in his line of work would be better able to keep up. Or at least fake it. "He has a point," Jahra said.

Beejee trotted across the counter closer to Sella.

"No," Sella said. She stroked Beejee's ear gently. "That doesn't necessarily mean it's magic. Anyone can pick a lock if they want to."

Cali beamed with pride.

Beejee batted Sella's hand away.

"This is true…" Jahra said.

Cali clapped, loudly. Koukie looked up from her resting place, but Jahra stayed still. "I got it!" she announced. "Let's wake up Tallam. Get him to recreate it tonight, before anyone's the wiser!"

Sella had to admit, it could work. Or, at least, it would definitely buy them some time. She turned to Jahra. "We need to get Tallam to recreate it. Quickly, and as best he can."

"But the real Golden Ladle has magic weaved into the metal. When the winner is announced, it will–"

"Doesn't matter. This gives us time. We'll find the real one before the end of the festival, alright? In the meantime, no one needs to know about the fake. At least, no one but us and Hazen."

"And Aadel and Cirian," Beejee added.

Sella took in a long, deep breath until her lungs felt like they'd pop. She breathed it out loudly, feeling her body go back to its, if not calm, at least less panicked, state. "We have to hurry," she said. "Let's see if we can find enough gold to make this work."

Sella spent the next few minutes going through every

drawer and collecting any spec of gold. She gathered a few kitchen items, a ring, and a small statue of a kelpie given to her long ago. She looked at it fondly for a moment before stuffing it into her bag. Memories would have to wait.

"At least credit me," Cali laughed as they headed out into the night.

"Sorry," Sella said, genuinely.

"It's okay," Cali said. "But once this festival is over, I want priority one to be finding a spell so I can talk."

"It's already a priority, even with everything for Opora going on," Sella whispered. Jahra was a good distance ahead of them, but she still didn't want him overhearing. "You have the people in your home, right? I know you'd like to communicate with them. I get it."

"I do already, kind of."

"Besides moving their items around and opening cupboards."

"Well, I did *slam* them tonight, actually," Cali said guiltily, as if she was admitting to a seriously heinous crime. "Just once. I felt bad after. That's when I came over."

Sella looked at her with a raised brow and a warm half smile. "Cali, you're doing your best. I need to step up. I know that."

Cali waved her hand. "You're trying."

She was. But Cali's words stung, all the same. Sella knew she meant them well.

Trying. The word made her feel small and powerless. All the magic she was able to wield without a wand, her fire… The fact that she had made a name for herself elsewhere after coming from a small nothing town… It all felt meaningless and useless when tasked with this.

A part of her mind told her that she messed most things up. That this was no exception. She pushed the dark thoughts aside with a shake of her head, instead, focusing on the quiet sound of her and Jahra's footsteps on the stone beneath them. Focusing on the absence of sound as Cali walked beside her.

The group rounded another corner and Jahra stopped at a silver plated door. In raised lettering, the sign above the door read 'Tallam's Smithy'. It began to swing a little on its silver chains as rain began to fall.

Sella had never been inside, but her mother had been on good terms with him, when she was alive. She remembered walking by it occasionally, admiring the silver plated door and the way it sparkled in the light. Tallam mostly kept to himself, as far as she was aware. When she did catch his eye at the market sparingly, he looked too tired to acknowledge her or even notice. She wasn't sure if that was because he was overworked, or bored.

"Well, knock," Beejee ordered Jahra.

Sella stepped up and did it for them. She knocked, loudly, twice, then pulled back and waited for the blacksmith to get ready.

After a long moment, Tallam opened the door, still in his nightclothes from the looks of it, and blinked at them with tired eyes. "The consultants?" he asked and then rubbed his throat to warm it. "Ah, just one consultant. And the assistant."

Sella smiled, she was glad he hadn't called her 'the kitchen witch'. Though, perhaps it was Jahra's presence that tipped him off as to their business there. She found herself suddenly wishing that Lohrna was with them so he didn't have to correct himself with the singular 'consultant'.

It only seemed right to have all of them there, and she missed her friend. She would love something like this. She wondered where she was now, if she was with The Society, whatever they called themselves.

"Can we come in?" Jahra asked. He looked down the street suspiciously, then up at the rainfall. "Please?"

Tallam looked up too and grumbled a bit to himself. He made way for them to enter and they all filed in quickly.

Sella let Jahra explain the situation. She simply sat with her back straight at the kitchen table and watched the interaction while listening to Cali's commentary. Her eyes looked about the room, landing on various metal oddities. Some hung from the ceiling on delicate hooks, others piled up at the corners or along the shelves over the wood stove.

She wasn't sure most of their purpose and couldn't even begin to guess at some.

Cali pointed to what looked like a vase with golden octopus tentacles reaching out of it at the counter. "What do you suppose this does?"

Sella shrugged, she hoped subtly.

When Jahra was finished, Tallam turned to Sella. "This does seem to be quite the predicament," he said slowly.

"We have gold," Sella said. She took out each piece of gold from her bag and set it carefully at the table. "I'm not sure if it is enough…"

"It's not," Tallam said. He looked to the vase with golden tentacles. "I will make the replica with this." He took the gold from the table in one swoop of his arm. "And with what I have here. I remember its details from the festival long ago. The replica will be good. It won't be magic, though."

"We'll find the real one before that becomes an issue," Sella promised.

Tallam nodded. He rose from the table, hands on his thighs to push himself up. "I'll get to work right away." He gestured to the door. "I wont bring it to Hazen's. I'm not known for my propensity to liquor. You'll have to deliver it."

Jahra stood quickly, knocking the table a bit as he did. "And how long will it take?"

Tallam looked at him with half closed eyes. "It'll be done before anyone's the wiser."

Sella smiled and rose from her seat as well. "Thank you, Tallam. Really, this is very kind of you."

Tallam nodded. "Anything to help Marra."

THE GROUP STAYED up most of the night while Tallam worked. They lingered at the table, drinking tea that Tallam had offered until the pot grew cold and Sella had to reheat it with her fire.

They stayed mostly silent. Beejee was half asleep on Sella's lap, Cali had disappeared. It was quiet now that morning mist began to roll in. From her view through the little window in the kitchen, Sella could see the darkness begin to dissipate. The smell of rain and rich herbal tea filled her nose.

She looked at Jahra. He sat in the chair across from her with his arms wrapped tightly around himself. His head hung just a little, eyes closed. A little snore slipped from his lips and he jostled his chin up for a moment, only to squint hard and nod back off. Sella smiled gently at him and took a deep breath.

She remembered him, vaguely, from before she left town long ago. He had been a small boy then. His face now had changed so much. It was longer, more angular, yet he still looked small to her. She wondered if he ever wanted to get out of Marra, what his dreams were, if he had any fluttering feelings for anyone in town. But she knew she'd never ask. He was quiet. At least around her. And she knew that she had a way of making people in town uncomfortable.

Still, her mind occupied itself with thoughts of the people in town. How she would imagine them in the big cities she traveled to. If they'd be willing to try a Kepilla coffee or remedy.

She sighed, realizing that she had forgotten her stick. Not that any Marran cared that she could wield magic without it. Not that they knew it was unusual. Still, now that Sediri and so many travelers were here, she needed to be careful. More intentional.

In all her journey through Orakan, she had never met an elemental witch who was anything but feared and ostracized. She had never met a witch who didn't have a wand.

Her fingers twitched, suddenly remembering the feeling of her mother's wand snapping in her hands. She heard the sound of breaking bark like a burst of thunder in her memory. The pieces were probably long decayed in the woods by now. She never went back to the place where she had faced off with Isra to collect their shards. It was better that the dirt and grass took the magic back.

At least, that's what she told herself.

The light was growing colder as the sun rose behind the

clouds. The patter of rain had stopped, the lanterns were out, and it was silent in the room.

Just when she felt her own eyes grow heavy and her head dip, Tallam pulled a chair from the table and sat. He held Jahra's shoulder with a firm grip and the young man awoke, blinking into the early morning light. "I'm awake!" he said quickly.

Tallam bowed his head. "It's done." From the pocket of his heavy leather apron, he pulled a golden ladle. He placed it on the table for all to inspect.

Sella and Beejee, now wide awake, leaned in.

"It's not bad," Beejee said.

"It's perfect," Sella corrected. "Thank you, Tallam."

Tallam watched Jahra from the corners of his eyes.

The young man was busy looking the ladle over in his hands. He held it so delicately, as though it were about to shatter at his fingertips.

"Incredible work. Marra is lucky to have you here," Jahra said. He put the ladle back down gingerly. "We owe you more than what we paid."

"Hey now, he said 'anything for Marra', let's not get ahead of ourselves," Beejee said.

"We can hear you," Tallam said slowly. "But I am glad to help." He rose from the table with a stiff groan. "Get this to Hazen's. And quickly or all my work will be for not."

Jahra picked up the ladle again, this time, more confidently. He wrapped it in a small cloth from his pocket and stuffed it into the interior pocket of his coat. "This will work," he said.

It sounded like he was trying to convince himself.

Calming Caffeine

Beejee was pacing the front of the store, tossing his head up to look out the windows occasionally. He grumbled to himself, as if entirely disappointed with whatever it was he saw, or didn't see, outside.

Sella was busy with customers, some humans, some Orkanians. She was explaining the signature blend, and the different options available.

Spice lover? Something sweeter? Earthy? Sella rattled the options for blends, noting that each held the same potency and effects.

As Aadel had suggested, customers did seem to be in need of coffee rather desperately. One human held a hand over their left eye, pressing into it gingerly as if they had recently been punched. Another looked like she hadn't slept at all in maybe two days. She lazily walked from shelf to shelf, inspecting the cubbies of potions but her eyes were glazed, as if she wasn't really reading anything, just trying to make a show that she was making an informed decision.

Sella caught Beejee's eye. He huffed again and went back to his pacing.

Once the customers were finally gone, coffees finished, and headache cures in hand, Sella moved to the front of the shop to look out the bay window with him. "Worried about the fake?" she asked.

Beejee said nothing. But his little front paw pressed into the cushion. His claws were extended. "Tallam's good. And if we haven't heard anything yet, I think we're in the clear." Beejee pressed his nose to the window, leaving a little gray smudge. "There she is!"

Sella followed his nose to Koukie walking down the street, tail held high.

She strolled up to the front door and pawed at it to be let in.

As soon as the bell rang, Beejee was on the floor, already facing off with the larger cat. The space between his shoulder blades puffed slightly. "Finally!" he scolded. "I have been up all night. And where have you been?"

Koukie meowed at him. She walked past casually as he had only simply said 'Welcome home.'

Sella bent down to stroke her fur as the cat made her way to the back of the shop. "What's going on?" she asked Beejee.

Beejee's tail flicked. "She's been out again with those alley cats. You know the ones."

"I don't," Sella began.

But Beejee was quick to continue, "She's been running around with these cats like she's a common stray eating mice for dinner. She forgets she's in the company of a great witch. It's unbecoming."

"Unbecoming or… are you maybe feeling a little protective?" Sella hypothesized aloud. She had never seen him care about the comings or goings of Koukie before. And certainly she had never seen him question her so brazenly. Koukie was much bigger than him, and she reminded him frequently.

Her familiar scoffed, but didn't fight it. Sella could feel his affection for her, his worry. It felt like an older sibling, or at least, stories she had heard about them. She scratched his back. "You're worried about her safety. It's okay to worry. But, she's her own cat. She's going to do what she's going to do."

"She's a grown cat," Beejee said, head held high. "She can look after herself. It's the *perception* of the thing."

"Mhm, the perception" Sella conceded. Beejee worried about perception quite frequently. But it usually had to do with her use of fire. Or her way of speaking a bit awkwardly, being stuck in her own head. She suspected that he was more worried about Koukie's perception than her own.

A warmth spread through her chest. The two cats had come a long way from the first night they met, though they still got into spats from time to time. Sella had to admit, it was nice to see Beejee concerned for something other than just the two of them, or their shop's finances, for once.

She looked across the store to the stairs leading up to their home.

Koukie gazed back at her knowingly, a smirk, if Sella ever saw one, on her face. The orange cat slowly blinked at her once, then trotted up the remaining stairs and out of sight.

It was only a moment later when she saw Aadel, wild graying curls and thin horns adorning her head, hustling across the street and toward her store.

Sella straightened and flattened her wrinkled dress with her hands quickly before the older woman came into the store.

Aadel, in a flurry, entered. She gave Sella one quick pat on the shoulder as she passed her and went straight to sit at a stool at the far end of the shop.

Sella hurried over behind the counter, worry creeping into the place where warmth had just been.

"A strong cuppa, my dear." Aadel patted the counter gently. She looked around the empty shop and tapped her chest. "Something to calm this racing heart. Add some honey, too."

Sella nodded, reaching for the calming blend. Hints of subtle lavender, sweet, rich honey, and earthy grounds filled the room. Sella heated the water with her hands. Her eye drifted to the fake wand at the counter. She really needed to get better about remembering it was there when out of towners were in, especially the humans.

"You heard about the… little debacle, I take it?" Aadel said once Sella had finished the coffee.

"Jahra told me. Did you hear our solution?"

"Hazen told me," Aadel said. She didn't wait for the coffee to cool before she took a long drink. "I think it'll work. That was good thinking. But, Sella. You *have* to find who did this." She turned to the empty stool beside her. "Cali, is there any way you can help with this? Use… your haunting skills?"

Sella rolled her eyes, though she immediately regretted it

and hoped that Aadel hadn't seen her. It was kind that she was trying to include Cali, even if she wasn't there. "She's not in right now," Sella said quickly.

"Oh," Aadel said. "This is her usual stool though?" You should get a plant to put on it when she's not here so we know."

Yes, 'we'. Meaning Aadel and Hazen. Other than them, most of her business was out of towners. But, she thought, it wasn't a bad idea. Except that she killed most plants she came in contact with for too long. Maybe she could get a little vase and seasonal flowers, she thought, since those were dead already.

Aadel leaned forward on the counter. "This is important," she said, pulling Sella's mind away from figuring out how to budget for flowers. "We need everyone we can on deck to help find this before word gets out."

Sella nodded seriously. She did her best to look concerned.

Yet, no matter how she tried to think about it, she just could not bring herself to care too much about a Golden Ladle going missing. But, she knew the elders cared, and that made her want to try. Still, a part of her was fine with it going missing. All the theatrics of a festival like this was so outside anything she cared to be a part of. Perhaps it was her sleepiness, or having to explain the oddities to an outsider as she had the night before, but she was fine with antiquated traditions fading away.

Instead, she said, "We'll find it. Lohrna and Cali and I."

"And me," Beejee said. "Not that anyone ever remembers me."

Sella rolled her eyes. A second time. Aadel was going to

whack her the next one, she knew it. Just like when she was a little kid. She did her best to recover. "He's feeling a way this morning, never mind him," she whispered to Aadel.

The coffee finally seemed to kick in. Aadel's posture softened. She let out a relieved breath. "I know you will work to find it… but," her mind suddenly seemed less frantic, her breathing, Sella noticed, began to slow. "Where is Lohr?" Aadel looked around the shop as though she missed her on the way in. "With the bees?"

Lohrna was often out at the edge of the forest tending to their bees. They had been left by her mother and produced the best honey she had had in all her travels. She suspected it was because of Lohrna's care and love that they kept producing even in the autumn and winter months. Lohrna wasn't a witch, but she had a certain kind of magic within her.

Sella looked down at the lavender honey in the little glass jar. Once again, a pinprick of pain blossomed where affection had just been. She looked out the window, then poured her own coffee. "Probably with the MIMOSAs?" Sella guessed as she leaned forward on the counter.

"MAMBOSSAs… They seem like good folks," Aadel said. "Shocking they're so open as shifters, though."

Sella flinched at the word in Aadel's mouth. It was Sella's fault, after all, that Lohrna was the way she was. Her fault for leading her into the woods that night. Her fault for not protecting her. They were so small…

Sella's fingertips sprouted fire and she retracted her hands quickly from her mug.

Aadel reached for Sella and her skin burned at the touch. Was she not frightened? Fire was dangerous, so closely tied to Sella's emotions that flickered unpredictably like candlelight.

But Aadel simply looked at the witch with kind eyes through her thick lashes. She had never blamed Sella for what happened. Never questioned any of it or judged her or her own daughter for it. She had been softer with Sella than her own mother had been. Sella never understood why.

Now, she looked down at Aadel's hands on hers and felt the same. Perhaps she'd never know how or why Aadel was not afraid of her. Why she loved her through it all.

"I'm glad she's found a place she feels that she can belong," Aadel said, patting Sella's hand with her own.

Sella smiled and blinked away the fresh tears that began to form in the corners of her eyes. She sniffed and then withdrew her hand. "You're right," she said with a shaking breath. "I'm glad she found someplace to belong."

"I said someplace she *feels* she can belong," Aadel corrected. "She already belongs."

Sella nodded. She brushed her eyes quickly with the back of her hands as the bell chimed and a few more humans entered, looking just as rough as the others had before.

Aadel finished her drink and set it down along with a few coins. She winked at Sella, so obviously that had the group been from Marra, they would have spotted it immediately. "I'll go see how Hazen is fairing at the tavern then," she announced entirely too loudly.

Sella lifted both hands, palms out to hush her, but she was already halfway out the shop. Aadel was stopped by one older man and pointed at the honey on a low shelf. "What kind is this?" he asked.

"That's the good stuff right there. From across the sea are you?"

The two engaged in a conversation that Sella could hardly hear. She was tired. She poured herself another cup of coffee. At least business was good. Or, better than she expected with Sediri fresh in town. She figured that the close proximity to the hotel probably helped her more than anything.

A few more customers with faces and horns she did not recognize entered. The shop was getting crowded. And, as excited as she was to have business, it began to make her heart quicken.

As her chest began to tighten, she felt the air growing thin around her. She tried to count the list of things on her mind, but only got to 'one' when Penya, the ancient hotel's proprietor, came through her door.

TEN

Seas and Desist

Sella had never seen Penya outside of the hotel. Oceans, she had never seen Penya out of her hotel *lobby*. And now that she really thought about it, she couldn't remember a time she saw her out behind her desk. She had, only on a few occasions, ever really seen Penya awake.

The old woman entered with a fiery spark in her eyes. She shuffled quickly past everyone in the shop, Aadel included, and went straight to the counter.

"Penya, how can I—"

Penya slammed a paper on her counter with a loud *thud*. "Do you know about this new kitchen witch in town?"

Sella's eyes shifted quickly to her customers. Thankfully, none seemed all that interested in them, except Aadel, and the man she was speaking with who were both leaning their bodies closer to the back of the shop to very obviously eavesdrop. She wanted to shoo them away but instead, she looked back to Penya with a customer service smile. "Yes, I know the other witch," she said calmly.

Penya tapped the paper on the counter with her finger urgently. "Well?"

"Right, yes," Sella said. She picked it up and read the header aloud, "Kepilla hereby demands the dismantling and slash or relinquishing of the siren statues in front of your place of business." Sella looked up at Penya. "You got this from the new kitchen witch?"

"Yes." Penya's bones creaked as she moved closer. "She says Kepilla owns sea monsters anywhere they set up one of their ridiculous predatory shops."

"You know about Kepilla?"

"I own a hotel, Sella. I *do* speak to my guests," Penya spat. "Are you going to do something about this or not? They cannot *own* a creature."

"I... I'm just a kitchen witch, I don't–"

"Well?"

Sella was growing incredibly frustrated with people cutting her off. She took in a long breath and waited for Penya. She stared into Penya's old eyes with what she hoped was a matched intensity and not just frustration.

Aadel broke their standoff. "Penya, what's this?" She took the paper from Sella's hands, a bit harshly. Her eyes went over the letter. They grew full by the end of the page. "I must say, it does sound pretty legitimate."

Penya spun on her heel to point a crooked finger at Aadel. "What do you know? Those statues have been there longer than you've been alive."

Sella's eyes bounced between the two women. She tried to keep her expression neutral, but she couldn't help that she was a bit afraid. She felt like a small child watching the adults get into a fight. These two were equally stubborn, though she was leaning toward Penya's victory here.

When she and Lohrna were little, one of their past times was snooping about the hotel. Penya had caught them once and held them inside the lobby until their mothers showed up to claim them. She had regaled them with the story of the two siren statues outside to keep them occupied. They had been made, she claimed, by an actual siren and were accurate renditions of their haunting songs. It was true that every time the wind blew, the statues did emit an other-worldly, eerie sort of song. Which was why everyone in town hated them.

"They are magic, and old, and I refuse to let them be moved," Penya said, interrupting Sella's thoughts.

Sella took the paper back. She looked it over. "Of course she can't–"

"I will *not* remove the statues. You have to talk to her."

"She will," Aadel volunteered for her.

Sella opened her mouth to protest but one of the humans who had been busy browsing came forward with an armful of goods. Sella glared at the two older women for a fraction of a moment before she put on her best fake smile. She motioned for Aadel and Penya to move away while she said cheerily, "Hello! What a wonderful selection you have!"

Aadel, somewhat begrudgingly, it seemed, pulled Penya along by her elbow to the far corner of the shop while Sella spoke with the customer.

The human, a small man with large eyes and even bigger smile, said, "I'm excited to see a witch's shop here. I was worried a small town like this wouldn't have what I need, especially in Orakan."

Sella sorted through his haul, pricing it all out in her mind. She wondered if she could upcharge since he seemed so enthusiastic. But she shuddered instead at herself. What a wicked thought. Beejee would be proud. "You're from across the sea?" she asked.

"Yes," he said. "And sorely broke. I can't believe they changed the location of the Opora last minute. Worse, I can't believe the other inn wouldn't refund my room."

Sella hummed in response. She wouldn't fall for it. The price was the price this time.

"Well," the human went on, "what's the deal with the other shop? The locals recommended you instead. Though the other shop does seem more... official." He turned, slightly, to the two women at the corner of the shop. "But, I'm surprised to see two witches in such a town as this."

"I'm the original," Sella said as she put the various bottles and powders into a small woven bag. "Come see me anytime..." She trailed off as she inspected the items. "What did you say ails you?"

The man smiled again and pulled the bag across the counter. "I didn't," he said, though not unkindly. "How much do I owe you?"

Sella said the total, with a little less than she would have charged normally. His story seemed to hit her harder than she thought.

The man paid and left without another word.

"Be sure to write down what you sold," Beejee said quietly, appearing behind the counter as if by magic. "Remember last time, that's what saved us."

Sella nodded and wrote down everything he bought and a description of the man.

The last few customers, as if emboldened by the man's purchase, queued up to buy their goods.

Sella wrote down every item, and every description, quickly until the shop was empty, except for Penya and Aadel.

They were still bickering a bit in the corner, Aadel looked casual about whatever Penya was flailing her arms about, but she said a quick comment here and there. Sella watched them in her peripheral vision and restocked the potions that the customers had purchased.

At last, the two ended their conversation.

Penya looked at Sella with hard eyes. "I'll expect to hear from you soon." She walked out of the door and hobbled down the street out of view.

Aadel chuckled a little to herself. "Penya and those statues. I'll never understand it."

Sella turned to the older woman. "They mean a lot to her," she said with a shrug. "But I've never heard of Kepilla trying to take down any sirens, statues or otherwise. They must be gaining confidence to be so bold these days."

Aadel glanced out the window, making sure Penya was truly gone. "Between you and me, I wouldn't mind them getting gone. Yes, they have a lot of history, but those darn things always sound so loud when it storms."

"I'm guessing almost everyone feels the same," Sella said. Herself included, if she was being honest. They gave her the creeps. "But, I think it's overstepping on Kepilla's part to try to take them down. We can't let them get away with something like that."

Aadel nodded. "I like that spark, Sella," she said.

ELEVEN

Dealing with Witches

SELLA HADN'T SEEN Lohrna all day. The store kept busy enough, much to Beejee's glee, so her friend only crossed her mind in the brief moments when the place was quiet and still. She wondered for a moment if she was being overly needy. If all the commotion of the festival, of Cali's new circumstances, of the missing ladle, was all catching up to her.

But still, she reminded herself, it was odd that Lohrna hadn't come in at all. Her anxiety prickled up a little as it occurred to her that Lohrna might even be angry with her. She hadn't been the most kind when they last talked. It was possible it was even worse than she originally thought. She reflected back on the conversation, and though it was recent, the details were fuzzy.

It had been a while since anyone had come in. She could close early.

She flicked her hand and the fires overhead and ambient music, gentle tinkling of ceramic cups went out. She turned the sign to 'closed' and grabbed the stick from her counter and walked up the steps to her loft. Each foot landed heavier than she anticipated, as though her boots were made of stone. She sighed and unlocked the door, slinking inside her cozy little space.

The large room was warm and inviting despite her negative mood. Already, the cats were curled up at the foot of the bed, halfway hidden in the piles of blankets. The fireplace cast a flickering glow, and… in the corner of her room by her wardrobe, stood a human shape, draped in a plain white sheet.

"Fancy meeting you here," the sheet said.

"Tides, Cali!" She hunched over a little as her body acclimated to the presence in her room being friendly, not threatening.

Cali removed the sheet quickly and was at Sella's side with a light laugh. She held Sella's back, just between her shoulder blades, and rubbed a little circle. "I'm sorry! I thought it'd be charming? Or at least get a chuckle out of you?"

Sella took in a deep breath through her nose. She stood up tall again, and Cali's hand fell away, semi-translucent.

"No," Sella said with a small laugh. "It was funny. I think. Also terrifying. I had a lot on my mind and didn't exactly expect to see that."

"I did get your heart racing though?" Cali asked with a raised brow. She bent forward a little to catch Sella's eye.

Sella's face burned. She turned to the kitchen and took off her boots quickly, trying to rid her stomach of the feeling that she was falling. "Yes, you certainly did that," she said as she crossed the floor with lighter steps.

Cali appeared by her side again, as if through teleportation. She looked up at Sella. "Do you have time to talk tonight?"

"Always, Cali. But it makes me worried you wanted to give me a scare before…"

"Not a scare. Necessarily," Cali explained. "An exhilaration. An homage to when we met. Or at least, officially met. Rather than me just showing up at your shop and you forgetting I existed."

"I'll never be able to make you forget that I was kind of a monster to you, will I?"

"Not a monster, just… mildly selfish. For good reason, usually. It's charming how much you're in your own head, once someone gets to know you."

Sella's half smile lit her face despite herself and the insult. "Have you tried the sheet trick on the new tenets of your place yet? I'll bet that'll do it."

Cali shrugged. "In a way, that's what I want to talk to you about. What's for dinner?"

Sella cast a quick glance at Cali. Her quick transition worried her. "I'm too tired to make anything. It was a busy day, thankfully."

"You have to eat something."

Sella looked around her. She grabbed a blueberry scone from the counter. She lifted it up like she was proud of it. It was stale, from the day before. It crumbled a little at her touch, but the little sugar crystals on top still glistened in the firelight, and it smelled fresh enough. She showed Cali, who huffed in return.

"Fine. At least it's something," Cali said. She flickered out of view, then appeared on the velvet loveseat in front of the fire. She motioned for Sella to join.

When they were both comfortable and Sella was mostly finished with the second scone, upon Cali's insistence, Sella prompted, "So, what did you want to talk about?"

Cali looked into the fires, the light danced in her eyes.

"And, why do I get the feeling you're stalling?" Sella asked.

Cali's legs curled up under her. She swayed her head from left to right as if stretching out her neck. "Sediri, the other kitchen witch…"

Sella's brows rose. "Yes?"

"She found me today," Cali said.

Sella turned her body to face Cali. She grabbed her hands carefully, afraid they'd disappear. "Are you alright? Did she try to banish you?"

Cali smiled. She squeezed Sella's hands back. "No, nothing like that. Maybe worse?"

"Worse?"

Cali's thumbs moved across Sella's hands. She looked down at them, as if she too, was feeling the weight of them. As if she were truly alive… here… for a moment. Her eyes traveled up to Sella's face. "She said she'll give me my voice. If I help take down your shop."

Sella flinched. Her hands slipped from Cali's.

"Obviously, I won't help," Cali added quickly.

Sella shook her head. "No. Of course…"

Of course Cali wouldn't help her rival. Of course she wouldn't take down her shop, the shop that had been there for a generation. But. If Sediri *could* help Cali… If she had some knowledge that Sella didn't… Then, what was any of her raw power for? What did it matter that she didn't need a wand? That she could manifest fire? What was any of it if she couldn't help the one person she wanted to most.

Her eyes bounced around the room, and she realized she was holding back tears that had begun to bud in the corners of her eyes. She didn't know what to say. She just knew it felt like she had slipped under water, and she wasn't sure which way was up. She tried to steady her breathing.

Her shop. Her mother's shop. The place she grew up, the place she fled to when she couldn't cut it out in the big cities. It was a refuge. A jail cell. A coffin. Her mind was spinning.

"Sella, I told you right way—"

Sella cut her thoughts off quickly before they could drag her down any further. "It's not that. I'm not angry or… upset even," Sella said, though her voice shook a little. She looked at Cali. As her gaze steadied. a tear slipped from her eye. She used the back of her hand to push it away quickly. "It's just…" She needed to say the next part quickly, before she could stop herself. "You should take that deal."

"What?" Cali pulled back a little. Her green eyes shimmered in the firelight, bouncing around Sella's face as if studying it.

"I'll do it," Sella said. "I'll close the shop if it means you get to feel…" More alive? More like a person? *More, more,* Sella's mind was thinking in layers, she couldn't grab just one. "I'll find someplace else. Sediri can have Marra."

A deep wrinkle formed between Cali's brows. She looked away. "Sella, you're being stupid. And, I don't want to be rude about it, but if I'm not, Beejee will." When her eyes reached Sella's again, they were fierce, alight from within. "You have a place here, and it took you some time, but you're finding your way. Here. Things are finally starting to work out *here*. It's not time to leave yet. We won't let her push you out. I won't let her push you out."

Sella's breath caught in her throat. She pulled her arms close to her body. "But what does it matter? The shop, money, any of my abilities? If you can't be yourself as you want to be, none of that matters. You chose to stay here, Cali. It's my job to help you now."

Cali rolled her eyes. "Your job? Really?"

"My responsibility."

"If you think that sounds better, it doesn't." Cali leaned forward again.

"It's not fair that only I get to talk to you," Sella said, her eyes locking in on Cali's. "It's not fair to you. None of this is. Don't you feel—"

"Annoyed? Stuck? Bored? Frustrated beyond belief?" Cali filled in the gaps. "Of course I do, Sella. But not with you. With the situation. I *like* talking to you. It's not a burden to do so. And I'd *choose* to spend most of my time with you even if I could talk to everyone else."

Sella pulled her legs up onto the couch. She looked into the fire, watched its flames dance. A long moment hung in the air between them. "I've been looking for a spell to help you, Cali..."

"I know you have."

"But I haven't gotten anywhere," Sella went on. "I can barely find any information about ghosts, let alone one... like you. I have no idea how to help you. And it's so painful that I can't. It's a short dock after a short dock to a deep plunge." Sella folded her legs up toward her chest. She kept her stare on the fire. "I… I can't help you. But Sediri can." She bit the inside of her cheek, hard. She wanted to stop talking before her voice betrayed her with the tremble she felt in her chest. She had no right to cry when it was Cali who really stood to lose in this situation. No right to cry when she was alive.

"None of this defeatist talk," Cali said brightly. "If you get into one of your moods, I'll have to haunt it out of you. Frankly, I don't want to have to stay up all night haunting you. Again." Cali pulled Sella's chin toward her to make eye contact. She held Sella there as she spoke. "You like having your clothes in the closet? Never again. They'll always be on the floor. Your cupboards closed? Say no more to that! I'll pinch your toes all night. Pull your blankets right off!"

Sella laughed, though her sinking feeling in her chest lingered painfully. "Please don't. I need the sleep," she said, pushing away another tear that fell from her eyes.

Cali moved closer to brush a lock of dark hair from Sella's face, but her fingers passed through, as quickly and touchless as a shadow. She smiled anyway and pushed her own hair behind her ears. "It'll be alright," she said. "We'll figure it out. I already told Sediri 'no thank you' anyway. I'll avoid her and her familiar whenever I can. And in the meantime, I'll keep honing my haunting skills to get those squatters out of my place."

"You mean the paying tenants?" Sella teased, finally feeling like they were getting back to themselves again.

Cali huffed, dramatically. "Once you find a way for me to talk, I'll be on the payroll somewhere. I'll buy them out."

"Working in the afterlife? I'm sure you can come up with more interesting things to do."

Cali's smile grew wicked. "Oh, I am sure I can."

Sella choked as Cali disappeared from view.

TWELVE

Pebbles and Other Hard Things

A sound like a pebble hitting Sella's second floor window woke her from her dreamless sleep. The loft was chilly and dark.

Sella turned over in her bed, pulled the covers up closer to her chin. She waited.

Another small pebble hit the window. The sign that Lohrna had used since they were kids for Sella to wake up, and usually, get into some kind of mischief with her. Sella had an idea about what Lohrna wanted to get up today. But she didn't want to participate.

"She's going to break it," Beejee tapped Sella's cheek with his paw, claws still sheathed. "Wake up."

Sella groaned and pushed the blankets off. She waved her hand and little flames burst brightly throughout the room. In the fireplace, the dying embers erupted into a roaring fire, fending off the darkness and the cold. She sat up and stretched, yawning loudly.

Beejee glared at her, as if her body's protest to being awoken so early was inexcusable. He hurried silently over to the desk and looked out the window below. He hissed at the figure below, even though he knew that Lohrna couldn't hear.

Sella gave him a quick pat and put on her boots. She was still in her crumbled nightdress. Beejee was right, she would continue to escalate her choice in rocks. And the window was old. She hurried down the steps to let her friend in.

"Practical Potions Consultants are open for business!" Lohrna practically shouted when Sella opened the door.

"Shhh!" Sella grabbed Lohrna's arm, doing her best to be gentle, yet forceful, as she pulled her into the shop. "I think we're supposed to be discreet."

Lohrna laughed a little. "Yeah, yeah. No one's awake yet. Come on, let's talk suspects!" Her friend bounded up the stairs and Sella followed behind her with hunched, sleepy, shoulders. "Can you brew me up some confidence, please?" Lohrna said when Sella closed the door behind her.

Sella raised a brow at her. She yawned. "Confidence?"

Lohrna nodded. "MAMBOSSA has been going well," she said. "But… I could just use the confidence. It's kind of a lot. And if I want to help solve the greatest mystery Opora's ever seen, I'll need all I can get."

Beejee and Sella exchanged a quick glance but stayed quiet. Sella got to work at her counter, heating the pot of water and searching her cabinet for the right proportions. Confidence. The idea of making a cup of it for Lohrna seemed so backwards. She found a small jar labeled 'I got this'. She added a few spoonfuls of the bright yellow spell to the pot.

The room filled with the rich smell of chocolate, hints of

cinnamon, and a lingering spice. Sella breathed in deeply and held her hands on the pot, enjoying the heat and the comforting aroma. She wished for her friend to feel about herself the way she felt about her. Powerful. Kind. Unique.

She hoped, for a fleeting moment, that none of her sleepiness or craving to crawl back into the warmth of her bed made it into the pot.

She opened her eyes, the metal of the pot glowing a faint red at her touch. "How *is* everything going with MAMBOSSA?" she asked, cautiously. The last time they talked about it hadn't ended well. She still tried to recount exactly where she went wrong, but couldn't find it. She wanted to tread lightly.

The blend was finished and she poured a large serving into a teal cup.

Lohrna took a deep breath in. She looked up at the rafters and sipped the coffee. "It's going. It's a lot of rules... Did you know there's a different fork for salads and side dishes? Anyway, what's in this? Something spicy..."

Sella noted the quick change in conversation. She knew there would be no fighting it. Lohrna talked about what Lohrna wanted to talk about. If it was one of her intense, various hobbies, or what spices Sella used, it didn't matter. The MAMBOSSA discussion would have to wait.

"Secret ingredient," Sella said quickly. It wasn't a secret at all. But she wanted to avoid giving her friend too much information and their conversation becoming so meandering they'd miss the rocky foundation. She sat across the table and held her hands in her lap. "Your mom told you about the fake ladle, then?"

Lohrna nodded. She took another long drink. "But I

don't think anyone's caught on yet. Hazen says it's a good replica."

Of course she had already talked to Hazen, Sella thought with a quick half smile. Lohrna had a way of getting things done in a way Sella had never been able to accomplish. "Well, that's good. Tallam's a professional, I suppose. I gave him every piece of gold I had. I'm glad he's put it into good use."

"Sorry about that," Lohrna said. "I heard you had to get rid of your kelpie?"

Sella nodded. "It was time. A gift from a different life," she said. "I don't want to remember banishing anything. Ghosts or otherwise."

Lohrna looked around the flat. She mouthed 'Cali'?

Sella shook her head. "She's gone for now," she said. She rested her chin in her hand and yawned again, trying her best to stifle it. She was grateful that Lohrna was here. Grateful that things felt like a time much more simple, and also more horrible— back when they were trying to solve Cali's murder. She remembered the three of them sitting at this table a year ago, coming up with theories, and swapping information.

It felt so distant. Like a faded memory of a dream.

Lohrna, unaware of Sella's tired mind floating away went on, "And apparently, the new witch in town is telling Penya her statues are 'intellectual property of Kepilla'? What even does that mean?"

Sella hung her head. She had forgotten about Penya. She grumbled to herself, then sat back up straighter. "That's what Kepilla does," she said. "They come into town and drive all the other magic out. Since they're called Kepilla, they probably want to avoid anything sea monster related getting customers confused… As if anyone would think the hotel is affiliated with them…" She looked up at the dusty rafters and sighed.

"Seems like a stretch. Kepilla are a silly legend," Lohrna said. "No one actually believes in them."

"That's why it's an especially dirty move on Sediri's part. She doesn't need to be so ruthless about it. I've never heard of them going this far about something like this. It's all so… brutal." She wanted to go on, to tell Lohrna that Sediri had tried to get Cali to turn on her, that her grackle was snooping about, that she had seen Branzo threaten her. But she waited. She didn't want to sweep her friend away with everything all at once.

Lohrna shrugged. "Well," she said, "everyone in town, the locals anyway, are all saying good riddance to the things. But Penya's in a state of distress about it. I never knew the old woman could even move like that. She's going around town telling everyone who will listen about it."

Sella bit her lip. She had seen Penya rise up and shout, just once. When Lohrna's arrest in the hotel lobby ruined her nap. Sella did her best to forget everything about that night. But like a slow tide, it kept creeping up on her when she thought she was safe. Even now, her fingertips burned as anger and fear flooded into her.

"Calm down," Beejee said at her feet.

Sella blinked, hard.

"What's wrong?" Lohrna asked. "You think Sediri did it, don't you? She's come to town, and trying to shut you down, take away the statues. I'll bet she took the ladle just to make Marra look bad."

Sella shook her head. She opened her eyes. "I don't want to blame Sediri for the ladle just because of my personal feelings about her. She'd have no reason to do that, not really. But I do need to talk to her and just see what I can figure out. At this point, the list of my grievances with her is growing long."

"I'll hold down that stupid bird while you talk to her," Beejee said. He jumped onto the table. "The awful beast has been flapping about town, leaving… *droppings* like he's a common pigeon. Disgusting. And, he's been harassing Koukie."

Lohrna's eyes grew wide. "Koukie? But she's the sweetest!"

Beejee looked at her with narrowed eyes. "I'm aware," he said. "The damn grackle has taken up a small war against the cats in town. I think some of them are trying to hunt him. As they would any bird. He should understand if he thinks he's above the common animal. Horrible familiar."

"Well, I mean, if he's defending himself, I guess I can't blame him too much." A little laugh escaped from Lohrna as she set her head in her hand. She looked at Beejee with an easy smile. "Poor Koukie, though."

Beejee stomped his paw. "It's a cat's right to hunt and prowl. The damn bird has got to be more reasonable. He should go perch somewhere high if he's so concerned."

Sella held her hands between the two, waving a little. "Can we get back to the stolen item that will apparently ruin the town? What did Hazen have to say?"

"Nothing really," Lohrna shifted effortlessly. Confidence was kicking in. "He had the place all locked up. And he's a light sleeper. He has a guess, but I don't think it's a good one."

"What's his guess?"

Lohrna finished her cup before answering. "Spicy. I love it," she whispered. Then, louder, she went on, "Hazen and Cirian say they know Branzo. Well, Cirian, mostly. He says he's kind of a pompous jerk, actually, and that he's probably bitter that they had to move the location of Opora from his town to Marra. You know, the decrease in revenue and prestige for his town and all that. They think he took it to make Marra look bad."

Sella thought about it for a moment. That wasn't exactly the worst plan, if he really was so concerned about fame and glory. She shrugged. "Seems like a good guess to me. If I was a mayor worried about these things… I'm just saying, it makes sense."

Lohrna sighed. "I don't know. I don't see it. But then again, I didn't see Isra being a cold blooded killer either. So what do I know?"

Isra. Sella's fingers grew hot remembering their ordeal a year before. A young witch with no one in town… She had murdered Cali when she saw her witch's mark, a curse leaving her face scarred to the eyes of any witch. Sella hadn't understood why she had resorted to such a drastic course of action then, and she still didn't all this time after. But, there was a part of her, her heart, she realized in that moment, that hurt thinking about her locked away in a cell, alone and unable to use magic.

None of it was fair. Not really.

"I trust your gut, though," Sella said at last. The words came out instinctively. She had said the first thing she could to break her thoughts. "But I have to admit, Branzo probably couldn't get in without a witch's help."

"True," Beejee said. "Let's arrest Sediri and be done with both scandals at the same time."

Sella flicked at his ear. "Alright, so Branzo wants Marra's reputation stained for taking the fame away from his town. That's a good lead. Even if he isn't responsible, maybe someone close to him is? Maybe a shifter?"

Lohrna's eyes narrowed. "What's that mean?"

"Not like you... I mean someone who can shift into something small, easy to get in and out of a place."

"It wasn't a full moon." Lohrna crossed her arms.

"Some can shift at will," Sella said. Her tone was careful. She looked away. "They don't tend to announce it, but I've heard of them in my travels."

Lohrna stood quickly, her arms down at her sides.

Sella's gaze followed them down to Lohrna's clenched fists.

"Right, *your travels*. Sometimes I forget about how much more educated and well versed you are on *my* experience. You got to leave this place and learn so much about shifters, huh?"

Beejee positioned himself behind Sella's legs. She felt his fur at her ankle, it felt like needles, like her skin was on fire.

"I'm sorry, Lohr—"

"No." Lohrna's fingers loosened. Her shoulders slumped. "You're right, you know more about this than me. You know a lot more about a lot of things. That's just the way it is." Lohrna looked away, eyes fixed to the floor. "And you don't trust the new shifters in town. No one does. I get it."

"It's not that—"

"No, Sella. It is." Lohrna picked up her coat from the back of the couch and threw it over herself. "It's fine. Lucky for you, I was the one that got bitten that night."

Lohrna's words hit her like a punch. Sella stepped back, practically tripping on Beejee's small body.

Lohrna went on, eyes fierce, "I'll see what they know. With actual tact."

Sella's mouth opened, then shut. Her hand was still outstretched as the door slammed shut behind Lohrna.

Beejee returned to face Sella with narrowed eyes. "Well, that went poorly," he said.

Sella deflated. She pushed away the sting of tears at the corners of her eyes. "Thanks, Beejee. Helpful." She melted into the couch and covered her face with her arms. She took a big deep breath in. As she exhaled, the little fires all quieted.

Beejee curled up beside her and purred gently.

"I keep messing things up," Sella grumbled.

"Try again tomorrow," Beejee said.

THIRTEEN

The Busy Bee Blend

THE WARM SMELL of cinnamon and apple spread through the small space as Sella pulled a tray of scones from the fire-fueled oven. She examined them, looking at each for any sign of imperfection, a burnt corner, or a stray apple seed. Finally satisfied, she placed them down on the counter under little cloths to protect the dark wood.

From the corner of the room, she heard a small voice. "It'll never not amaze me how you can hold hot things like that without a cloth to protect you."

Sella smiled, though her heart had skipped at Cali's sudden presence. "I'll take it. I need a win today," she said.

"That bad?" Cali asked. She drifted toward the kitchen with a kind smile. Her green eyes were narrowed, though. As if she was prepared to fight someone.

Sella wondered for a moment if that ferocity was truly for her. Her heart felt like it had expanded in her chest. She breathed through the rush, filling her nose with the sweet aroma of her all night baking session. She looked back at the scones before her stomach grew any more giddy. "It wasn't a great evening," she said at last.

Cali leaned across the counter. "I'm listening," she said.

Sella shook her head. "No, tell me about your night. How are the tenets?"

"And where is Koukie?" Beejee demanded. He jumped up on the counter to face the ghost with a stern expression that only a cat could truly muster.

Cali's brows rose as her gaze shifted to Beejee. "I'm not sure. I figured she'd be here."

Beejee snorted, a small, silly sound from his little pink nose. Still, he faced the round window as if completely disinterested.

Cali looked back at Sella and shrugged silently. "They're not getting the hint," she said. "I can't seem to do much there though. I can't get a sheet over my head at all. Or even move too much around… I think they think it's just drafty in there with all the slamming cabinet doors. It's infuriating."

Though, to Sella, her tone sounded more amused than anything. She offered, "It sounds infuriating, for sure."

Cali waved her hand. "They have a terrible decorating style too," she said. "It's so… not cozy in there. Not like here."

"We'll figure this out, Cali." Sella said as she sprinkled small crystals of sugar on top of the scones. They caught the firelight as they stuck to the dough, making each one shimmer.

"What's in them?" Cali asked, changing the subject as usual when things got too close to anything really going on with her. She sniffed them dramatically. "Oooo, cinnamon apple."

"And calm," Sella added.

Cali nodded. "Good call. The old folks here need it."

"And so do I," Sella said. "Lohrna was over last night…"

Sella spent the next few moments explaining her evening with Lohrna to Cali. She tried to keep it neutral, but she knew her words were charged despite herself.

Cali's mouth drew into a thin line. "Sella," she said. It sounded like scolding.

"I know," the witch countered, hands up. "You don't need to tell me I didn't handle it well."

Cali smiled, a little wickedly. "That wasn't what I was going to say," she said. "I was going to say that sounds like a tough situation. On one side of the thorn, you're right. You do need to figure this out sooner than later, and it *is* possible for shifters to change outside the moon cycle. So your theory could make sense. Aaaand, on the other side, yes, you could have been more considerate in your wording. And, to her credit, at least in Tollintal, it's really, really rare to hear about a shifter who can change like that. But I suppose most of them take the suppressant potion there."

"No, it's really almost unheard of in Orakan too." Sella hung her head over the scones. She rolled her neck and sighed. "I don't know what I was thinking."

"Can I make a suggestion?"

Sella looked up through her lashes. "Go for it."

Cali leaned in closer. She reached for Sella's closed fists. "I think you're feeling a bit worried about Lohrna. And the reasons for that are complicated. You're missing her, maybe even preemptively, because she talked about going away with the society. You're jealous, too."

Sella raised a brow.

"Yes, you are. I know you. Tell her you're sorry, and ask what she found out. She loves you. And… maybe more," Cali added mischievously, "she loves a good mystery. I think she'll be excited if you are. She was the one who pushed you to take Benka's job in the first place."

Sella knew she was right. Cali often was. She felt the ghost's cold touch on her fingers and closed her eyes. "I wish Opora was over already."

"Days to go. And another witch to deal with until then."

"Ugh," Sella's lids squeezed shut tighter. "I do not want to think about Sediri and her ridiculousness right now."

"Then don't," Cali whispered. "Think about my problem for now. How to make me more… real. The answer is out there. And, if it helps, I seem to come alive around you."

Sella felt a light touch at her jawline, like the tickle of a spider's silk landing on her skin. Then, she felt a shock on her lips. Her blood crackled. Her eyes flew open and Cali was inches from her, a simple laugh already escaping from her as she shimmered out of sight.

Cali was gone and the emptiness of her disappearance felt like standing at the edge of a cliff. Like there was just the vastness of the end of the world and nothing but the ocean head. Like she wanted to jump, but she knew it was impossible. Like she couldn't quite comprehend the scope of what she saw. The empty room. Expansive in its plainness. "What..?" Sella started, lifting her hands to her face.

"That was a kiss, you idiot," Beejee said from across the room. "Finally."

. . .

SELLA STARED at the customer with a blank expression. She hadn't been able to shake the feeling of heat in her veins from her all morning. Not that she actually wanted to. But it felt like she was swimming through murky water. She was sure she knew where she was going, but she couldn't see the destination yet.

She had gone over the conversation again and again. Reimagined the spark at her lips again and again. She had puzzled through every word that she could remember, trying to figure out what had happened, and why. Why then? Was it a custom in Tollintal that she didn't know about, like their weird way of shaking hands?

The customer, a human, blinked at Sella with a confused look. She looked behind her, then back again. "So about the potions?" she offered cautiously.

"Sorry!" Sella said quickly. She was holding two separate potions, one labeled, 'Busy Bee' the other 'Get Things Done'.

"What's the difference between the two?" the human asked again. Her tone was sweet, but her brows knit together as she spoke, as if trying to see just how far out to sea Sella had drifted away.

Sella held 'Busy Bee' up to the light that shone through the shop window. It glittered gold. "This one is honey based, you add it to your drink and it provides a quick, but stable productivity." She held the other up, its dull color looked sad by comparison. "This one is for serious productivity. Hyper-focus. If you have a deadline to worry about, this is the one you need."

The human held a finger to her chin and hummed. "I

like the idea of both… But perhaps hyperfocus might not be what I'm really in the market for." She trailed off for a moment, pausing at length as her eyes bounced between the two. "You have some really interesting options here. Kepilla down the way is just selling coffee to go with the basics mixed in. No ambiance like in here." Her eyes moved to the little tables where a few customers, mostly Orakanians, horns and antlers adoring their heads, sat chatting. The sound of music and clinking cups filled the space with warmth and heart.

To Sella, at least, today the shop felt like home.

Thank you," she said, trying to stifle the grin at her small victory. "I pride myself on my unique and effective blends." She gestured to the counter behind them. "I'm also selling cinnamon and apple scones infused with calm."

"I'm calm enough, that's the problem," the woman said without missing a beat.

Sella thought for a moment, looking between the two potions. "I have an idea, if you're willing to wait," she said.

The woman nodded and Sella turned quickly toward the other end of the shop. She ducked behind the counter and found an empty bottle. She combined the two potions together, watching the brilliant yellow fade to a deep amber. She shook it and then rose from her squat. She adjusted the metal pot until it was firmly in her grasp. She breathed in deeply, smelling the sweet scent of honey, and felt her fingers warm as she set the intention.

Productivity. And… bravery.

Whatever this woman was looking for, she was sure that she was too. Sometimes when people said they were calm but had a lot to do, what they actually were was anxious. There was a point when the to-do list, instead of panic, reached a state of serene acceptance that absolutely nothing at all would get done.

She was certain she was right. She had seen it in the woman's eyes. Heard it in her quick tone. She wasn't calm at all. She was on a river of calm, battered about by stones of worry.

Honey and clove filled the air. A few customers turned their noses toward the back of the store as Sella opened her eyes. She smiled. "I think *this* might be what you're looking for," she called to the woman.

The human smiled back. "It does smell amazing."

Sella poured her a cup, then packaged up the remaining potion in a small velvet bag, a recommendation from Beejee to make their sales feel more prestigious.

The woman smiled brightly at the bag. "How cute!"

The cat might have been on to something.

She left coins on the counter and sipped from the cup without any of the cautious hesitation that most Marrans did when they drank her coffee. It was nice to see someone just taste it without the long glance at her as though it may be positioned. "It's good," she said brightly. "Thanks for the speciality blend."

"Anytime." Sella was busy pouring herself her own mug. She needed the extra boost. So much had happened in such a short time that she hadn't even realized she had become paralyzed. Warmth and courage flowed into her as she drank.

Between Sediri and the ladle, things felt like they were

closing in around her. But as she drank her cup, an idea began to form in her mind. One she was actually mad at herself for not thinking of sooner. It was a long shot, but she knew what she had to do.

FOURTEEN

Always Awful, Always Wise

THE SHOP WAS COMING to a close and the night festival began to sound loudly in the streets. Sella peaked out from the door and down the cobblestone road where a crowd was forming and heading toward Hazen's tavern. She squinted but couldn't recognize any of the faces. The locals had probably already made their way to the tavern, eager to claim their usual seats.

She shut the door and locked it with a flick of her wrist.

"It was a good day," Beejee said from his pillow at the bay window. His nose was pressed up against the glass, watching people pass by. "We could stay open late. Capitalize on the… stumbling crowd."

Sella raised a brow at him. She swatted her hands on her long black shirt, shaking off various powders that had accumulated there throughout the day. "No, I actually have something I need to do, and it's urgent."

Beejee turned to her. "What could you possibly have to do other than see the winner of the latest fish off?" His tone was sarcastic but she knew his question was serious none-theless.

"I have to go to The Library. Tonight," she said quickly before he could interrupt. She was already halfway to the end of the store.

"The Library? It closes at dawn, you'll never make it in time. And why do you need to go to *The Library?*"

Sella took the steps up to their room two at a time.

Beejee was right behind.

"I need to see if I can find a spell to help Cali," she said as she opened the door and began to rummage through her wardrobe for a clean dress. "She's relying on me to help her and I haven't been able to find anything here. If I don't figure this out soon–"

"What?" Beejee demanded. He stood on her bed to get a better look at her. "She'll what? Disappear?"

"She told me Sediri came to her," Sella said. She suddenly stopped, realizing only now that the bravery she felt was mixing with fear. She was worried. And confused. But this was a chance to save her shop and bring Cali her voice. At least, there was the possibility of an answer now, no matter how slim the odds. She had found nothing in her books, or her mother's. Seaglass hadn't been any help. But this? It was something.

"What did that witch want?" Beejee asked once Sella calmed herself. He looked her in the eyes and waited.

"She said she'd give Cali a spell to make her stronger, give her the ability to talk to non-witches." Sella paused. She hung her head a moment, considering the options. "If she helps take me down."

"She'd never–"

"It's not that," Sella cut in. "I know she wouldn't. She told me as much…. It's not that."

Beejee jumped from the bed to the couch. He caught her eyes and tilted his head. "I understand," he said solemnly. "But you won't make it in time tonight. I know you think it needs to happen tonight, but we still have time until the festival is over."

"I don't know what else to do…" Sella said. Her voice broke.

Beejee pushed his head into her hand dangling at her side. She rubbed his chin as he did and smiled a little though the tears. "Go tomorrow, before sunset so you actually get there with time to spare," her familiar purred.

"Tomorrow's already too late. We're running out of time—"

Beejee, still looking out the window, cut her off, "You won't be able to go now. I'm glad you finally came up with a plan, but the timing is wrong. Besides, even if you made it by tonight and had time to find what you're looking for, you'd be back by mid morning. Long after the coffee rush."

Sella sighed. "That hardly seems like it matters right now, though."

Beejee went on, "Have Lohrna help me with the shop. That way, you have a way to start talking to her again. I'll get the information out of her about the shifter society. Since you bungled the job so badly."

Sella grumbled in response.

"You know she'll take any chance to talk *my* ears off."

Sella chuckled despite herself. She tucked a lock of dark hair behind her pointed ear. "Yeah, that's probably true."

Lohrna had been trying to win Beejee over since they

were small children. She knew Beejee loved her, even if he faked hostility. Now that he could talk, Lohrna was determined to get him to admit it. It would definitely sweeten the deal if it was just the two of them running the shop, even if Sella wasn't on her bad side at the moment.

Still, they hadn't had any disagreement or miscommunication like this since they were little. Then again, she had been gone a long time.

Beejee went on before Sella could go further down her thought spiral, "She likes feeling useful. Part of the problem is that you made her feel like she was only useful to you as a shifter. Not as a friend."

Sella looked down at her familiar, brows raised. "You know, sometimes, you're awfully wise."

"I'm always awful, always wise." Beejee trotted to the round window. "Oh good, Koukie's here. Tell her what you just said so she'll listen to me and break things off with the alley cats."

Sella folded up her clean dress and set it on the writing desk to let the fluffy orange cat in.

Koukie squeezed through the opening, fur expanding her to twice her size in one big poof once she was through. She looked up at Sella and meowed.

Half of her wondered, for a moment, if Beejee had delayed just so she wouldn't forget their dinner. She patted the other cat on her back and her tail went up.

"I got you," she said quietly as Beejee began to scold her.

"You're late for dinner, *again*. And you smell like trash. Clean yourself."

Koukie only meowed lazily at Sella, then passed Beejee like she wasn't listening and rested by the fireplace.

"Everyone ignores my genius!" Beejee yowled.

"Not me this time," Sella said as she scooped bits of left-over chicken onto plates for the cats. "You're right. Your plan is better."

"Finally someone with sense! Do me another favor and go see what terrible noise is outside and secure Lohrna to watch the shop tomorrow."

Sella placed the food on the floor. "You got it," she said.

And while she had the burst of inspiration and bravery, she decided to find the new tenants at the tavern too.

FIFTEEN

Don't Fight the Undertow

THE TAVERN WAS FULL, as usual, but the MAMBOSSA was easy to spot. They clustered like a school of fish in the corner, as if they were safer in numbers. When one moved, the others followed in a pattern.

Sella caught Hazen's gaze and decided to ignore the group for now. She'd need to check in with him, and get a drink, before she was ready to talk to them.

"Did I miss the winner of the day's challenge?" Sella asked as she squeezed into an opening at the bartop.

Hazen smiled behind his thick beard. "Some human named Erena won. Caught twenty three fish in the day…" He trailed off as he poured Sella a glass of wine. "Remember when we Wyldes used to win all of these challenges?" It was a rhetorical question, Sella knew. She simply nodded as he went on. "The humans are really stepping up this year."

A half smile crossed Sella's lips. "Humans are amazing," she said. "Just think of Cali."

"True," Hazen said. "I know she's around… In whatever form she's in now. But I still miss her telling me my papers are all in disarray. Or that I'm bad with my coin."

"Speaking of," Sella said as she leaned across the counter a little. "Which one of these folks are the new tenants that moved to Cali's old place? A little odd that there's new actual tenants, not just travelers, don't you think?"

Hazen's back straightened, he scanned the crowd. "They keep to themselves. Some folks from the north, if I remember what Ovina said."

"Can you tell me about them?"

"No, I don't know much. But they're over there," Hazen gestured with a tilt of his head. "It's been hard to keep things straight. Right after they moved in, Opora was announced."

Sella turned to see two Orakanians huddled together at the end of the bar. One was standing, arm around the other who sat hunched over in the stool. Both looked a little sleepy, with visible bags under their eyes. The woman in the chair tossed her choppy yellow hair from her eyes, it tangled in her small antlers and the other woman fixed it carefully with long, graceful fingers. She smiled at the one in the chair warmly, her own horns reached up to the ceiling from either side of her head. Her bright blue eyes flicked to Sella's as if sensing her stare.

Sella tried to make it look casual, as though she were simply surveying the room. "I'm guessing they would've been the talk of the town if Opora hadn't happened," she said, sipping her wine as she looked purposefully away from the two. "It's weird someone moved in right before all this."

Hazen scrubbed a spot on the counter with a damp rag.

"Marra is a lovely town," he said. "After all, I settled here. Cirian seems like he's planning on staying a while. Maybe the festival will inspire more people to stay here once it's done."

"That's true. I guess I never really asked how you came to be here," she said. The realization made her cringe. "Cirian just refuses to tell me his story."

"My story for a night when I'm not the host," he said, looking down the bar at a few people trying to get his attention. Hazen ran a hand over his beard. His eyes shifted to the golden ladle behind them.

Sella's glance followed. "It's fine," she whispered. "Don't fight the undertow."

"Just float," Hazen nodded, his body seemed to relax finally. He took in a deep breath and turned to Branzo, who was still atop a table, telling some kind of story that required both hands flailing about in the air. "I'm not sure about this one," he whispered, continuing to ignore the few out of towners trying to refill their drinks.

Sella twisted her body around to get a better look at the mayor.

Branzo was gesturing madly, shouting about something that was clearly fascinating to an eagerly listening group. But she couldn't make out what he was saying among the din around them.

She shook her head. "He's definitely something," she murmured through her cup.

Hazen was already pulled away by another customer when she turned back. She sighed. She wasn't sure how she was planning to make her way to the other end of the bar and say hello to the two who had just moved in.

She thought about just passing by, accidentally bumping the standing one on the shoulder. But what would she say? 'Oh, sorry! By the way, does your new living space feel haunted, because it is'? Or, 'Hello, sorry I was staring. It's just, I know the ghost haunting you. She wants you out'?

Sella looked down at her cup. Nothing was right. There was no really good way of doing it. But she owed it to Cali to try. She downed her cup, slid it to the edge of the bar so Hazen wouldn't need to reach for it. She made her way through the crowd to the couple at the end of the bar.

Sella kept her gaze low, but she couldn't help but notice that the blue eyed woman was watching her. This wasn't going to be smooth, or easy.

She felt her heart begin to beat faster as she pushed through the last set of bodies to them. She and the other woman's eyes finally locked. The woman on the stool turned, her hair falling into her eyes as she did. "You're the local witch?" she said before Sella could even begin.

Sella's heart slowed, though her hands grew warm. She nodded. "I am."

"Our house is haunted," the woman said. "We need a banishing spell."

Sella let out her breath. The way to start the conversation was, as it turned out, easy. "I know. But I'm sorry, I can't banish this ghost."

"Then we'll go to the other witch," the woman with blue eyes said. She held her grip on the bar tightly.

Sella's vision tunneled. "You can't!" she whispered. She leaned in closely, steadied herself and went on, "The ghost that haunts you… she's special to this town. Everyone here, the locals all know and love her. Please, let me talk to her, don't go to the other witch. She's not from here. She won't understand."

The woman on the stool looked up at the other. "A *local* ghost, Ipla? That's exciting." She sounded genuine, despite her tired expression.

As if the ghost would be anything but local.

Ipla, with eyes as fierce as before, looked from her partner to Sella. Her shoulders sank a bit. "Who are we kidding? You were our last hope," she said. "We talked to the landlady and she just said it's 'part of the house's charm.' Apparently, all of the other homes on that street are not quite suitable for long term living."

"Yes," the other woman said quickly. "Plus, she's rented out all the others for Opora. And when we called her out on it, she said it's only because they're short term rentals."

"You won't go to the other witch, then?" Sella asked, one brow raised.

"No," Ipla said with a heavy head. She looked down at the floor for a moment, then her intense stare was back on Sella. "We already asked her…"

The other woman jumped in after Ipla trailed off. "She said it's outside of the contract she holds with whatever ridiculous company she works for," she spoke with a breathy but quick voice, it reminded Sella of the shallow creek in the woods. Quick, quiet, clear. "She also *heavily* implied she thought we might be secretly spies for the company. But at least she gave us a discount coffee for our troubles."

Sella could laugh. It wasn't unheard of for Kepilla to send what they called 'poltergeist patrons', folks who would come into shops specifically to ask for things off menu or for practices to occur outside of the shop walls. Sediri must have been genuinely worried that Kepilla was watching her closely if she turned them down, even knowing what she knew.

"Neither of us will be able to help you the way you're expecting," Sella said. "But there's other ways I can be of service." She caught Hazen's attention and held up two fingers, indicating to refill their drinks.

He nodded back and got to work.

"This round is on me, alright? I'm Sella, and I'm sorry we're meeting on this note… I'm the original witch here. My mom used to own Practical Potions and Honey. I can make you speciality blends to help calm you in the home. And, I can see the ghost who haunts you. She's known here, and beloved. I promise we can make this situation work for everyone."

Both women simply looked at Sella. From behind her, she heard Branzo's loud voice booming. She glanced behind her to see him now violently waving a butter knife to a captive audience. It was clearly quite the story. Sella rolled her eyes and turned back to the two.

Hazen placed the three mugs of frothing liquid in front of the group and Sella fished out a few coins from her pocket. Hazen winked at her as he took her silver and moved on.

At last, Ipla took her mug. "I'm Ipla," she said. With her free hand, she held the shoulder of the woman beside her. "This is Rizan. We'll take you up on that speciality brew."

"Even though we've heard a thing or two about spots," Rizan said with a light, bubbling laugh. She rubbed one eye and sipped her own mug. "We'll need something to help sleep through slamming cabinets."

Sella did her best not to flinch at the mention of *The Incident*. She tapped the counter with her fingers gently and then picked up her mug. She pulled it close to her chest. "Come by soon, I'll craft the perfect blend for you both, I promise."

"We'll hold you to that," Ipla said, kindly but firmly.

Sella nodded. "Have a good evening," she said and turned back to face the roaring crowd. All at once, the noise of the large room filled her ears. She noticed Sediri on the far wall talking, what appeared to be begrudgingly, to a fisherman. She had a bored expression but the fisherman was holding her elbow and waving his drink about.

She saw Branzo, now wielding two butter knives aloft on the table, his captive audience beginning to look more and more like they were actually held hostage.

A few locals clustered by a high table, squinting at the scene like everyone around them were made of worms.

Sella took in a breath so deep, her lungs stung. She tried to focus her attention. Not everything needed to be dealt with right now, no matter the sense of urgency she felt in her bones.

Now, it was time to talk to Lohrna, if she'd have it. She glanced back at MAMBOSSA and found Lohrna at the outskirts of the group. Her friend was looking at them all expectantly, bouncing a little on light feet as each of them took turns speaking. She reminded Sella of a lost child, eagerly looking for acceptance among adults. She felt a stab in her heart but pushed through the crowd anyway.

For all she knew, she was entirely misreading the situation. She had done so before and paid the consequence. She tried to keep an open mind as she came closer.

"Hey, Lohr..." she said quietly when she reached the edge of the group. She held her glass with both hands, thankful to have something to do with them so she felt less awkward.

"Good evening," Mims answered.

The group parted for him so that it was just him and Sella staring at each other.

"Hello," Sella said. She pulled her glass closer to her body and looked up at him with what she hoped was a neutral expression, despite her annoyance. "Good to see you, Mims."

"Sella," he said with a tilt of his head. "How is the evening treating you?"

"Lovely, thanks." Her eyes narrowed as she glanced around his massive frame. "If I could borrow Lohrna for a moment?"

Mims smiled, but it didn't quite reach his eyes. Unlike when Cali did the same, however, his expression felt sinister rather than trying to avoid a difficult subject.

Sella squared her shoulders. In her hands, the ceramic of the cup warmed.

His eyes flicked to her hands, then back up to her. "Of course," he said, moving slightly so Lohrna could pass. "We'll save the pleasantries for another time, then."

Lohrna waved to the group gleefully as if she had witnessed nothing but a casual conversation and not what Sella perceived as the start of something dark. She joined Sella and the two of them maneuvered to the other side of the tavern. As they passed Branzo's table, she overheard a loud part of his tale.

"Those pixies were coming back in swarms every new moon!"

Sella picked up her pace. She wasn't sure she cared to hear where this story was going. If it was about Penya's hotel or something else, she was in no mood for pixie talk.

When they reached a more quiet space by a large pillar, she turned to Lohrna who was already talking, "I haven't really learned anything—"

"That's not what I wanted to say, actually," Sella smiled gently. She looked down at her feet. "I was actually wondering if you wouldn't mind tending to the shop with Beejee for a few hours tomorrow. We can't close with Sediri in town like this, and I need to run an errand."

Lohrna looked at her quizzically, she cocked her head slightly. "Are you being purposefully vague so I have to talk to you more?"

"Is it working?"

Lohrna stared at Sella with stern eyes for a moment.

Sella's blood turned cold. She waited.

Then, the corners of Lohrna's eyes crinkled. "Oh, fine! You win! What's the secret mission?"

Sella explained her plan as Lohrna listened attentively. "Good plan, good plan," she said. "But, do you really think The Library will have a spell for you? It's not exactly their thing."

"No, it's not," Sella said. "But, folks have been known to collect witch's spell books. Maybe there's one in there. It's a long shot but I have to try."

Lohrna nodded. She tapped a finger at her chin. "Yes, you do have to. And yes, I'll help you with the shop tomorrow. Any excuse to talk to Beejee."

Relief flooded into Sella's joints. She felt like she could collapse as all the pent up tension suddenly fled her body. This conversation felt like them again. She was grateful Lohrna never held her anger long. "Thank you," she said. She wanted to add: For the help. For forgiving her. For being her friend. But Lohrna was already on to her next wild thought.

She turned, a mess of black curls narrowly missing hitting Sella's face. "Pixies!" she hissed, though no one around her could hear. "The pixies! Bring a pixie with you!" She turned back to Sella. "That Branzo is insufferable, but he's got the right idea. Well, he gave me the right idea."

"I don't think I want to bring a pixie with me anywhere, let alone in The Library."

Lohrna grabbed one of Sella's hands quickly. "No, remember the story my mom used to tell us about the hotel? About Rukus, the pixie."

"I think that's just a story," Sella said.

"It's worth asking," Lohrna squeezed Sella's hand. "I'm not mad at you right now but you're in deep waters."

"Fair enough," Sella said. "I'm with you."

"Come on, let's go see Penya."

SIXTEEN

The Art of Finding the Unfindable

Sella and Lohrna stood before the large double doors of the hotel. It was the one building in all of Marra that looked entirely out of place. It reached tall over the town like a watchtower. The gray stone and tile roof contrasted the red and brown brick of the buildings nearby with their cozy thatched roofs and stained glass windows.

The two siren statues at the entrance began to sing a low, creepy song.

"Time to go in before it rains," Lohrna said as she pushed one of the doors open. She led the way inside quickly just as a droplet landed on Sella's brow.

The hotel lobby was vast, warm, and bright despite the dark chill that had begun to settle in outside. The ceiling entryway stretched up two stories, with white beams across the top accented by vibrant green vibes that wove their way down as if they were stretching for the warmth below.

A large fireplace covered all of the left wall with a tall iron guard surrounding it. Stacks of dusty, old books were grouped just far enough away from the flames in piles a little too high to be stable. Carefully placed signs hung from each stack with ornate lettering no longer reading 'free to good home' as they had all Sella's life, but now replaced with entirely too expensive pricing.

Out of towners, seemingly all who were not at the tavern, were lined up beside the fire chatting and drinking from glistening ceramic mugs. Sella eyed the cups closely for the signature stamp of Kepilla. But Lohrna ushered her to the other wall before she could spot any.

In the small desk, Penya sat with crossed arms and a sour expression. She glowered at them. "Well, what have you done about my statutes?" she asked before either of them could even start with a 'hello'.

"Nothing yet—" Sella started.

"But! We will promise that the new witch won't touch them, *if*," Lohrna said, stressing the 'if' at length, "you help *us* with something."

"Does it have anything to do with the golden—"

Lohrna's hands flew up, waving wildly as she hushed the old woman. "Penya!" she hissed. "No, it doesn't. Tides! Keep it together. Not everyone is…" She winked dramatically. "…in the know, you know?"

Penya waved her own wrinkled, frail hands back. "No one is listening anyway," she said. She looked at Sella. "Your mother put a spell on this desk. I can hardly hear a thing out there, and they can't hear us here."

Sella's ears twitched. Now that Penya had mentioned it, it was true, she couldn't hear any of the chatter, the crackling fire, or … anything. It was unnervingly quiet.

Lohrna exchanged a glance with Sella. "Well, that explains how you're able to sleep through everything and anything…" she mumbled.

Penya frowned. "I'm old. I need sleep." She crossed her arms again. "Now if only your mother had made an actually useful enchantment so I *could* hear when someone is snooping through my office."

"Snooping through your office?" Lohrna prompted. "What happened? Pixies get your office?"

Penya spit, a small little *tut* sound. "Don't be worrying about my pixies. Or my office. The spell works too well. That's all I'm saying." She thrust her head up to get a better look at them as if they were the ones who had bothered her things. "What do you two need help with?"

Sella's eyes narrowed slightly. She wasn't so sure that the comment about her office was nothing. Penya's office had been disturbed? She was about to ask when Lohrna smiled brightly and said, "Actually, just a pixie. We know you have never been able to get rid of them here. We're looking for just one."

Penya grunted in reply.

"The pixie named Rukus?" Lohrna went on. "The one who can find lost things."

"I know who Rukus is," Penya said gruffly. "What do you want with the pixie?"

Lohrna paused and shrugged. "Um… To find a lost thing?"

"And if I help you find him, you'll save the statues?" Penya eyed them both. "Not just 'help'. You'll do it."

"Promise!" Lohrna said. She nudged Sella with her elbow.

"Promise," Sella echoed.

She had been making a lot of promises this evening. Each one was a drop of water, slowly drowning her.

Penya stood with a labored breath. "Rukus can only be found if you're not looking for him," she said. "And he can only find lost things that you don't know are lost."

"Only the first part complicates things," Lohrna said without hesitation.

Penya's eyes narrowed. "We'll need to find someone who has lost something that they don't know they've lost."

"And someone who doesn't know they're looking for the pixie," Lohrna said. "Got it. Well, this sounds like something we could use Cali for."

"The ghost?" Penya came around her desk. She moved toward the fire and as they followed, the gentle hum of conversation, tinkle of ceramic, and crackling fire filled the air again.

Sella looked around her, amazed at the magic she could neither see nor sense. Of course her mother had created such a spell. She wished, for just long enough that felt guilty, that she was there now to help. Chances were, if her mother didn't know the spell to help Cali, she'd know how to make it.

Penya was shuffling along until they reached a man with little goat horns who was holding a book delicately. "Well, are you going to purchase that?" the hotel proprietor demanded.

The man looked at her with his mouth slightly open. He seemed too stunned at Penya's abrasiveness to speak. He mumbled something inaudible and set the book back down.

"I'll charge the room," Penya said and shoved the book back into his arms.

The man looked at the book, then to the group. "Oh, um. Thank you… that's convenient."

Penya grumbled, then moved on. "Well, go get your ghost," she said with a grunt. "I'll be here."

SEVENTEEN

High Value Socks

"So the plan is for me to steal something from Aadel. But none of you can know what it is?" Cali asked. She was wearing a sheet over her head at the table while Sella and Lohrna sat opposite. "Also, it's good to see our plan worked and you two are back to being friendly," she added, though in a whisper as if Lohrna could hear.

Sella's jaw softened.

Beejee jumped onto the tabletop. "That's right," he said, ignoring her last comment. "And then we'll offer Rukus a jar of honey for its return. It'll draw him to the room with all of us, and Aadel there."

"Does it need to be a high value item?" Cali asked.

"Not specified," Beejee said.

"But also he can't be found if we're looking for him? That's where I'm lost," Cali said as the sheet moved a little with her voice and small movements.

Lohrna took a sip of her tea and looked at the sheet with a smile. "Pretty brilliant, right?"

"I'm still stuck on the last part," Cali said, raising one hand beneath the sheet to get Lohrna's attention.

Sella leaned in. "We offer the honey in exchange for the lost item at the same time that Aadel comes into the room. Since she's not looking for either him or the item, she should be able to see him."

"And.. honey?" Cali asked. "He'll show up for honey?"

"Pixie lore says they love their sweets. I think it'll be a good option. Honey is only sold at my store, after all," Sella said.

"And, Sella's mom put up warding to keep pixies out," Lohrna added. "So Practical Potions and Honey can't be raided. Plus, the old house is guarded by the magic that, that–"

"The one that only lets me in," Sella said. "So honey is hard for them to come by. I think it'll work to entice him."

"But how will Aadel know what to do with him?" Cali asked. "Wait, what *are* we going to do with him? Put him in a sack or something?"

"Or something," Beejee grumbled under his breath. Louder, he said, "That's where I come in. I'll be there to watch Aadel's reaction. Once she sees the pixie, I pounce."

"In, what, the general area? That's not a *great* plan."

Beejee's chin thrust in the other direction. "Fine, I'll bring Koukie too."

Lohrna's smile grew. She finished her drink and stood. "Alright, this is odd but should work. Once the cats–"

"*Familiar* and a cat."

"–have caught the pixie," Lohrna ignored him, "we'll all be able to see him. At least, according to Penya. Once they stay still long enough to see them, you can't unsee them.

Which…" Lohrna tapped her chin. "That actually might be annoying. Do you think that it's really forever that we'll be seeing pixies?"

Cali shook her head, though Sella couldn't tell if it was in humor or because she thought the plan was terrible. She bit the inside of her cheek and tried to study the outline of the face beneath the white sheet. But it gave no indicators. Determining Cali's mood was sometimes like looking for a singular piece of seaglass along the smooth pebbled shore. It was always a small thing, a crease between her brows, a slight downturn of the corner of her mouth, a tilt of her head so minor that not a hair would move out of place. Under the sheet, Sella missed all the subtly.

"What do you think?" Sella asked, tired of her own mind spinning in on itself. She'd have to trust that Cali would be honest and not merely optimistic.

"It's odd, but I don't see why it can't work," the ghost said at last. "I think bringing Koukie is a good idea. Eight paws are better than four. But, do you think he'll want to work with us after we set cats on him?"

Sella glanced at Lohrna, she translated.

"I'm bringing *a lot* of honey," Lohrna said. "We'll make it up to him."

Cali laughed and the sheet billowed lightly. "Maybe bring some wine, too," she said. "Poor little guy."

"Going to The Library to find any information about ghosts like you is already basically an impossible task," Sella said. "Having someone who can find things lost to time can only help our odds."

Cali nodded. "It's worth a try. I'll go try to summon the strength to steal from Aadel."

The sheet fluttered to the floor and Cali was gone.

GETTING Aadel into the hotel room the following morning was a part of the plan that Sella had not considered. She stood outside the door in the predawn light with Beejee at her feet. The familiar looked entirely bored with the whole situation.

"Just tell her you have urgent ladle business," he said once he realized Sella was just standing at the door.

Sella knocked the door, once, twice. "I don't want to give her false hope that we found the ladle," she whispered.

Aadel's door swung open just as Sella was about to give it a third and final knock. "You found the ladle?" Aadel gasped.

Sella pinched her brow. "No," she groaned. "I'm sorry, that's still out at sea."

"Well, the tide's rising," Aadel whispered as she moved aside for Sella to enter. "Come in."

"Actually," Sella began, but Beejee was quick to interject.

"We need you at the hotel," the familiar announced. "Penya's called a meeting in room 203."

"A meeting?" Aadel asked. She came back into view in the doorway.

"Yep," Lohrna's voice called from within the house. "Hustle! To the hotel!"

"You know about this?" Aadel turned to her daughter. "And you're up early..."

Lohrna secured her cloak around her shoulders and lifted her mother's onto her smaller frame. "Well,

MAMBOSSA teaches us that we need to not sleep in, lest we appear lazy," Lohrna said.

Aadel shrugged her cloak on and glanced at Sella. "Hmm," was all she said.

The four made their way quickly to the hotel in silence. Sella wished she had brought them travel mugs with coffee. It was a silly oversight and she imagined fondly the first few sips of hot liquid on her lips.

Once inside the hotel, Aadel finally asked, "So this really isn't about what I hope it's about?"

Sella shook her head. "Sorry. But I hope to get a lead on it soon."

Aadel looked uncharacteristically skeptical as they climbed the stairs to room 203, the only empty room in the hotel, and from Penya's description, the only uninhabitable one.

The door opened and Sella immediately saw why. The room was full of boxes and stacked piles of various items from floor to ceiling. The window was completely blocked by a collection of porcelain plates and teacups so only small rays of the early morning light seeped through the cracks to illuminate their way.

Sella looked around the room, her eyes catching on a loose paper here, a stack of what appeared to be only left shoes there. She stepped into the room, what little space there was to enter, and Lohrna and Aadel followed close behind. They both huddled behind Sella as if a monster was about to leap from behind one of the boxes.

The witch summoned a flame in the palm of her hand to better light the way into the room. At her ankles, she felt

Beejee and Koukie join them. She glanced down at the two cats and then looked at Lohrna with a nod.

From beneath her cloak, Lohrna pulled out a jar of glittering honey the size of her fist. It was wrapped in a little pink bow. Sella smiled at her friend. It was a nice touch.

"What's going on?" Aadel whispered, holding onto the back of Sella's dress, pulling her back just a little.

Lohrna shut the door behind them and Sella's fire grew.

Lohrna said, a little loudly for the small space. "We've brought a jar of lavender honey. In exchange for my mother's missing item."

"Missing item?" Aadel held Sella's back tighter.

Beejee and Koukie had both jumped up onto separate boxes at varying heights. They were watching Aadel intensely.

"It's okay," Sella whispered to the older woman. "Don't be frightened."

"It's *really good* honey," Lohrna said, sweetening the deal. "Happy bees by the edge of the forest. Surrounded by a forever bloom."

There was a sound like a little crackle of fire. And suddenly, chaos erupted.

Aadel shrieked, she pointed at the space in front of her with wide eyes.

A wool sock, crocheted in red and gold, fell to the floor in front of them.

Both cats launched themselves through the air, hitting each other, and something else, that was also screaming.

Koukie meowed, and Beejee cried, "Be still, pixie!"

"I just want the honey! Unpaw me!" a little voice from the floor called out.

Sella bent down to get a good look at the little creature under Beejee and Koukie's paws. "Are you Rukus?" she asked.

The pixie, squirming beneath the cats, looked just like, and yet nothing like, the illustrations she had seen of them in her studies. He was small, about half Beejee's size, with long, spindly arms and legs that thrashed about, trying to pull at the cats' fur with clawed hands and feet. Except, his feet were also hands. He was covered in a layer of soft looking blue fur, stripped with brown throughout. Sella grimaced slightly at the sight though tried her best to keep her face neutral. She moved her fire away from her face so it was harder to tell her expression.

"We'll let you go once you hear us out," Beejee said through his sharp teeth.

Aadel clasped her hands over her mouth. "Oh, my sock!" she gasped.

"He can only find things you don't know are lost," Lohrna explained, poorly. "Cali stole it."

Aadel nodded as if it all made sense.

Sella looked back to Rukus. "We'll let you go in a moment, and the honey is yours to keep. But, there's much more to be had," she said calmly. She scratched behind Koukie's ear and the orange cat purred, then released Ruku's legs. "Thank you for finding the sock. We have another favor to ask. In exchange for more honey than you can eat."

The pixie narrowed all four almond shaped eyes that took up the majority of his head. He barred tiny sharp teeth at her. "I can eat a lot," he grunted. Behind him, brown furred wings fluttered, thumping the wood floor in a fren-zied tapping.

"Don't doubt my witch's promise," Beejee said, pushing the pixie harder the louder the wings flurried.

Rukus' eyes shifted from Beejee to Sella. "More than I can ever eat?"

"I promise," Sella said.

EIGHTEEN

Shortcut to The Library

"You're sure you got this?" Sella asked. She looked at Beejee with concern etched into her forehead.

"Our sales will be better with me at the helm," Beejee said. "You're awkward. It puts people off."

Lohrna flinched dramatically at Beejee's insult. But it hardly phased Sella.

Lohrna pumped a fist in the air. "Yes, it's fine. Go show that witch we mean business!" she said, a bit too confidently.

Sella wondered for a moment if she could bottle that level of self-assurance and enthusiasm.

Impossible.

Sella did her best to look half as bold as her friend. She gave each of them a little nod, then slipped out of the shop and into the crisp late afternoon air. She pulled her cloak around her shoulders tighter. It wasn't truly cold out, but beneath the fabric, she hid her satchel, and a sleeping Rukus inside, close to her body.

Her eyes scanned the groups of travelers who were wandering the street admiring the architecture, from the looks of it. But eyes fell on her, some lingering for what felt a little too long. It felt like everyone around her knew what she was up to.

"I'm coming too!" Cali appeared beside Sella just as she exited the main street.

Sella jumped at the suddenness. "You're killing me," she breathed.

Cali gasped, eyes wide and her hand over her heart.

"Oh, I'm sorry!" Sella reached for her quickly but only found smoke as Cali's form vanished.

"I'm kidding," Cali appeared at her other side. "I like sneaking up on you too much to ever stop… No matter how insensitive your phrasing."

Sella straightened, then tapped her bag gently. She felt a light tap back. "You want to go to The Library with me?"

"Hello? I was a bookkeeper."

"Dealing with numbers and paperwork," Sella said as they turned another corner. "Not these kings of books."

Cali shrugged. "Yes, but this is a magical library that only opens at night *and* is run by vampires? I *have* to come."

"The vampire stories are just things kids here tell to frighten one another," Sella explained. "But The Library *is* only open at night. Some of the books in there are too precious to be exposed to the sunlight, even through tiny cracks in the stone. So during the day it sinks underground."

"Sounds suspiciously like something a vampire would conjure to explain their odd hours. I like the vampire lore better," Cali said.

They entered the edge of the woods, the sound of the ocean grew louder.

Cali hopped over a ring of mushrooms as they crossed

the threshold of the woods. Though she'd do no damage, it was always sweet the way she went out of her way to not step on plants or disrupt anything along her path. Except for Sella's peace.

Sella smiled to herself. She hoped the ghost would never stop haunting her.

Cali went on, "Either way, a library that sinks into the ground or is run by vampires… it sounds interesting, and we have a pixie guide? We don't have *anything* like this in Tollintal. I came across the sea because I wanted to see more. No offense to Marra. Orkan is this incredible island to us. So, now I'm going to go see some of it. With you."

"We won't see much for a while," Sella said. "It's just woods here."

"We don't have woods where I'm from either, just desert," Cali said.

"Well, I hope you enjoy the walk. But, the better news is, there is a shortcut."

"A magical shortcut?" Cali tilted a little to catch Sella's eye.

Sella nodded. "How'd you know?"

"Educated guess," Cali said. "Marra is isolated. Altha is far enough, then, I'd assume, to not make it by foot before the close of *The* Library." She paused, looking around them at the tall trees waving slightly in the salty breeze. "I wish Beejee were here so he could call me suspicious for knowing so much."

"He would, too. But I think he's getting more used to the fact that you just do research. And, as you say, make educated guesses," Sella said. She ducked to avoid a branch that hung a little low. "The shortcut is a bit far still. Are you sure you're up for the walk?"

"I like your company," Cali said. "Oh, we can talk ladle theft!"

Sella's cheeks flushed. She looked ahead intensely. "I'd like a break from all that for now. Tell me more about Tollintal, if you don't mind. There's a lot of humans in town for Opora. I want to be sure I understand the customs."

"Still thinking about the Dimas handshake debacle?" Cali prompted. "You have got to let that go. That was a year ago and you didn't know."

"I'm not *not* still thinking about it. I don't like making awkward missteps…"

"You just don't like social interactions in general, especially if you think you're being offensive," Cali said. Her tone was light but the words stung.

"I don't know a lot of customs from across the sea," Sella said. She stepped over a log and Cali followed. "Compared to people in Marra, I'm well traveled, but I'll admit…" Sella paused. She stared at the sky through the leaves of the trees with a small squint. "I feel like a fraud sometimes."

"I think that's normal, Sella," Cali said, pausing beside her. In the silence, she heard a pattering of rain on the branches above. "But I wish you saw you the way I saw you."

"If only," Sella said. She began to walk again, a little faster than before.

The light was getting darker as the sun began to set.

Sella looked back, wondering how Beejee and Lohrna

were doing. If Beejee had scratched at her yet. If Lohrna had decided to throw up her hands and leave. Possibly for good. MAMBOSSA wouldn't stay after the festival, Sella knew.

She peaked into the satchel to see a still sleeping Rukus. She closed the flap over again gently.

She was stalling. She didn't want to ask outright. But talking of customs and… seeing her differently? Sella had to know, and she knew since it was Cali, she'd have to ask bluntly. She paused and turned toward Cali who stopped in turn.

Cali smiled at her but put her arms at her hips. "Why'd we stop again?"

"Back at my place…when you… when…" Sella started but lost her thought as it left her mouth. She looked away, the feeling of dread creeping up in her gut as she thought about how to ask.

"Oh!" Cali said cheerily. She grabbed Sella's hand. They were solid, for now. "When I kissed you?"

Sella felt her blood turn hot in her wrists and neck. She nodded. "Is that… Just why..?"

"Because I wanted to see if I could. Your eyes were closed, so I figured if I couldn't, you wouldn't see me fail at our first kiss. That'd be embarrassing, and I've had enough embarrassment in life that I don't need any in death. I'd have died twice!" Cali's expression turned hesitant. Worry lines formed between her brows. "Was it weird? Should I have asked?"

Sella shook her head quickly. Stands of dark hair slipped from behind her horns. "No, not weird, I just didn't know…"

"I like you, Sella." Cali squeezed Sella's hands. "The circumstances are strange, I admit. But... I thought this," her fingers lanced between Sellas and she shook them a little, "was a bit... you know, obvious?"

"To everyone but me, I think." Sella sighed. Relief, excitement, joy, and even a little sadness flooded through her.

"And... you like me, right?"

"Cali this past year, I've grown to care more about you than–"

Cali laughed, her hands began to fade. "You're a codi, sometimes."

Sella smiled back. The word itself, she did not know, but the meaning was clear. She had once again thought herself into sadness and frenzy when she hadn't needed to. She hoped the term meant that she did this in an endearing way. She made a mental note to ask what a 'codi' was when her mind could focus.

"And I like that about you," Cali said. "But you don't have to tell me everything with so many words. Just tell me that you like me too."

"I do."

"Then, come on," Cali said, her laughter still chimed through the air as she disappeared. "Let's get this pixie to *The Library*!"

Sella shook out her arms. Her limbs felt like heavy metal had settled into her bones but the excited feeling in her stomach remained. It fueled her forward. "Shortcut's up ahead," Sella said.

"Lead the way," Cali said as a little shimmer lit the space beside Sella.

. . .

SELLA STOPPED at a clearing in the trees. The forest had darkened but the light of the nearly full moon illuminated the empty patch of grass in a silver glow. Sella stepped within the circle and Cali, semi-translucent in the moonlight, followed.

Sella reached a hand into the bag and touched the pixie inside. His fur-like skin was velvet against her fingers, then, a sharp sting pinched down on her hand. "Ouch!" She pulled her hand out, the flap of the satchel flung open as she did.

The pixie peered out from the depths with his four fierce eyes that seemed to be glowing from within like little embers in the dark. He shook a fist at her. "Watch your hands, *kitchen witch!*"

Sella sighed. She wished people, even pixies, would stop using those words like an insult. She examined her hand where a row of half moon puncture wounds blossomed with beads of blood. She pinched at the bite mark, but it healed before she could really examine them closely. She glared at Rukus. "I have to be touching you if you want to travel with us," she said.

"I don't *want* to do anything with you. But fine." He held out a tiny hand for her to grasp. Spider leg-like fingers wrapped around her thumb gently.

She held out her other hand to Cali. "Just in case the same applies to ghosts," she said.

Cali laughed. "Oh, Sella, any excuse to hold my hand, I see." She grasped Sella with a firm hand, though the rest of her body was still mostly shimmering.

Sella blushed and closed her eyes, feeling the magic of

the clearing begin to put pressure on her feet slowly, then creep up her legs and body. It felt like being slowly submerged in a warm bath, soothing, gentle, but just slightly uncomfortable as it moved up to her neck and over her head. She held her breath and felt the sudden drop in her stomach.

When Sella opened her eyes, she was at the entrance of The Library.

It was a large, looming building that seemed without end, as if it stretched forever into the clear, star-studded sky. Stained glass windows on each floor depicted images of books, candles, and though she didn't point it out to Cali, vampires. The images looked much like anyone else, especially in the glass. But their skin was clear among the color, their open mouths full of shark teeth.

A small sense of pride filled her for a moment. She was grateful that her mother had long ago carved this path for her. Back when she had been an adventurous reader. Back when things were easier. Before everything had been burned.

Cali jumped out of Sella's grasp, breaking her thoughts. "That was amazing!"

"It is," Sella acknowledged. "But, we also lost about three hours of our night. It's not really a particularly fast way to travel, but it allows us to not be exhausted when we arrive."

"Interesting…" Cali mused. Her eyes were locked on a stained glass window, but which one she was focused on, Sella couldn't be sure. She hoped it wasn't one of the vampires.

The pixie in her bag was less excited about the whole

thing. He poked his head out from the bag. "Let's get on with it, then," he grumbled. His voice was so small that Sella felt a chuckle escape her. Rukus, despite himself, sounded like a small child about to throw a tantrum.

Sella quickly climbed the steps to the small red door. The building itself was impressive, but the door always struck Sella as out of place. Just a plain red door among ancient brick and gaudy glass. A little red door leading to so much beauty and knowledge.

Sella's mother had said it was because wisdom came from unlikely places. But the rest of the structure seemed to go out of its way to boast. So Sella was never really sure which it was. Wisdom from small places, or showing off that knowledge was only for those who felt they belonged among such an impressive structure. Now, she thought, perhaps it was both.

"Stay hidden," Sella told the pixie as she closed the bag.

Beside her, Cali flickered for a moment, then vanished.

Sella slipped inside quickly where a man stood at the desk at the end of the small hallway. He looked up from his reading, a scroll that Sella could not decipher, and nodded at her.

"Good evening," the witch said as she approached.

The man looked her up and down before a moment of realization spread across his face. "Sella?" he asked.

She smiled back. "You remember me."

"How could I forget? Ever since *the incident*," he said, though his expression remained one of calm nostalgia. "You are welcome to the library, so long as you are alone. I recall that was the agreement." He swept his hand and a hidden door behind him opened. "Seven hours to closing time."

"Thank you," Sella said with a small bow of her head. She tried to not look suspicious, kept her hands away from her bag beneath her cloak, and eyes forward as she passed him.

Success.

The door shut and they were left in the entry of the library without a guide or aide.

An expansive round room before them was lit brightly by what seemed like thousands of candles atop candelabras of all sizes. From the ceiling many hundreds of feet up, a large multi-tiered chandelier hung like vines creeping down the length of the main hall. It spread light and warmth throughout the space along its golden branches. A few drops of white wax fell to the center of the room.

The space was huge, built in a big circle, and filled with books and scrolls, all meticulously organized in high bookshelves. Dark wood ladders at various heights clung to the walls on rollers. Jetting off the main room were several hallways, all lined with books. They led to little sitting rooms, or other large spaces where books and scrolls waited to be read and loved again.

One of the halls led to the stairwell, but it changed every so often, so she figured Rukus would probably have to travel through the main hall up to the other levels. It was risky, but she knew he was fast, and hard to find, even if you were looking for him.

Sella smiled, remembering Lohrna once getting on the tallest ladder and zooming throughout one of the main, and very crowded hallways, until she hit a bookshelf at full force, knocking it, and several others in its path down. For once, an incident in question, had not been her doing. But she was famous by association and forbidden to ever come back unless she was alone and quiet. She was grateful now. It seemed to have its perks if the door keeper had remembered her all these decades later. The check in process here was usually, if she remembered correctly, a lengthy nightmare. And they would probably need every bit of the several hours to find anything of value.

Sella began to preemptively consider just how strong she should make her coffee in the morning when a light tap on her shoulder reminded her to get moving.

She nodded and made her way to the end of the room where a hallway, lined from floor to ceiling with hardcover leather books, led to a smaller room. It was empty, save for the several large plants by the glittering, colorful window. She lifted the flap on her bag and Rukus flew out with shimmering wings already beating rapidly.

"Alright, we're looking for a spell. A scroll, probably, but maybe a book. Or paper within a book," she told the pixie.

"So descriptive, you should be a novelist," Rukus drawled. He shifted from above her head to just below her nose. "I'll find you missing materials, whatever they are. It's your job to sort through it and see if it's what you're looking for."

Sella took in a deep, long breath. "That's fair enough," she said. "Try not to wreck anything while you're out."

"That's an offensive stereotype," the pixie said as he flew out of the room so quickly that Sella's eyes lost track of him.

Cali's disembodied voice whispered beside her, "He and Beejee should be friends."

Sella snorted. "Don't tell either of them that. I can only handle one sarcastic creature at a time." She sat down at the window on a big, purple plush chair and pulled a book at random from the shelf. She flipped it over in her hand, feeling the worn leather on her fingertips. She opened it and the spine crackled like the last wood in the hearth. The earthy smell of rain and warm dust filled her nose. It tingled, making her sneeze.

"The Life and Times of Erameth Bellpaver?" Cali read the title aloud. "Who's that?"

Sella shrugged, turning the book over again. "I'm not sure. I just wanted to feel a book in my hand. It's been longer than I would like to admit." She looked up and surveyed the floor to ceiling shelves around her. "Anything you want to read?"

Cali flickered into view at the far wall. She stood on her tiptoes to have a better look at a series of books, all red leather spines and gold lettering. She disappeared from view, then appeared again, crouched down suddenly in a different place. She pointed to a book at the bottom shelf. "This one?"

Sella rose from her seat and examined the book. She read the title aloud in a whisper, "Kelpies: Keeping for the Undereducated and Illinfomred?" She raised a brow at the ghost.

"What? We don't have kelpies across the sea…"

Right. Just… wyverns.

Sella had longed to ask her more about them in the past year they'd spent together. But even now, she kept her mouth shut. That was a sore spot for Cali, whether she admitted it or not. Cali was always so happy, she never wanted to press on something she knew would hurt her. And her family seemed to be at a very painful point.

So instead, Sella picked up the book and flipped to the first page.

"Read it to me?" Cali asked as she faded away like smoke.

Sella cleared her throat and began to read.

RUKUS HAD COME into the room over and over again. Each time, moving so quickly, it was as if he had simply teleported. He held up a scroll, a book, or some random sheet of paper torn from the pages of an ancient text.

Nothing was what they were looking for.

Sella's eyes grew dry and they began to sting with strain. Her voice was getting croaky from reading aloud. Her body was heavy with the need for sleep. Cali, too, seemed tired. Ghosts, she had learned long ago, did in fact, need rest. But if it was a carry over habit from life or some actual need, she still wasn't sure.

Sella blinked, so long she was sure she had fallen asleep for a moment when her chin hit her neck. "I'm awake!" She sprung up from her seat.

In front of her, Rukus hovered with a page in his hand. "Clearly," he said dryly. He shook a few small papers in Sella's face, so close they grazed her nose. "The Library is closing in a few minutes. We need to clear out."

"What piece of flotsam did we find this time?" Sella plucked the papers from his hand. She examined it with sleepy eyes. It was torn pages from a scroll, not a book. It looked like it was ripped right from the middle, and then shredded haphazardly. She looked over a few of the words on the first scrap, but they held no meaning to her at all.

"This was a waste," she grumbled and folded the papers carefully.

"The papers were lost. Lost things can be valuable," Rukus said, indignantly.

Sella glanced slowly at the pile of other discarded found items. "Mhm, just like red socks," she mumbled. She stuffed the pages into her satchel anyway and hoisted herself from her chair. "Alright, let's get going."

"You tried," Cali's voice said. "That's what matters."

Sella felt tears prick at her sleepy eyes. She had tried. She always *tried*.

"Let's go home," she said quickly before her voice quivered.

NINETEEN

Into the Sea

It was nearly morning when she arrived home.

Beejee was waiting for her by the circle window over-looking the street below. Koukie was sleeping soundly by the fire. She didn't wake when Sella shut the door, though she seemed to close her eyes tighter, somewhat annoyed when Sella flung her boots off and they landed on the wood floor with a loud *thud*.

"We had a great day of sales at the shop. Not that you care," Beejee said once Sella flopped into bed. He curled up by her head on his own pillow and placed a paw on her cheek.

Sella simply grunted in response.

"Did you find anything helpful?" Beejee asked at last.

Sella grumbled back, "Sleep first. Talk after…"

Beejee growled but they both fell asleep before either could say anything else.

.   .   .

MORNING CAME TOO SOON. It was Koukie who had woken the household with cries for breakfast. She even jumped onto the bed to paw at Sella's arm when she didn't rise at her loud meows.

Groggily, slowly, Sella rose and opened the window for the cat to leave and find something to eat on her own. She could hardly be expected to make a meal in her current state.

Koukie glanced at Sella disapprovingly before she slipped out onto the roof and disappeared into the morning fog.

Sella hardly cared that the cat was mildly upset with her. Koukie would recover. She stumbled back to the edge of her bed and fell back onto the sheets with a loud bounce of the mattress. "Why does it always feel like we're swimming against the current?" She flung an arm over her face.

"Well, I think we're pretty strong swimmers, if you ask me," Cali said, confidence in her voice that Sella thought was entirely unearned. "For example, we had a great plan! Did it work..?" Cali paused, but not long enough for an answer. Not that Sella would give her one. She answered it herself, "No. But it could've!"

Sella opened her mouth, eyes still closed. No words came out.

"We did get a lot of random papers and books, which was... I'll admit, it's less than interesting."

"Where is this going?" Sella asked.

"Well, I think maybe there's still something to be gained from the experience," Cali said, still far too bright and chipper for the early hour. "What's the folded up papers? Maybe it's like a clue or something? You know how the protagonist of the story always gets the clue at the last possible moment?"

Sella raised an eyebrow at her. She pointed to her satchel at the end of the bed. "Help," she said pathetically.

Cali huffed, then slid the bag a fraction closer. She sighed, a quick breeze chilled Sella's skin. "This is harder than it looks, you know," she said.

Sella rolled her head to one side and looked at the bag with one eye closed. She wormed her way to the edge of the bed and opened the satchel, pulling the papers carefully out. She sat up at last, and arranged the torn pieces on the bed so they lined up.

It formed a series of short lines. The rhyme was easy to follow, like a children's verse. But as she read it, her chill sunk into her bones. "It's a love poem…" she said quietly, reading it again slowly to herself. "I guess someone must have lost it."

"And destroyed it… That's so sad," Cali said. She moved closer to look over Sella, crouching down so low her chin rested delicately on Sella's shoulder.

Sella turned her head just a little to watch Cali's green eyes scan the page. She moved her head slightly away at last, letting Cali move in closer. She felt her nose and cheeks burn but blinked away the feeling of closeness as best she could.

The ghost whispered the poem aloud from the beginning:

Your light guides me through the door
All the way down to the rocky shore
Here, I feel your touch like stinging salt
And I know it's all my fault

I can hear the sirens' song
Though their voices are long gone
If I should fall into the sea
Will your light take care of me?

"Oh, this is tragic," Cali whispered. "Do you suppose the person who lost this is…" She paused, reading over the poem again. She turned to Sella, her chin finally landing on Sella's shoulder, pressing down with weight that felt so real. Cali's face shifted slightly to catch the witch's gaze. "If Rukus can only find things that are lost. Things that people don't know are lost..? Is the person dead?"

"Yes," Sella said carefully. "The paper looks old. They're probably gone."

"I'm not sure if that's worse or better…"

"I would think better, but what do I know?" Sella folded the papers back up. "Maybe the sea is looking after them."

Cali laughed. "I don't think the sirens are known for that."

Right. Sirens. Not known for being forgiving, just as she was sure Penya would be unforgiving if she didn't hold up her end of the bargain.

The creeping feeling of dread was worming its way heavily back in Sella's heart. Their night had been completely wasted. Another day and no closer to any solution to her growing list of problems. She had to find the person who stole the ladle, and quickly. But most importantly, she needed to find a way to make Cali more visible, or at least vocal, to others.

While Cali had said she would never dream of working with Sediri, Sella knew that it was really only a matter of time before she would have enough. It had been a year. A ghost could only take so much.

Oh, and of course now she had promised Penya that she'd put a stop to Kepilla removing the sirens.

Sella groaned. "There isn't enough coffee in the world."

Cali put both hands on Sella's cheeks. She looked down at her upside down and shook Sella's head gently back and forth. "None of this now," she said. "You're a witch. Start acting like it."

"Kitchen witch?" Sella prompted. She wasn't used to anyone saying it like it was a compliment, let alone without the 'kitchen' modifier.

"Certified!" Cali said with a wink. She pressed her lips gently to the tip of Sella's nose, then let her face go. She stepped back so Sella had to stretch her neck to keep track of her. "Come on, you and I both know you're more than just a kitchen witch."

"Don't tell anyone."

"I'd like the option to, though, in case you cross me."

Sella's eyes softened.

"None of that, I said. Plenty of time to overthink later. Let's open up the shop. Make some extra strong coffee for us and maybe a speciality 'Be Nice to Everyone' blend for the festival goers. Something tells me things are going to get rowdy as the competition stiffens."

Sella took a deep breath in and pushed herself from the bed. No sleep to be had for now. Now, it was time to get to work.

TWENTY

He's a Mess

BEFORE SELLA HAD a chance to flip the sign to 'open', there was already a banging sound on the window. A loud, insistent, frantic, sound.

Sella's brow furrowed as she looked from outside the window to see Sediri, and, to Beejee's dismay, her familiar perched on her shoulder. Sediri waved through the window like she was on fire.

The early morning air was cool when Sella opened the door. Fog slithered in at her feet as Sediri flew in and slammed the door behind her. "He's dead!" Sediri shrieked before Sella could even open her mouth.

Sella's mind went blank. The witches, and familiars, stared at each other for a moment, as if she hadn't said a thing at all.

"Who's dead?" Cali asked, appearing from behind Sella's shoulder.

Sediri gasped, hand held over her chest. A long lock of dark red hair fell over her shoulder as she suddenly thrust herself forward, pointing a long finger at Cali. "Don't do that, ghost!" she scolded.

"You get used to it," Sella said calmly, though she knew that so far she still hadn't. She turned back to Cali, who handed her the stick. Sella tucked it quickly in the folds of her skirt as Sediri regained her composure.

The other kitchen witch straightened her back, the bird on her shoulder fluffed his feathers with a small, quick buzzing sound. "Sella, are you a consultant or not? Branzo is dead!"

"Branzo?"

"Branzo!" Sediri said. "He's dead. Right outside my shop. This is a mess!"

"*He's* a mess, or *it's* a mess?" Cali asked. She was still standing behind Sella, but her curiosity seemed to be getting the better of her.

Sediri took a long, deep breath in as she blinked slowly. "Both?" She turned to Sella quickly. "Look, the mayor of a prominent town—"

"Not *that* prominent," Beejee interjected.

Sediri went on as if she hadn't heard him at all. "--is dead! In front of my shop! You have to help me. You *know* how this looks."

Sella sighed. She did. It looked bad. Really bad.

"Why would we help you? You're trying to run us out of business!" Beejee asked what Sella, the darkest part of her, thought.

The grackle squawked at him.

Sediri's eyes narrowed at Beejee. "Because if this festival turns into a feeding frenzy, they'll be blaming the witches first and last. We're the chum and you know it."

Sella folded her arms across her chest. She wasn't so sure they'd go after *both* witches. At least, the Marrans wouldn't come for her this time.

Probably.

Most likely.

"Did you do it?" Cali asked bluntly.

Sediri looked at the ghost swiftly, eyes already burning.

Cali ducked closer to Sella.

"I did *not* kill him," the other witch said. "Does it look like I'm faking this? The man is dead, and bloody. I couldn't overpower him even if I wanted to." She gestured to her thin frame as if that alone was enough to clear her name. "Besides, I'm just a kitchen witch. What am I going to do but poison someone? And he was..." She paused, eyes looking up as if she was remembering seeing his body.

Sella shuddered. She probably was picturing that in horrible detail. She wasn't sure she wanted to see it.

Sediri continued, "He was definitely... *not* poisoned."

Sella raised a brow at her. "I hear you, but how *exactly* do you want our help?"

"Is it too much to ask that you solve the crime before everyone wakes up?" Sediri asked, her voice was light, almost as if she was joking. When she got no response but their blank faces, she went on, "Listen, just help me run damage control before folks chase both of us out of town. I'm sure whoever did it is long gone."

Beejee and Sella exchanged quick glances. First the missing ladle, now a dead mayor? Sella doubted the two were unrelated. Whoever did this would probably stay until the end of Opora.

They had until then, at least, to figure it out.

"Alright, fine," Sella said.

Beejee hissed.

"Let's go see the crime scene," Cali said, a little too eager. She squeezed Sella's arm, urging her forward.

THE SCENE outside of Sediri's shop brought back flashes of finding Cali's body. Sella shuddered as they looked over the body. Cali's death had been significantly more peaceful, a quick and painless poison. Whatever had happened to Branzo had been swift, but it was no easy, immediate poisoning. Sella looked him over with a hand over most of her face. She peeked again at the body through her splayed fingers.

Beejee, meanwhile, bravely sniffed at the pool of blood. "No poison smell that I can pick up on," he said. "But then again, he's wearing *a lot* of oils…" The familiar scrunched his nose as he sniffed again. "Far too many."

The sun was just beginning to rise over the rooftops. Rays of pink filled spaces that just moments ago had been in shadow. People would be waking soon.

Sella took in a deep breath and then looked at Cali, who was peering ghoulishly over the dead man's face. The ghost pointed to his head and nodded. "Must've been quick, at least," she said, gesturing at the wound at the back of his head. "Maybe he was super intoxicated and fell and hit his head? Or someone whacked him and he didn't see it coming… Which is a nice thought, I guess. I appreciate that I didn't know I was going to die."

Sella's brows rose. She removed her hand at last and steeled herself. She looked more closely. The gash was deep and dark. His eyes were still open. He was dressed in the clothes he had been wearing last she had seen him. He was on his back.

She did her best to memorize the details before she said, "We should probably move him. Before everyone gets up and sees this."

Sediri and her grackle nodded frantically. "Yes, please."

"You have to help," Sella said. She stood taller.

"I *what?*" Sediri squeaked.

"Come on, kitchen witch," Beejee said to Sediri.

Sella smirked. It was nice to hear, for a moment, something that had been thrown at her as an insult before. It felt as if he was proud of her fire. For a moment.

"This is one of those times I think I'm glad I can't help," Cali said as the two witches grabbed either end of the large man. "Wait, why isn't he a ghost?"

Sella grunted as she held Branzo's legs a little higher. She gestured with her head to where she was leading him and began walking backwards.

Sediri followed, holding his arms hooked under her own.

"I don't know," Sella said, straining a little.

"The better question is, why are you?" Sediri asked Cali.

A response never came. As they rounded the corner, so did Aadel and Cirian from the opposite direction.

A loud gasp broke from Aadel's mouth. Sella could hear it from down the street, so loud she was certain at least a few people in the apartments above the shops had to have woken up.

Sella felt her blood turn hot in her veins. She looked at Aadel, then Cirian, who stared at her with equally wide eyes, completely frozen in his place.

"This isn't what it looks like," Sella said quickly, dropping Branzo's legs a little in her hurry to shuffle closer to them.

The two Marran's hurried down the cobblestone toward the witches. "Branzo?" Aadel gasped again. This time, luckily, through her hands. She looked over the body, eyes scanning him quickly but thoroughly. She turned to Sella. "What happened? Did you… Did you have a good reason?" Her hands were trembling as she lowered them from her face.

Sella felt her cheeks flush, her heart quickened. "No, Aadel, we didn't kill him. Sediri found him like this."

Aadel looked at the other witch. Her eyes suddenly narrowed. Wrinkles around her mouth deepened as they thinned into a tight line.

"Aadel," Sella repeated through gritted teeth. She shuffled her feet to keep Branzo's legs up. "She found him like this."

Cirian pushed through Aadel, shouldering Sella out of the way. His large arms looped above Sella's as he grabbed hold onto Branzo's legs. "Alright. She found him like this. What's next?" he asked.

Sella stepped aside and pointed to a narrow alleyway. "We take him to the office."

Cali hurried to Sella's side. "I don't think our little 'content with a life of paperwork, wants to stay out of everyone's business', Jahra, is going to be terribly happy about this."

"Jahra will… just have to be fine with it. It is part of the job," Sella said aloud.

Sediri looked confused, but simply grimaced in reply. She shuffled forward as Cirian led the way.

Behind them, Aadel kept close to Sella. She looked up at

the witch with a suspicious expression. "You're sure she's not involved?"

Sella glanced at her for a moment, but they all kept pace and she didn't want to be too loud. "I don't think so," she whispered.

Aadel exhaled. Though, for disappointment, disagreement, or some other frustration, Sella wasn't sure.

The street was still empty when they arrived in front of the jail and tiny offices where the previous detective had run his operation.

Finally, one thing had gone right.

Sella unlocked the door with the twist of her hand and ushered the group, body and all, inside. "Put him…" Sella thought for a moment. She wasn't quite sure. "Put him in one of the jail cells?"

"Sella!" Cali scolded.

"There's beds in there?" Sella shrugged, half heartedly defending herself.

Cirian only nodded, then did as he was instructed. He led the way to the hallway.

"Is no one going to take a turn carrying him? Really?" Sediri said as she passed Aadel, Sella, and Cali.

"You find the body, you deal with the body," Aadel said as they, and the body, disappeared into the jailroom.

Cali smiled at Sella knowingly.

Sella waved her away.

"Sella, you better keep your focus where it ought to be," Aadel said, her tone hushed. "The bigger mystery is the ladle."

"What?" Sella's disbelief was clear in her tone.

Really? This generation was unwell.

"Branzo… Well, he was a bit of a menace. Always talking *so* loudly," Aadel said, matter of factly, as if that alone was enough to kill him.

Sella rubbed her temples as Cirian and Sediri came into view again in the narrow hallway.

"What now?" Sediri asked.

"Coffee," Sella and Cali said.

TWENTY-ONE

Rude, Actually

A LIGHT RAIN was beginning to fall.

Inside the potions shop, Sella hoped, morbidly, that the water would wash away any trace of blood on their route to the jail. They had been careful, but she was also distracted, and a little frantic. Time ran out to retrace her steps to truly double check before she had to open her shop and try to assume business as usual.

The last thing they needed was a frenzy.

She had pulled a stool from the other side of the counter to sit on and was staring blankly at the coffee pot until her head began to droop.

"Sella?" Cali prompted. She was attempting to nudge Sella's coffee cup closer to her with no avail.

Sella blinked hard, then grabbed the mug. "Thanks," she said with a small smile.

Cali leaned across the counter, hovering gently over her own deep purple mug. She breathed in loud, eyes closed.

Sella's gaze drifted from Cali's closed eyes to her lips. The tips of her ears and nose burned and she looked away. She should be trying to figure out what their latest conversation meant. Trying to puzzle what to do next. How to make Cali feel loved, and happy, and safe. But instead, they were both breathing in steam that smelled like burnt, bitter ground coffee beans.

Sella had infused the drink with strength, but that had a strong, acidic flavor and she was dreading taking another sip. She straightened her back, she closed her eyes tight, and downed her cup. Taste was for calmer blends.

"Aadel's probably told half the town by now," Cali said, awakening Sella at last. She turned to the front of the empty shop and tilted her head to look out the bay window. "No one's come in. They must think you're busy in here consulting."

Sella opened one eye. "I feel busy," she said. "If that counts."

"Not really," Cali said, though not unkindly. She sat back down at her own stool and then rested her chin in her hand. "Do you think there's any chance that Branzo will come back as a ghost and just tell us who did it?"

Sella shook her head, though she knew it was at least partly a joke, she was too tired to filter herself. "I don't think so. If he's not here already, he's probably gone."

"To the place where wine flows from fountains and there's always chocolate scones on white table cloths," Cali said wistfully. She perked up a little, a finger raised. "But! They don't stain!"

Sella smiled gently, remembering what felt now like a lifetime ago when she had made up what she thought an afterlife would be like just to make Cali smile. When Cali had asked her what she thought and she had first been honest that she didn't know. Just knew it did, in fact, exist.

When Cali had frowned, Sella made up an idea of what it might be like. Something idyllic where the ghost could really eat and drink and be merry. But no matter how they talked about how much better things would be on the other side, Cali had chosen over and over again to stay here.

Sella could still hear Cali's laugh, see her sitting on the rock above a quickly flowing creek as Sella described the fictional afterlife. It was a place Sella hoped was real. But the truth was, Sella didn't know what it was like on the other side. She liked to imagine those who came before her were happy and eating well.

Cali went on, unaware of Sella's thoughts, "I'd say 'lucky him', but I still quite like it here. Even if there's no chocolate."

"Maybe after Opora, we'll go to your home. Where there's chocolate," Sella suggested. She watched Cali carefully. Cali hated talking about home, but imports of chocolate were rare. Sella saw her opportunity and took it. "It could be fun to see your home. I'd like to see those plants with spikes on them. And a clear blue sky every day."

Cali shrugged. "Eh, Tollintal isn't all that great. Come for the wyverns, stay for the chocolate. Hope you don't dehydrate."

The corners of Sella's lips twitched. She wasn't sure what about any of it was funny, though. Exhausted, she looked down at her empty cup.

The bell above the door nearly flew off its hinge as Lohrna entered the shop, already in a flurry. "Branzo!"

Sella stood up slowly. Her body ached. All she wanted

was to turn to liquid and seep through the cracks in the floorboards, become one with the dirt and not rise until this whole thing was over. Still, she did her best to look awake and alert. "Yeah," she said as she poured Lohrna coffee into a yellow mug. "What're the people saying about it so far?"

Lohrna came up to the bar and shook out her wild curls.

Cali dodged the droplets and moved a few seats over. Sella pushed the ghost's mug to follow her at the farther stool. Maybe a plant wherever Cali was sitting would be a good thing after all. It'd be less for everyone to frantically try to manage when they came in.

Sella moved Lohrna's mug closer to her friend. She was glad she was here, despite the shuffle. She missed Lohrna and her way of always seeing things as they were. The way she drew Sella out from her own thoughts without any judgment or concern. She just saw Sella as she was.

"Well, MAMBOSSA is horrified," Lohrna said quickly. She held the mug close, but didn't drink. "They said that murder is—"

"Let me guess," Beejee said, suddenly leaping onto the counter. "Is it 'what separates us from animals'?"

Lohrna nodded. At last, she took a long sip. "Sorry, Beejee. Animals can be incredible in so many ways," she said at last. "I think the society just feels that it's important to separate ourselves." She shook her head, hands up. "Anyway, that's not the point. The point is, some people are already pointing fingers."

"None in my direction, or yours, this time?" Sella asked.

Lohrna shook her head. "Not yet, at least. We're lucky there's so many newcomers in town right now." She leaned over the counter closer to them. Her voice lowered, though the shop was empty, "But it is freaking some people out. A few contestants have dropped out of Opora already."

"Seems fair." Sella nodded. "I mean, some golden spoon isn't worth death."

"And some are saying the most awful things," Lohrna went on, ignoring Sella's flippant attitude. She ducked a little to look at Beejee, as if he would be the one to really understand the situation.

Beejee looked into her eyes soulfully.

"Apparently, Branzo wasn't exactly well liked," Lohrna told him. "Despite his audience out and about. A lot of people were really upset that he left his town when they were in need. You know, with the plague and all. Even more are talking about his shadowy reputation from his past."

"Presently, I'll say he was too loud for my taste," Beejee told her.

Lohrna nodded, taking a long sip of her coffee. "Always trying to draw in a crowd. Who does he think he is? The King?"

"Rude, actually."

"Really rude."

Sella watched them closely. Leaving the two of them to run the shop for a few hours seemed to have done what decades of getting into mischief never quite accomplished. Sella knew Beejee loved Lohnra, in his own way, but to see them like this? Her heart felt full for a few beats until dread began to take root, weaving its way into the center of her chest. Her eyes drifted to Cali who offered her a warm, knowing smile.

Lohrna followed her gaze to the empty stool. She raised a brow suspiciously. "Cali?" she asked.

Cali and Sella nodded.

"Cal!" Lohrna cried, arms raised as if she was about to hug the ghost.

Beejee bared his teeth. "Back at your obnoxious ways, I see."

"Wait!" Lohnra slammed her palms on the counter. "So, how's Jahra handling this?"

"Not really sure." Sella shrugged. She poured herself another cup. "We… kind of left the body there. And a note."

Lohrna shook her head. "A note?"

"He can read," Beejee said, like that justified leaving a dead body for the paperwork lover to find.

Lohrna's mouth hung open, shocked, it seemed, at their response. She slid her mug closer to the pot and Sella refreshed it with the steaming liquid to the brim.

"It was the best I could do," Sella defended herself, though not well. She stumbled over her words and didn't sound confident at all. "We had to get it… well, him… out of the street quickly and carry on, at least outwardly, business as usual. I did promise Sediri I'd help her. Call it professional courtesy."

"Mhm. And we're *certain* she didn't do it? My mom says you're sure. But, Sella. You're *sure*?"

"Pretty sure? He was hit over the head."

"Like, really hard," Cali added. "Sediri isn't exactly a giant."

As if Lohrna could hear the ghost, she said, "Yes, she's little boned and he was tall, but–" Lohrna paused, looking up. "Don't you think she could get one good hit in, if she had planned it?"

Sella stared at her, her brows raised. "I mean… Maybe? I think if she planned it, it'd be better followed through. Why kill him in front of her shop? Why ask me for help?"

Lohrna conceded, hands raised in defeat. "Alright, maybe not even *planned* it, like it was on her mind. But maybe it was something thought about, briefly? As a possibility and she was ready, even if most of her didn't know it?" Lohrna raised a hand in the air and swung it down quickly onto the counter. "Just like, *wham*! She didn't know she wanted to, but she did it. Something heavy in her hands and she just went for it!"

Sella pulled back. "Yeah, I know Sediri," she said. "I don't think… *wham* is in her vocabulary."

"Sure, you know her, but not as a suspect. As a rival. One you at least seem to kind of respect."

Sella and Beejee both hissed.

"Fine. You hate her. But don't think she'd be able to over power him. Even with my genius idea of it being a only half baked murder with some kind of weapon…" Lohrna eyed both Sella and Beejee as if she was on to something great.

When she was met with only blank stares, she sighed. "Any other clues?" Lohrna asked.

"Didn't seem like there was a struggle," Sella said, trying to leave out any personal feelings she may have. She tried to be objective. "He wasn't disheveled or anything and he was laying there like he wasn't running from anything. There was less blood than you'd probably expect at the scene, which is odd."

"That does seem weird."

"It's possible he was moved," Sella suggested. "Maybe to

put the blame away from whoever did it? The gash was pretty big. It would've bled a lot."

Lohrna looked up, as if picturing it in her mind.

Sella went on, "He had red marks on his arms, though. It looked like a reaction or something."

"Maybe to one of Sediri's potions? Maybe that's why she killed him. Trying to keep it from getting out?"

Sella shook her head. "I just don't see it. I don't think that's reason enough to really kill someone. At least, I'd hope not."

"Alright. I hear you on that, but I don't think we should rule her out just for that. No offense."

Sella had to agree. Her friend was right, so was Cali. It wasn't impossible that Sediri had done this, it was likely she also wasn't without motive. Could she have really done something like this, though? Even if in the heat of the moment?

Sella tried to recall any time she had seen Sediri angry, truly angry in the past. Yes, she had heard her raise her voice, even point her sharp nailed fingers at people aggressively. But she couldn't recall ever seeing her hit anyone or throw anything. When they had run that shop together, the worst Sediri ever did was act better than her and correct her when she would deviate from the recipes.

"Do we think it has anything to do with the stolen ladle?" Lohrna asked after the long pause in the conversation.

Sella shrugged. "Two crimes at the same time. It's weird. But, also, there's a lot of new people in town, and a lot of motivation for either crime, I'd think."

Lohrna sighed. "You're right. I want them to be

connected. It'd be easier that way. But I don't know if they are."

"My gut tells me it is," Sella said. "But I don't know and I have nothing to go off of. With all these people in town, there are a lot of motives. A lot of means…"

"But limited opportunity," Lohrna said. "With Branzo, he had to be murdered in a kind of tight window from when people were out on the street to when Sediri found him early in the morning. Plus, the ladle was stolen right under Hazen's roof. He was asleep, sure, but he says he would've woken up if someone was rummaging around in there."

"True," Sella said. "But picking a lock isn't difficult. It's more the stealth they'd need to get the ladle once they're inside that I'd be worried about."

"So we need to find the sneakiest person in town," Lohrna said, rubbing her hands together.

Cali shrugged. "I think we need more information before we really can say if they're connected or not."

Sella set her jaw tight and bent down to fetch a Clarity Blend. It was all just a bit too much now. She needed something extra.

Beejee curled up on the counter. The tip of his tail flicked.

The bell above the door chimed and Hazen stepped through.

TWENTY-TWO

Seaglass and Secrets

HAZEN LOOKED AROUND, an expression of mild confusion on his face. "You've been crowded since the start of Opora," he said. "Where is everyone?"

Sellas's eyes flashed to Beejee.

Great. Just what she needed: her familiar on her case about sales.

"No crowd today, it'd seem. You heard, I'm sure, about Branzo," Sella said, gesturing him in. She poured him a cup of coffee in a long and thin ceramic travel mug. He had been so busy since the start of the festival, she was certain he couldn't stay.

"About the mayor of the other town? Yes, I heard… terrible thing, that," Hazen placed his coins on the counter and took the cup with both hands. "So about this ladle, then," he whispered. "Any clues on finding it? You don't think the culprit already fled town, do you?"

Sella blinked. "What?"

"The fool who stole the ladle?" Hazen leaned in closer,

he set the mug down. "Do you think they already left town with it?"

Lohrna scooted his to go cup closer to Hazen. She motioned to it. "Clarity?" she suggested.

"You're worried about the ladle thief?" Sella asked, ignoring Lohrna for now.

Hazen didn't seem to even notice Lohrna at all. His eyes were locked on Sella, he looked intense, as though he were pleading with her. "Well, of course," he said. "What kind of monster would–"

"Hazen!" Lohrna cut in, pushing his cup now directly into his hands. "Someone had been murdered! *Branzo*, the mayor, has been murdered!"

"Oh, he was rude and awful anyway," Hazen said with a wave of his hand. "And not kind to shifters, let me tell you."

Sella rubbed her eyes with her palms. This was so unlike his response to Cali's death, where he had told anyone who would listen about the value of her life, about how even though she was a stranger to most of them, she was loved and cherished and deserved to be alive. Sella was at a loss.

Cali touched Sella's arm, it was cold, and hot, at once. She opened her eyes and looked up at the ceiling, focusing on the dusty rafters. Too dusty. She'd have to do a deep clean soon.

Beejee, thankfully, spoke for her, "Who cares about some ladle? It's a gold spoon. We already made a new one."

Hazen turned to the cat, a few curls spilled over his ram horns. "I'm surprised at you," he said. "The ladle is a tradition dating back generations."

Beejee narrowed his eyes, about to retort, just as the

door opened again and Ovina and her sister, Kartha, strolled in. The town weavers, and landlords, specialized in both weaving complicated textiles and outlandish gossip. Sella was surprised to see them here, now. They rarely came in, except to get occasional remedies. And it was always with one literally pushing the other inside.

Ovina, with Kartha close behind, shuffled up to the counter.

Sella watched Ovina, dangerously close to Cali's stool, with wide eyes. Cali squeaked and disappeared as Ovina sat in her spot.

"Good morning," Hazen said with a tip of his head.

Ovina huffed. She ignored him entirely, except for a quick sideways glance. She tapped the counter with her walking stick. "Sella, Lohrna, when are you two going to solve this case?"

"He just died this morning!" Lohrna threw up her hands. "Have some heart for us! We're doing our best."

Kartha waved a finger at her, quieting her. "Who died?" she asked.

Lohrna's mouth hung open. She closed it quickly, then blurted, "Branzo!"

Ovina rolled her eyes. "Yes, yes. Such a travesty."

"No," Kartha cut in, "we meant the real crime here. The missing Golden Ladle."

Sella hit her forehead with her open palm. Of course. The damn ladle.

Kartha, either not noticing or caring about the witch's exasperation, went on, "You have spent too long prancing about the shop and doing nothing to find it and return it to where it belongs. You have to find it and make it your priority. It'll be the shame of Marra if word gets out!"

"Who *doesn't* know at this point?" Sella uttered under her breath.

Beside her, Cali shimmered into view. "Maybe Ovina killed him," she said with a laugh. "I don't trust that walking stick."

Sella's eyes darted to Cali, then back to the group.

"She wants to draw attention away from the ladle so she kills the only person no one in town would miss but would be big enough to start trouble," Cali went on, her tone teasing. "Think about it."

Sella simply sipped her coffee, watching them all and waiting for the effects of the cup to really kick in for herself.

Lohrna was leaning over Hazen to talk to Ovina with a raised finger. She looked like she was scolding the old woman, but Sella could hardly hear. She left her body drifting away, blissfully, into disassociation. Her mind was clear and calm.

Hazen broke her serenity with his booming voice. "Let's just have them focus on one mystery at a time. First the ladle, then Branzo."

Sella deflated but her focus was clear. "I have to close the shop today," she said quickly, cutting in on their squabbling. "Sorry, everyone. I have to go."

The group eyed her as if she had just spoken a made up language.

Beejee's tail flicked.

Sella waved her hands, ushering them out. She spoke quickly, before she could second guess herself, "Go on. I have to close. Goodbye."

Hazen cast a sideways glance at Sella, but stood up without fuss. He tapped the coins on the counter and nodded at her. "You got this, Sella," he said. Then, he turned to the sisters. "Come on, now. The shop's closed."

SELLA STOOD before a small house cradled at the bottom of a little mossy hill. Rows of faded white box beehives in front lead the way down a small path to the front door. But her eyes were scanning from the right, where tall lush trees loomed over the clearing, to the left, where a small drop off led to the ocean.

The sound of the waves hitting the rocks, the breeze through the leaves, the hum of the bees, all created a kind of music to Sella's ears. The sound of childhood. Of warmth, and comfort.

And yet. It sounded like screaming.

Amid the din, magic glimmered in their air surrounding the house. The faint sound like chimes in the distance, hinted at a deep, powerful magic protecting the house. It was locked, and would not open for anyone but Sella. And only if she had a quiet mind.

Sella had been back here a handful of times since they had solved Cali's murder. It had been for a number of reasons, though many felt like an obligation. The creature inside the house seemed to pull her back slowly, every so often, like a tide slowly rising.

She was just a small swimmer trying to fight the waves. The Niminé was an undertow taking her away into the deep.

It was time to come back again. But this time, to ask for help.

She held Beejee in her arms. It was one of the few times he allowed her to do so, here at their childhood home. As if he was a kitten and she was a small child, and everything was simple enough that a girl could hold a cat. He nuzzled into her neck and Sella took in a deep breath of the fresh salt air. She exhaled loudly, and felt Beejee's pur deep within her chest.

The music faded, and Beejee jumped from her arms onto the grass. "I'm looking forward to hearing what the Niminé has to say," he said.

"You're sure you don't want to come?" she asked.

Beejee thrust his head up. "No, I'm fine here."

Sella sighed and left him behind. He never wanted to come in. But that must have meant he felt she wasn't in danger in the creature's presence. Even if sometimes she felt like she might be.

The inside of the house always seemed to be just as she left it. Colorful light shone through the stained glass windows. Magic in the home made it look as though the outside was sunny and warm, even when it was overcast and chilly.

A cozy table decorated with a lace cloth and two cups of tea on either side waited for her.

Seaglass sat in the chair facing Sella with a mug in their hands. The Niminé, a legendary sea dwelling creature, had made their way to the shore long ago, and, apparently, rarely, if ever, left. At least, it was always home when Sella came by.

Always ready.

Seaglass was small, half Sella's height or so, but deadly looking. Thread thin limbs lead to fingers that moved swiftly. Sharp nails adorned each finger like a cat's claw. When Seaglass smiled, rows of shark teeth filled their face. Silver, pupiless eyes seemed to look everywhere, see everything, and stare straight into Sella's thoughts at once.

Sella could never quite decide Seaglass' age, or gender, if they had one at all. But fine wrinkles at their forehead and smile lines revealed it was at least older for their kind.

Most likely.

How Seaglass knew her mother, and why they had promised her to watch the house after her death remained a mystery. But Seaglass never spoke bluntly, always in riddles and questions and metaphors. Sella had come to peace with the possibility that she would never know its origin or true intentions. She had to trust, blindly, that the creature of myth would not harm her in her own childhood home. She had to trust that when they spoke, it was with the intention of being kind no matter how maddening the conversation felt.

But now, she needed help and she had to trust that her Clarity Blend had led her here for a reason. It seemed the kind of help she needed now was the kind that only a super-natural entity could provide. Even if their words would be deeply, deeply frustrating.

Seaglass smiled and gestured for Sella to join at the table. They had placed a steaming mug at the empty seat.

Sella breathed in deeply, doing her best to maintain the calm. The magic protecting the house was powerful. Even here, she could hear its faint chimes as her breath quickened as it often did when she had to approach the Niminé.

The magic would expel her if she got too anxious or heated and she couldn't afford to waste time trying to get back in again.

She took another long breath through her nose. The air smelled of lavender and sugar and dust. Of sunlight on skin and freshly wet earth. It was pleasant and overwhelming at once.

Sella took the chair opposite of Seaglass and stared into the mug. It was one of her mother's tea recipes, she was certain. But the memory was as tangible as the silver steam. It slipped through her mind quickly and was gone.

"Fine day we're having," the Niminé said, holding their own mug closer. "Too bad tomorrow it will rain."

Sella took her own mug and closed her fingers around the hot ceramic. She waited a moment, then took a long drink. It tasted familiar, but it wasn't exact. Something was missing, or miss proportioned.

"I never can get Tria's recipes quite right, it seems," Seaglass said once Sella swallowed. "I suppose she took her secret ingredients with her when she left this world."

It was true. Every time Sella visited, Seaglass would try to recreate a new recipe that her mother had made during her childhood. It never turned out just right.

It could be that the recipe was wrong, or, Sella suspected, both their memories that failed them and no matter what, it would never be the same. Remembering was funny like that. Always just out of reach, clouded by time. She was different now than she was then, than she would be in a moment. Nothing would ever be the same.

Sella breathed in the steam and closed her eyes, trying to access the memory itching at the corner of her mind. No matter how she searched, she could not scratch it. She breathed out, and let it go. "Seaglass," she said, locking eyes with the Niminé. "Can you help us? Someone's been murdered during the festival."

Seaglass simply blinked at her.

Sella continued, "Is there a spell, or… anything? Maybe if I could just talk to the victim–"

Seaglass tilted their head to the side, cutting Sella off. "His death is simply a symptom." Seaglass waved a hand, fingers clearing the space as if from cobwebs.

The air felt fresher. Sella breathed deeper.

"If he's gone to the other world, then he has gone," Seaglass said. "We cannot bring him back."

"But if–" Sella's hands clenched around her mug. Her fingertips warmed. "If even for a moment, isn't there any way–"

"Quiet your mind, Sella," the creature interrupted her with a voice that seemed to echo in Sella's mind. Out loud, Seaglass said, "Pushing for answers always leads to more complicated questions."

Only with you, Sella wanted to say. She kept her mouth shut, her eyes down at the table.

Seaglass seemed unfazed and went on, "Did you find how to open the rose spell yet?"

Sella shook her head. "I'm still afraid I'll break it if I try to open it," she admitted. It had been a year since she received it, along with another scroll to help Beejee talk. She sensed within the rose spell's words was something deeply powerful. But if she opened it by force, it would rip the scroll, and the magic would be gone.

Seaglass nodded, understanding, it seemed. "Yes, it can be hard to know when the time is right. But remember, time is simply a river on which we are all floating to the singular destination. It leads to the ocean and crossing the ocean takes a lot of time. In that way, it is a circle."

Sella wanted to demand that Seaglass speak plainly. Instead, she took another sip and waited. She'd have to try to decipher the riddle later.

Seaglass ran a finger in a circle on the wood of the table, their sharp nail left a mark along the wood grain. They rested a hand over the circle, and the mark was gone. "Perhaps you will travel across the sea someday, too. And take your familiar with you. I know he longs to see the other side of the world. And what a wide world it is."

Sella could whack her head on the hard wood surface. It was always riddles and questions with Seaglass. How her mother could stand it was beyond her. Seaglass made it sound like they were close when she was alive. But Sella couldn't fathom it.

She looked at her mug and tapped the ceramic lightly with her fingertips. There must have been something in this conversation that was meaningful. Something she could use.

"Alright, thank you, Seaglass," Sella grumbled at last, coming up empty on all thoughts as to what this conversation could possibly mean. Seaglass didn't have a spell to help them, not this time, and that was what mattered. She slurped the rest of her drink loudly.

"Magic has a kind of music to it, if you remember to

listen and still your mind. You cannot hear the windchimes when the hurricane is crying out."

"I guess not," Sella said.

"I think you'll find what you're looking for soon enough," Seaglass said with a smile full of sharp teeth.

Yeah, Sella thought. This house had magic she could hear. And it always wanted her out.

TWENTY-THREE

Enter at Your Own Risk

ON THEIR WALK BACK, Sella decided that the only kind thing to do was to check on Jahra. Or, really that she'd be a monster if she didn't have the decency to at least go explain things to him. The poor young man was, while employed by the King as a detective assistant, at his core just a rule-following kid who seemed to only end up in the one place someone like him could in their small town.

She knew he had seen Cali's body when it washed ashore a year ago. She hoped this was, at least, a bit less traumatizing.

"Maybe he didn't even go into the cell," Beejee suggested at her side.

Sella shrugged. "The note was pretty clear to only go at his own risk."

"Then do we *have* to go? It'll look suspicious."

"We do have the new sign saying we're part of the detective team. Petty crime happens at events like this. It'll look like we're… actually doing our jobs. Besides, I'm sure almost everyone knows by now."

Beejee grimaced, his teeth exposed, as though he had just smelled something absolutely foul. "Our job is magical beverages and pastries and remedies. That's what pays."

"And honey?" Sella suggested.

"Ah, yes. The retirement honey," Beejee said sarcastically.

Sella frowned at him, but didn't argue. He was right. At least, in that regard.

But she knew she was on the moral high ground. The right thing to do was check in on the poor man and at least see if he needed any calming blends.

When they made it to the building at last, the street was just crowded enough that she hoped no one would even notice the two of them slipping inside casually.

Jahra was pacing down the hallway when they entered. He spun toward them with wide eyes. "This is so bad, Sella!"

Sella stepped back, worried for a moment that he was about to cling to her like a frightened child. But instead, he kept his distance, going back to pacing.

"Marra is going to have *a reputation*," he went on. "One murder last year, now this? A prominent member of the region's leadership? Dead!" He turned back to her, hands clasped together. "*Please* tell me you have a lead on the Golden Ladle."

Sella shrugged.

"No!" Jahra cried, holding his head with his hands. He paced the hall again. "I'm sending for Benka. We need expert help here."

"Don't," Beejee cut in, his pride clearly wounded. "We can handle this."

Sella raised a brow at him. It was a quick change of heart from a moment ago. But that always seemed to be the way to get him to do something he didn't want to do. Just tell him he couldn't.

"Oh, who am I kidding?" Jahra said sadly, seemingly talking to himself. "By the time he gets our letter and makes it back here, it'll be too late. The festival will be over and we'll all be shamed. Tides… do you think I'll lose my job?"

Sella gathered her thoughts, her back straightened as she did her best to convey an aura of confidence. "Jahra," she said, her voice even and kind as she could make it. "I'm going to go make you a calm blend, alright? Just… Maybe take the next few days off. Stay home. You don't need to be here with Branzo… with the body."

Jahra ran a hand through his hair, his sleeve snagged on one of his horns and he had to tug it free. He looked frustrated at it all, his face was contorted like he was about to scream. Instead, he took a deep, long breath in. "Can I trust you to handle this?" he asked at last.

Sella nodded. She backed to the door and opened it slightly.

"It'll be two silver for the calming blend," Beejee said as he slipped out the door.

Sella looked back at Jahra and, with a frown, shook her head. "Free," she mouthed silently.

With the coffee delivered, Sella sent the frazzled assistant to his home. He could do the necessary paperwork there, and he was in too much of a panic to focus anyway. Sella hoped the calm blend would get the poor man to take a nice long nap despite the caffeine.

She spent the rest of the day pretending that everything

was fine and serving up potions and beverages as if nothing was amiss. For the last few hours that the shop was open, no locals came in. She felt a refreshing lightness at every person being a stranger. No one knew who she was, or what they wanted to get. They browsed the shelves as if everything was interesting to them, and she got to believe, at least in part, that everything really was fine. That there was no stolen magical item. No murderer right under their nose. That this was simply a stroke of good luck that the festival was in her small town and she was excited to be there.

She could lie to herself for a little while. It was a good day.

OF COURSE, the feeling of fake serenity didn't last into the night.

It was after closing. The shop was empty and swept. The little floating fires had all been put out, leaving the room dark and a little cold. From the bay window, folks passed by slowly. They came and went from Hazen's tavern. None looked within the shop.

Sediri and Sella were staring at each other from across the counter like two predators having a standoff. Both their bodies were tense, their eyes narrowed slightly.

Both familiars looked ready to fight.

At last, Sediri spoke, "Well, have you heard anything?"

"About what?" Beejee feigned confusion.

On her shoulder, the grackle flapped his wings.

Beejee strut across the counter to really look the other familiar in the eye with teeth bared.

Sella interrupted them before it could escalate further, "Nothing pertaining to you, or your shop."

"Well, you need to solve this fast. I'm responsible for opening this store here. It *can't* fail."

Sella threw her hands up. "That is the worst motivator, Sediri. You're trying to shut me down! Why would I help you if that's the biggest compelling reason?"

"It's not personal, Sella. It's business."

"Wouldn't it make the most business sense for us to let you take the fall, then?" Beejee hissed.

Cali cut in, appearing from the empty air like a flash of light, "Idea!"

Both Sediri and Sella jumped back. Sella's hand was wrapped around her chest, her heart raced loudly in her ears. "Tides, Cali!"

"Sorry!" Cali whispered to Sella. She turned to an equally frightened Sediri but went on as though the other witch was not gasping at the air like a fish out of water. "How about this? If you agree to drop the whole thing about the siren statues, we'll keep working on the case."

"What?" Beejee and Sella said in unison.

Cali nodded at them. "Penya's up in a frenzy about it. And you promised to take care of it. Besides, it's not right to strip Marra of its history." She turned back to Sediri. "Stop threatening to take the statues, leave the old woman alone, and we'll work on this with you."

Sediri's back straightened. She smoothed the front of her dress, then looked at the ghost with half closed eyes. "I can't do that," she said.

Cali huffed.

"You are obligated to solve this case, Sella," Sediri said,

focusing her attention back to the other witch. "You are a consultant. Do your duty or I'll report you to the authorities. *The real* authorities outside this filthy fish town."

"Hey!" Beejee yowled.

Sediri's bright eyes flicked back to the ghost. "Instead of trying to make ridiculous deals, ghost, think about *my* offer. I wouldn't put my trust in this one," she said, eyes flashing to Sella. "She's a selfish mess and–"

"Get! Out!" Cali screamed.

A burst of wind blew around Sediri and Majla. Sediri grabbed her hair and held her familiar close. She looked at Cali with wide, frightened eyes, and the wind stilled.

"Get out of this shop," Cali said, her chest puffed as she breathed in deeply.

"Think about it," Sediri said again, regaining her composure. She turned on her heel and the bell above the door chimed as she left.

Sella sank behind the counter. She snapped her fingers and the door locked. "What a disaster."

Cali crouched down beside her and rested a hand on Sella's knee. "I won't even consider her 'offer'," she said with a small smile.

"Thank you for defending me." Sella let her head fall.

Cali laughed. "Of course. Sorry I got a bit angry, though. There was probably a better way of handling that."

Sella shook her head. "I like the fire," she said at last.

Cali's eyes narrowed playfully at Sella. "Except when it's directed at you."

"Even then."

"The audacity of that witch, though. My request was simple and easy, right?"

Sella shrugged. "Maybe not. Maybe the company has a bigger hold on her than we know. She doesn't want to do anything to upset them."

Cali hummed. Her thumb followed the curve of Sella's knee. "And to think she'd try to make that offer to me again. In front of you."

"Maybe you should consider it, though," Sella said.

"I want *your* magic to help me." Cali squeezed. Her voice grew quiet, she whispered, "I just want you."

Sella felt a cold finger under her chin slowly pull her face up. Cali held her gaze, and then her hand turned to mist. The corners of her eyes wrinkled as the smile reached her eyes. She leaned in close, and disappeared just before their lips touched.

Sella waited, one hand outstretched.

Cali's voice, light like chimes, sounded, "It's hard to haunt. Go see Lohrna and come up with a plan to help everyone. I'll be upstairs when you get home."

Sella felt the sting of tears prick at her eyes. She closed them tight, then curled her legs close to her chest. Cali was gone. The void of her presence felt like the impossibly small feeling when the clouds parted and Sella gazed in wonderment at every inch of the night sky filled with stars.

"That woman is a poltergeist," Beejee said. His voice brought Sella's body to the ground. He rubbed his head into the back of her hand. She knew he meant it well. Pride radiated through him.

Cali had defended her. As best she could. Even with everything piling on her, Sella felt safe and warm. Cared for.

TWENTY-FOUR

The Runner Up

SELLA RELUCTANTLY FOLLOWED the crowd coming out of the hotel and tavern as festival goers made their way to the market. As she passed the siren statues, they hummed a low song. She shivered, and glanced up at the sky. Past the rows of colorful flags and banners connecting the businesses, the stars were hidden behind a layer of low hanging clouds.

Seaglass was right. It was going to rain.

And Cali was right. It was her job to help however she could.

At her feet, Beejee trotted alongside her. "Yes, yes, the decor is delightful," he said. "Let's keep moving."

Sella picked up her pace, but continued to trail behind one of the large groups. Her eyes scanned the backs of heads for Lohrna's antlers. But most of the crowd seemed to be human. It was an odd feeling to suddenly be in the minority.

The town square was huge. Vendors, all Marrans, had all reopened for the night market. Colorful lanterns hung from booths and tall metal posts, illuminating faces with soft shadows as they passed by. Expressions ranged from excited, to fearful.

While no one seemed particularly sad about Branzo's death, it was still a shock and by now, she was sure everyone knew about it. A murder, even if they didn't know the details, even if they didn't like the person, was still scary. Sella understood.

Beejee, less so.

"Idiots," he hissed under his breath.

Sella exhaled. She tried to ignore him, remembering instead her annoying conversation with Seaglass just as a few light raindrops began to fall. Magic had a sound… But Branzo hadn't been killed by magic. At least, not a magic she knew of. Probably not one Sediri could manage either. She wondered if it meant she needed to be more open and listen better.

With a furrowed brow, she turned into a crowd and listened, waiting for something to spark a flame within her. But she only made it a few feet into the market when she heard, "Good evening, Sella."

She turned to face Mims, immaculately dressed as, it seemed, he always was. He held his hands in his pockets stiffly.

So, no handshake this time. She wondered briefly if Cirian had kissed him.

He nodded his head to her as if prompting her to speak.

"Good evening," she said at last as Beejee brushed up against her ankles. He trotted off quickly into the market, leaving her in the crowd. "Where is Lohrna?"

Mims smiled but Sella felt anything but warmth from him. "She's with the others in the group. They are doing community service. It is always best practice to leave the community in a better way than we found it."

"And you? Are you too good for community service?"

He chuckled, hands remaining firmly in his pockets. "No, nothing like that. I am here to make sure our presence will be welcome. It's only two nights until the full moon."

"You have your suppressant potion, though," Sella said, as if he didn't remember.

Mims nodded. "Indeed, but some places, especially small towns," he emphasized with a terse nod, "are less than educated on the matter. I take it you, in particular, are more open?"

Sella didn't like where this conversation was going. She hated how he was able to turn her questions back to her. And how he seemed so entitled to an answer. "Tell Lohrna to come find me. When she's done with her service." She dodged his question less gracefully than she would have liked but she said what she needed to and that was what mattered.

Mims looked like he was about to say something else when a loud, booming voice broke through the crowd.

"Sella!" Cirian cried out, throwing a thick arm around her shoulders.

Mims, looking visibly flustered at the show of affection. He backed up slowly. "Enjoy the festivities," he said, then slipped into a passing group like a shadow hiding in the dark.

Sella shrugged Cirian's arm off her. "Hi there," she said. "Seen Beejee around?"

Cirian laughed, held his drink aloft and then gestured at the crowd. "A little cat in all this? No. But I have seen this bird," he pointed with his free hand at a nearby post where Majla loomed, surveying the square.

Leave it to Sediri to not trust her to get the job done.

"He's eyeing me suspiciously," Cirian said, gaze locked on Majla.

"He eyes everyone suspiciously, don't take it personally," Sella retorted quickly. She pulled her cloak around her chest tighter.

Cirian put his arm over her shoulder again. Sella stiffened, but he didn't seem to notice. He ushered her along to a vendor, the flower seller in town. His booth was crowded with various gourds and red and yellow flowers, but empty of customers.

Sella glanced to the far end of the square where Hazen had set up a temporary table and was selling drinks. She looked back up at Cirian. "Everything okay?"

"Any word on the… well, you know," the flower vendor, a tall, lanky man with thick goat horns asked in a hushed tone.

"The… spoon?" Sella asked.

He nodded.

"No, Ralka, I don't have any information for you on the spoon." Sella said quietly. But she wanted to scream. How did everyone know about the damn Golden Ladle? And why did no one care about Branzo?

"Have you considered the new witch as a suspect?" Ralka asked.

Sella glared at him.

"What about that society that's come in?"

Cirian, arm still around Sella, growled. "Come on,

Ralka," he said in a low tone. "None of that bigotry talk. I won't hear it."

"But they—"

"You've met one shifter in your life, and you know she's gold," Cirian said.

"A man's been murdered!" Sella's whisper cut through their back and forth. She waved at Ralka but he seemed unfazed.

"Yes, but…"

She turned to Cirian with narrowed eyes and pulled him around the flower booth and into a back alley. "Alright," she said once they were alone in the shadows. "Out with it, tell me what you know about Branzo."

Cirian took a causal drink from his cup as if he hadn't heard her. He looked up at the sky with a slight shrug. "Not much to say. He was a self-serving, silly, dangerous man… And. I will miss him, I suppose."

Sella raised a brow at him.

Cirian sighed, and Sella realized she had not heard this kind of exasperated sound from him before. He had blown into town while she was away, spending money, making friends, and taking life entirely too cheerfully since.

This version of him? This was new, at least to her. "He was my cousin," he said with a shake of his head. "And I will miss him."

Sella felt as though the ground beneath her had suddenly shifted. "Branzo was your cousin?"

Crian laughed, his usual joyful mood returning quickly. "Yes, he was. And what a foolish man he'd always been."

"I'll find who did this and get justice for you," Sella said. She grasped onto Cirian's sleeve. "I promise."

"I know you will, Sella," he said. His face grew grim. "But promise you'll find the person who stole the ladle too? Hazen's been so worried…"

"I'll do my best," Sella said.

"I trust your best." Cirian turned back to the vendors, the bright and bustling square. "Any leads?"

"I feel like the ladle and the murder are connected, but I can't figure out how. Whoever stole the ladle did so without disturbing anything at Hazen's. Or waking him. And what motive? To bring Marra down? We're hardly a pinprick on the map."

"Coin?" Cirian suggested. "It'd be worth *a lot* of money."

Sella considered it. A magical relic with a long history, made entirely of gold. Yes, that would be worth a lot. Was it possible Branzo had debts? If so, then, where was the ladle? She bit her bottom lip, her mind raced, but her thoughts were impossible to hold. She felt steady for a moment, then the waves crashed into her, knocking her down again. Branzo and Sediri knew each other, at least a little. But she didn't want to ask her too many questions outright and she also didn't want to just set her sights on her simply because she and Branzo had a disagreement once.

"I'll see if I hear anything tonight," she said at last. "What do you think about the MAMBOSSA?"

Cirian's eyes narrowed slightly. "Sella, I'm surprised at you. You know shifters aren't shifty. MAMBOSSA seems like they're trying really hard to make a good name for themselves. They're going out of their way to make everyone comfortable even though they're here for a short time. I don't think any of them would risk it for a ladle."

"Perhaps," Sella said. "Mims makes me feel uneasy."

Cirian shrugged. "Yeah, that's fair." He guided Sella out of the alleyway and back into the warm glow of the festival. "Doesn't make him a thief, though."

"Or a murderer," Sella mumbled.

"That's the spirit!" Cirian slapped her back so hard she lurched forward.

Sella looked up at him with a harsh glare just as Beejee scampered up to them.

"Let's go," he said, motioning with a tilt of his little gray head. "I think I may have something."

Cirian nodded to them both. "Go on, then! Solve this thing!" He was making his way to Hazen's table before either of them had a chance to say goodbye.

Sella followed Beejee through the crowd, weaving and dodging arms and bodies as she went. Her familiar was in a hurry.

They stopped at the other end of the square in front of a group of humans. One of them, Sella recognized from her shop earlier. She smiled gently at her and the human grinned back brightly.

"Tell her what you told me," Beejee demanded loudly above the noise of the festival.

The human woman's smile grew even bigger. "I'll never get over this! A talking cat!"

"Witch's familiar," Beejee corrected.

She took a sip of her beverage quickly. "Amazing!" She turned to Sella. "I was saying to my friends here that your Practical Potions blend was so much better than Kepilla. I'll admit, I shopped at both to get a comparison."

"Oh," Sella said, trying to not sound so dejected. She

expected it to be something more, though a part of her swelled with pride at the compliment. "Thank you," she finished her thought quickly.

"Well, it's true. Better coffee flavor and better remedy," the human woman said. "Besides. I don't want to gossip but…" She lifted her long sleeve shirt, revealing a series of red, angry looking stripes across her forearm. "Do you have a cure for this…?"

Sella squinted in the dim light at the marks. She opened her hand and waited.

The woman placed her arm in Sella's grasp and let her turn it over, inspecting it closely.

She had seen marks like this before. On Branzo.

"I think it's a bad reaction to Woodwort," the woman said. "They use it back home in a lot of recipes. But if you rush the distillation process, some people get this reaction. I'm one of the lucky ones sensitive to it."

Sella's brows furrowed. She let the woman's arm go. "What's the cure? I'm sorry, I've just never seen this. I would have thought it was a reaction to… something else." She wanted to say poison, but stopped, not wanting to scare the woman.

"I was hoping you'd tell me," she said. "I've had this reaction before. It goes away in a few days but there is a way to speed up the healing. I don't know the ingredients, though. I'm not a witch." She said it all very kindly, a tone Sella was unaccustomed to when the word 'witch' was used.

"I'll see what I can do to help," Sella said.

The woman thanked her and turned back to the group.

Sella maneuvered through the crowd again in a daze. There was a lot to chew on that she had learned this evening, but she knew she had to stay to support Hazen. At least, until they announced the event's winner.

"I'll go this way," Beejee told her, slinking quickly through legs and under booted feet.

"I'll go this way, I guess," she whispered, though he was already gone. She wandered over to Ovina's booth where she and her sister were showing off a quilted blanket to a few Wyldes, but faces she didn't recognize.

A human stopped beside them. Sella recognized him as the man from the shop who had been so secretive about his purchases. Sella watched the interaction closely, lingering on the outskirts of the group and pretending to be very enthralled with the fruit stand next to them.

"What intricate work," the man said to the weavers.

Sella's ear twitched. He had a way of speaking that made her feel uneasy. But she couldn't exactly fault him for it. There was nothing really about him that was offensive. She glanced his way to see him running a hand down the quilt as the two Wyldes beside him backed up a few steps.

"It takes a lot of hard work to make these quilts," Kartha said proudly. "This one shows the history of Marra."

"And a rich one it is," Ovina said dramatically. "A humble fishing town, to a port for those from across the sea. We even have our own kitchen witch."

"Now, two," Kartha added.

"And our own ghost."

Sella's hands burned. They have some nerve talking about her as if they hadn't accused her of murder just a year ago. As if they hadn't booked Cali's old apartment knowing full well she was still there.

"Ah," the man said. "Yes, this town has a lot of intriguing marketing for a little port, at least. The hotel has been advertising itself to be one of a kind. And charging accordingly."

"We don't haggle," Ovina said, rather defensively. She pulled the quilt from his hands and folded it up.

"Perhaps you'll have two ghosts now that Branzo has also been murdered?" the man said, as if that was a recovery.

Sella looked at them from the corner of her eye.

Ovina and Kartha were glaring at him.

"He's dead," Ovina declared. "That's the only official statement. We don't know it's murder."

"Official statement from your kitchen witch?" he asked. He turned to Sella, "Any updates, consultant?"

Sella flinched. She was never as sneaky as she thought she was. "I am a certified kitchen witch," she said. "And the King had approved the paperwork. I'm an official consultant too."

"I never doubted," he said.

Sella's eyes scanned him from head to toe. He was so... ordinary. Nothing about him was offensive or out of place. "What did you say your name was?" Sella asked. She held out a hand, the custom of Tollintal.

The man took hers and shook it twice. "I didn't," he said.

Sella let him go quickly. Her annoyance was bubbling over into heat in her palms. She took a deep breath through her nose, hopeful he wouldn't notice. "Well, then," she said awkwardly. "I'll come by the hotel if I need to speak with you."

The man smiled, a kind expression despite his secrecy.

"I don't like humans," Kartha spat after the man made his way into the square.

"About that," Sella said, turning to face the two older women. "We are going to need to talk about terms of lease once the festival is over. Ipla and Rizan can't stay in that unit. It's haunted."

Ovina crossed her arms. "Go solve the bigger mystery here, kitchen witch," she said.

"Does the big mystery have to do with soup?"

Ovina and Kartha nodded. "Go on," they waved her away like a little kid who had overstayed their welcome on a front porch.

From the middle of the square, Hazen's booming voice quieted the crowd. "Tonight, we honor our lost leader! Branzo was a..." he trailed off, his eyes looking over the crowd cautiously. He moved a hand to his eye to play it off like he was getting choked up. Sella knew better. "Branzo was a strong leader and a pillar of the community. We celebrate him tonight and wish him well into the afterlife!"

A few people in the crowd clapped, some weakly, others a little too enthusiastically. Sella tried to pinpoint where each sound was coming from and gauge people's faces. But it was impossible to make out where in the large crowd the noises came from.

A small breeze blew and the lanterns overhead swayed, casting shadows about. She gave up and focused again on Hazen.

"And tonight, we announce the winner of today's gem hunt! The goal was to find lost gems hidden among the shore and I am pleased to announce the winner is none other than our very own Lohrna! Come on up, Lohrna! Where are you at?"

The Marrans in the crowd went wild, cheering and hollering. But Lohrna was nowhere to be found.

Hazen looked around. "Lohrna? Don't be shy! Come on up!"

Sella stood on her toes to see but she couldn't catch a glimpse of her. She would be thrilled to know she won. Finding rocks and gems was one of her favorite hobbies. She felt a pang of sadness in her heart. She was still with MAMBOSSA then? Missing this?

"She's not here!" someone from the right shouted. "That means it goes to the next!"

Hazen scratched his forehead. He waited. "Lohrna?" he called one more time. There was no answer but the murmur of the crowd. Hazen's shoulders looked heavy. He announced the runner up, some name Sella didn't recognize.

The crowd cheered again but all Sella felt was defeated. She hoped at least Lohrna got to keep the rock she had found.

Beejee and Sella left the festival early. They could hear the little flapping wings of a bird following them home but every time they looked up, he was gone.

TWENTY-FIVE

Reactions and Remedies

"So… Sediri hit him over the head after he had a bad reaction to an ingredient, then? Maybe they got into a fight and it has nothing to do with the ladle at all?" Cali sat on the countertop. Her legs swung gently. "I guess that could make sense. She'll do anything to make her shop successful. And if people are getting reactions to the ingredient, then it would absolutely hurt her business."

Sella hesitated. She was working over a boiling little kettle, using all the heat from her hands that she could to warm it without the bubbles bursting over.

Outside, it had begun to rain harder. Sella's eyes moved to the window, and she wondered, for a moment, if the festival was still continuing in the rain. If Lohrna got to enjoy any of it at all.

She snorted. Community service.

"Everything okay?" Cali asked, leaning down to catch Sella's gaze.

The witch nodded. "Yes, I just… want to be sure I get this right," she lied.

From the corner of Sella's gaze, she saw Cali's mouth twitch.

She never could quite get away with a lie to Cali. Or, more likely, to anyone. She knew she wore her feelings on her face no matter how stoic she wished she was. She took in a deep breath and watched her own eyes in the reflection of the kitchen knife she held in her hands.

"You're worried about Lohrna?" Cali pried.

Sella's forehead wrinkled. She focused on crushing just the tip of the long brown root on the stone slab. "A bit, I guess."

"I understand," Cali said. She wandered over to Sella's side, casually, as if she was merely passing by. But she stopped and stood on her toes to look over Sella's shoulder. "You're a good friend, Sella. Even though you don't feel like it."

Sella grimaced a little. Her ears turned hot. She glanced behind her, then back to her potion. "Thanks," she said at last. She pressed down on the root with the side of the knife. It made a dull crackling sound just as the fire in the large hearth grew bolder.

"This looks complicated," Cali said. She moved to the other side of Sella and leaned in to watch closely.

"Well, I want to do right by this person affected by one of Sediri's blends…" She trailed off, knife still pressed down on the root. "Do you think Sediri is capable of killing someone?"

Cali shrugged. "Physically? Maybe not. Mentally? I don't know. She seems like she would do whatever it takes to keep her shop open and make it a success here. Asking me to turn on you at least shows a poor judge of character, doesn't it?"

Sella felt a cold touch to her chin as Cali's hand directed her gaze. The ghost smiled gently. "It's frustrating, being dead," she whispered, her hand lowered slowly. "But there's always the sheet."

Sella felt a small laugh escape her. She looked at the wardrobe, remembering when Cali had first shown up at her home, a sheet over her head, glasses outlining her face. Sella's cheeks reddened. "I'll find the spell."

"I know you will," Cali said. She pressed up and kissed Sella again, but it was only as if mist had touched her. The ghost pulled away, a smile on her lips, and sad eyes searching Sella's for something she couldn't quite find. "Which is why Sediri is either terribly desperate or terribly unobservant if she ever thought I'd betray you."

Sella reached out, the tips of her fingers grazed a solid form of Cali's hand, but... it wasn't skin. It felt like stone. She looked down at their hands. Touching, but not quite. Holding, but no warmth. She took in a deep breath to still the tears forming in her eyes. "Calisyali..."

TAP.

The two turned to the window. Past their faded reflections, an orange blur filled part of the space. The cat scratched the window again, claws clanking dully on the glass.

Sella couldn't help but smile wider. She squeezed Cali's hand and then went to the window to let in a wet, and angry looking Koukie.

The orange cat scampered across the writing desk, dripping droplets of rainwater along the way before she hopped down and shook out her fur.

From his place by the fire, Beejee opened one eye and said, "About time, you feral stray. I ate your dinner, by the way. If you want food, you better be home on time."

Koukie licked her paw as if she hadn't heard. But still, she meowed gently as her paw cleaned her face.

Beejee's ear twitched. "She says Lohrna's outside," he translated. "And that the alley cats are going to get that grackle yet."

Sella gave Koukie's head a quick but gentle pet. "Be careful, Koukie. Familiars have magic, too." She rose to her feet and said, "I guess we better fill Lohrna in."

TWENTY-SIX

Practical Potions Detective Agency

THE THREE SAT at Sella's table. A pile of freshly baked mini muffins were stacked in the middle, filling the loft air with the sweet and nutty smell of spices and pumpkin. It made the rain outside feel far away. Here, they were warm and safe, and well fed. Opora and all its chaos was down below, a world away.

Cali sat by Sella with a floral patterned sheet over her head, a pair of Sella's reading glasses, and what Sella assumed was a large smile on her face beneath.

Lohrna was groaning to the point of near profanity as she stuffed another bite into her mouth though it was clear she hadn't finished the first one.

Beejee looked on, horrified. His mouth was agape, exposing his sharp teeth. He looked at Lohrna, then the tray of muffins, then back.

"These are *so* good, Sella," Lohrna said, midchew. She sighed, lending back in her chair. "Oh, oceans and seas…"

Sella's brows rose higher. "Are they starving you?"

Lohrna opened her eyes, swallowed, then said, "Seems

that way. There's *so many* rules." She straightened up in her chair and listed them with her fingers counting along. "We can't eat everything on our plate. It makes us look gluttonous. So we have to leave at least several bites *of each* food item. Turns out we can eat meat. Just not meat after dark or the week of the full moon. It makes us look predatory. We can't use our hands. For *anything.* They eat their scones with forks. Do you know crumbly eating one of Hazen's old *scones* with a *fork* is? It's impossible to get anything in your mouth! You look foolish and can't eat it so you may as well not even bother! Then, you can't wear red or black or white the week of the full moon. Apparently, those are hostile colors and we don't want to appear hostile. You have to open doors for people. Every time. And you can't sneak through, so if there's *all the people*, you're stuck there, holding the door *for eternity.* You have to fold your napkin–"

"Take a breath," Beejee cut her off. "We get it. Lots of rules. And stupid ones at that. Remind me why you'd want to join this group again?"

Sella shook her head at him.

Lohrna took another mini muffin and used it as a pointer to enunciate each word. "Forks. And. Scones. Are *not* friends." She ate the whole muffin with one big bite. When she finished chewing, she said, "They're so secretive, too. As the newest member, I have to basically be a master manipulator to get anything out of any of them."

"I wouldn't exactly call you that," Beejee said under his breath.

"Me either, friend," Lohrna didn't miss a beat or seem to take any offense. "I know my limitations and I'm not exactly subtle."

Beejee seemed taken aback. He cocked his head at her.

"But, I did find out that all of them shift involuntarily during the full moon... Except for Mims. Who can change at will."

Cali started, "Mims? How did you–"

"He told me like it's some kind of thing to be proud of!" Lohrna said. "This guy can shift into his form whenever he wants. But somehow he's better than us because he's a, and wait until you get this... a mouse."

Sella's eyes closed slowly. "A mouse?" It was hard to imagine someone like Mims, large, imposing, a quiet yet scary leader, as... well, a mouse. "Every full moon, he turns into a mouse?"

"*And* he can do it at will," Lohrna added with a raised eyebrow. "He thinks it means he's mastered the control of the condition." She turned to Cali. "And he thinks he's somehow less... less shifty because he's not something scary. Idiot."

Cali laughed, and though Lohrna could not hear it, she noticed the ripple in the sheet.

"Right? Cali gets it." Lohrna pointed to Cali. "Ridiculous."

"But if he's a mouse–" Beejee began.

"He could have stolen the ladle," Sella finished his sentence.

"I don't disagree, and that occurred to me, too." Lohrna leaned forward in her seat. "But why would he? We're missing a motive."

Sella tilted her head, considering. "Is MAMBOSSA hurting for finances?"

Lohrna shrugged. Her fingers grazed the edge of

another mini pastry. She moved a large grain of sugar between her thumb and forefinger. "Hard to say. No one's talked about coin, but they don't seem like they have jobs, really. And they travel all throughout Orakan as far as I can tell."

"That could be it," Cali said. "The Golden Ladle would be worth more money than they'd need to finance their travels and stays."

Sella nodded. "Maybe Mims was trying to fund their travels," she translated.

Lohrna's gaze shifted to her. She was still fiddling with the sugar but her stare was intense. Sella felt an unease within her. She tried to maintain calm as she did with the Niminé, though she felt like she was suddenly on unsteady ground and could stumble into a dark pit at any moment.

She chose her words carefully, "He may have had good intentions. But… stealing is not the right way."

Cali's head, beneath the sheet, turned to look at each of them, then back again. She was waiting for one of them to flinch.

Lohrna blinked slowly, then nodded. She leaned back in her chair again. "You're right. It'll hurt Marra if it's discovered that the ladle went missing during our watch. But… will it be discovered at all, even if we don't find the real one? How good is the fake? Is it passable as it moves to the next town in a year?"

Sella breathed out a sigh of relief. Lohrna wasn't angry with her.

At her side, Beejee folded up on himself, finally content to loaf on the counter.

"It's a good fake," Sella said. "But witches, and maybe

some older Wyldes will be able to tell it apart. The original is fused with magic. This one isn't."

"Can you recreate it?" Lohrna asked. "The magic, I mean."

"I don't think so," Sella said honestly. "It's old magic. Beyond my skill level and ability."

"Not elemental," Beejee said, eyes closed.

Sella glared at him.

He opened one eye, looked at her, then closed it.

A year later, and he was still getting used to the fact that everyone could understand him. Any kind of magic other than that of a kitchen witch was shunned in Orakan. Many didn't even approve of kitchen witch's magic. Elemental magic? That was something they actually needed to keep quiet about.

His tail flicked.

"Old magic, right," Lohrna said, skirting past the obvious tension. "So… not what you can do. Not now, at least," she added optimistically. She paused, eyes darting as she considered what seemed to be a thousand thoughts while she bit into another muffin. "So then we definitely need it back before the end of Opora. Which is… two days from now."

"On the full moon," Sella added.

Lohrna sat up a little straighter, but said nothing. She had always turned down Sella's offer for suppression potion. Now that she was with MAMBOSSA, though, Sella wasn't sure if she would finally take it.

Part of Sella wanted to ask what she was going to do. But she knew it was best to wait for Lohrna to come to her.

Lohrna was always honest. She'd tell Sella when she was ready.

Instead, Sella changed the subject, "Well, I think we have our suspect for the missing ladle. We have the way he could've done it unseen and without looking like a break in. And we have a good motive."

Lohrna nodded. "Makes sense. I wish it didn't, though." She sighed and let her head fall over the back of the chair. "MAMBOSSA has a lot of annoying rules. But… I would hate for them to be sinister. Even if they think it's for the right reasons. I just…" She sat back up straight again. "Oh, never mind. Do you think we can try to handle it quietly?"

"We'll definitely need to handle it carefully," Sella said. "One, so folks don't blame the whole society needlessly. And two, so they don't know we made a fake."

"That *would* put Marra on the map, though," Beejee said.

"I don't think we want *our* name associated with anything else scandalous," Sella said. "We really can't afford another incident."

Cali nodded. "Sediri did call you 'wand breaker'. So word has gotten out about Isra…"

Sella's forehead hit the table. She felt like she had been kicked in the gut.

Of course Sediri would use that insult. And of course it wasn't to her face. If she could defend herself, she'd tell Sediri that it was her mother's wand, not Isra's. That Isra had used it for evil. That it was a good thing that it was snapped in two and lay decaying on the forest floor.

Sella groaned as she felt a gentle pat on her back. The touch pulled her back into her body and out of her mind.

"Hang in there," Lohrna said kindly. "We'll get Mims on his own and confront him. Very quietly. Very mouselike."

Sella smiled, despite herself. "Alright," she said. "Can you try to get him to come into the shop? Maybe that could work as a quiet place where it wouldn't look too suspicious like we're questioning him."

"I'll try to get it done before the stew competition tomorrow night," Lohrna said. "He's pretty invested in MAMBOSSA winning that one. He says that if the folks all see that they can make a good home cooked meal, then our reputation will improve. Something about it being a sign of old hospitality."

"I mean, that's something," Sella said, sitting up finally. "I'm not saying all his ideas are amazing, but Marra does love their food."

Lohrna slapped Sella's back, hard. She turned to Cali with a wide grin. "Practical Potions Detective Agency is back!"

TWENTY-SEVEN

The Alley Cats of Marra

THE NEXT DAY WAS QUIET. Except for a few regulars stopping in to inquire about the missing ladle, there was little movement in or outside the shop. Sella rested her chin in her palm, feeling an odd kind of sadness that had begun to settle in her ribs, slowly weaving its way deeper into her lungs until her breath grew shallow.

Branzo seemed like he was kind of a ridiculous person. But was he actively harmful? Cirian had called him dangerous. She had no idea if that was true, but it felt strange that no one seemed concerned that he died, that they might be next, or that a killer was on the loose. Even the out of towners barely seemed to care that a major death had occurred during the course of the festivities.

Sella stood up and shook out her dress. For now, she'd have to come to terms with it. He was gone and not missed at all, and that was that. Still, two murders in her small town after lifetimes of peace felt like it was definitely too much. She needed to find whoever did this. Even if no one seemed to care. Even if a part of her, the darkest part, didn't care either.

When night fell and Lohrna had not come in, though, worry rooted deep within her.

"I'm sure she's fine," Beejee said as they waited by the door. "She can take care of herself."

Sella crossed her arms. She looked out the window and saw the faint shapes of people making their way from Hazen's to the town square. The stew competition would be beginning soon.

They squinted out into the night just as a tall figure approached. The bell above the door chimed and Lohrna came in, already huffing.

"I can't find him anywhere!"

Sella unfolded her arms. She ushered her friend into the shop. "That's odd…"

Lohrna threw off her overcoat, it landed on the floor and Sella was quick to scoop it up.

Beejee scampered up alongside them. He looked up at them, tail raised high. "Maybe he's a mouse," he suggested. "You said he could shift at will. Might be that he's up to something nefarious."

Lohrna stopped, she looked down at Beejee. "You may be right," she said. "But… How do we track down a mouse?"

Beejee nodded to a sleeping Koukie cat, curled up in a large orange fluff ball on the counter. "Finally put this menace and her alley cats to good use," he said. He jumped up onto the counter and swatted her ear gently, but with enough force to cause her to hiss at him. "Yes, yes, I know I could be more tactful," he said to her. "We're looking for a mouse. One that behaves differently than other mice."

Koukie slowly stretched, then yawned, little pink tongue curling in her mouth. She straightened, then meowed.

"She says she'll gather the filthy strays."

"I don't think that's how she said it…" Sella folded Lohrna's coat over her arm as she eyed the two cats carefully.

"I'm paraphrasing."

"Well, thanks, Koukie!" Lohrna said brightly. She gave the orange cat a quick scratch and followed her to the other side of the shop, opening the door for her as she left.

"I'm proud of her," Cali said, appearing in the doorway.

Lohrna let the door shut, passing quickly through Cali's form.

The ghost let out a small squeak. She shimmered out of view, and back, this time, much deeper in the shop.

Sella's face softened. "Hi Cali," she said, mostly for Lohrna's benefit.

Lohrna followed Sella's eyes to the empty space in the middle of the room. "Oh good, you're here! So, I wasn't able to find Mims, but Koukie's on the case! We should probably get to the festival, though. I know the competition will be starting soon and it's not like we will find any clues to either crime sitting here."

"She's got a point," Cali said with a laugh. "Let's go see what we can find out. And I want to smell some stew."

"You may regret that," Sella said under her breath as they stepped out of the shop and into the crisp, damp air. "It's all fish stew."

Cali waved her hand. "That's alright, I think it'll be an aroma adventure."

"I admire your commitment to seeing the positive," Beejee said, though his tone was begrudging. He walked with his head turning about like an owl, watching for any sign of Mims or Majla.

"Coming from you, Beejee, that is the highest compliment," Cali said. "I'll take it."

Lohrna leaned in a little as they quickened their pace down the cobblestone street, passing rows of connected homes on one side. When they passed the emerald door, Cali's home, Lohrna asked, "So, Cali, how goes the haunting?"

"Thanks for asking!" Cali said brightly. "I'm getting absolutely nowhere and it's the worst."

"There's that positive attitude," Beejee mumbled.

Sella snorted at their delivery. She wished Lohrna could have heard. "She said it's going terribly," she conveyed to Lohrna. "But she said it quite happily."

"It's for comedic effect," Cali said, raising a finger to drive home the point.

They turned the corner and entered the market square.

People gathered around rows of booths where large pots, all steaming and some bubbling, were placed. Little tags below each one indicated a number, rather than the name of the person or group competing. Sella had to admit, that did make things more fair. She had been, albeit very minimally, concerned that the Marrans would all just vote for each other.

She made eye contact with Hazen who gave her a quick, concerned expression. She knew he was wondering about the ladle. She shook her head quickly and moved on deeper into the crowd. She caught bits of conversation here and there as they moved together from one booth to the next.

"-- not too worried about it."

"-- word on who will take over?"

"Whole thing's rigged anyway."

"He got what was coming to him."

Sella's eyes shifted to that voice. Whoever said that, it sounded promising. But she couldn't decipher who had said it. Got what was coming to him? A chill ran up her arms.

A few heads away, Sella spotted the woman who had requested the potion for her Woodwort marks. She gave Lohrna and Cali a silent signal that she was moving in an unexpected direction, then made her way to the group.

The woman turned to look up at her when she approached. She grinned brightly.

"Hi," Sella said, feeling awkward. She fished out a small vial from her skirt pocket and handed it to her. "I'm not sure this will be terribly effective, but hopefully it helps."

The woman took the small glass vial. "Thank you! If it doesn't work, do I get my money back?"

"Oh," Sella took a small step back. "No. No charge. I'm not really sure it will work."

The woman looked down at the liquid. "It's okay, it's not like it itches, anyway." She put the vial in the bag slung across her chest carefully. "Tell you what, if it works, I'll buy a cup of coffee from you. If it doesn't... Well, who are we kidding? I'll still get a cup as a 'thanks for trying' offering."

"Sounds like a plan," Sella said.

Beside her, Cali flickered. She looked at the woman, then to Sella. "Who's this?" she asked.

Sella gave the woman a nod. "What's your name?" she asked for both Cali and herself.

"You can call me Malici," she said, kindly. "I noticed our names from across the sea can be hard for you folks to pronounce."

Sella smiled. She wasn't wrong. "I hope the remedy works, Malici."

"Yeah. Me too," Malici laughed.

Sella made her way back to Lohrna with Cali at her side.

"A coffee and free remedy?" Cali huffed.

"Malici seems nice. Why? Are you–?"

"Jealous? No," Cali said, entirely too fast. "After all, who can compete with a ghost?"

Sella felt a stab in her heart. Cali said it like a joke, but she knew her better. Cali was feeling off. Hurt. And if Sella thought the reason was silly or not, it didn't matter. In the end, it hurt that Cali was dead. Sella slipped her hand into Cali's, though her fingers passed through with ease. "No one can compete with you because you're you," she said.

Lohrna raised a brow at her. "Why thank you."

Sella blushed. "Come on," she said to both of them. "I think I heard something about Branzo over there."

But no matter how they circulated and listened, the night only grew louder and sillier until at last, Hazen stood on a chair, and called out loudly, "Judges! Take your ladles! The tasting will begin momentarily!"

Sella stood on her toes to make out the several dozen judges, each with a small golden ladle in their hand as they gathered behind the tables.

"Thank you to Tallam for the tasting ladles," Hazen's

voice projected. Beside him, a very uncomfortable looking Tallam waved, then his shoulders slumped back into himself. "And a thank you to all who entered the competition–"

Sella didn't hear the rest of his speech. At her feet, Koukie meowed loudly with a brown, thrashing mouse caught in her jaws. "Oh!" Sella tugged on Lohrna's sleeve. She pointed to the ground quickly, then to the alley where they could quickly get out of sight. "Hurry!"

Koukie led the way, tail held high.

Next to her, Beejee was showering her with praise, sprinkled with, "Of course those flea infested cats were no help. Told you they were the worst."

Koukie chirped with the mouse still dangling from her jaws.

"I refuse to believe that plan worked," he said in return.

The group slipped into the alley. Away from the noise of the festival, and the warm glow of lanterns, Sella felt the cold on her skin begin to prickle. She knelt down to the two cats and the squirming mouse. "Are we sure this is him?" she asked.

Beejee sniffed the mouse. "Yes, it's definitely him."

"Do we... bring him somewhere?" Cali asked. "Won't he be... indecent?"

Sella blinked. She hadn't thought of that. "Um, Lohr? Can we borrow your coat?"

Lohrna's head cocked for a moment, then her eyes grew wide. "Oh, yes. Absolutely." She removed her coat and held it high in front of them. "Alright, Mims. We got you fair and... um, lawfully. So by order of... our authority?"

"The King, technically. Benka put in the paperwork," Beejee corrected.

"Yes," Lohrna went on. "By order of the King, you have to unshift and explain yourself this instant." She shook the coat for good measure. "Come on, now. Don't make this weirder than it has to be." She closed her eyes tightly and shook her coat again.

But nothing happened.

They waited.

Sella stood up. "Beejee, you're sure it's–?"

The smallest crackle, a light popping sound, echoed in the small alley.

Koukie dropped the mouse and stepped back.

Sella watched, half in horror, half in grotesque intrigue, as the sound of snapping bones grew louder. The mouse twisted and contorted, growing larger, less hairy, with each snap. The sound reverberated in her ears and made her stomach twist. But at last, it was over.

Mims stood, tall and wide, eyes glaring at them. He took the coat swiftly and shrugged it on. It looked ridiculous on him, far too small, and dainty on his frame. "Well," he said with a shrug. "What is it you want to know?"

TWENTY-EIGHT

The Salt Incident

THE GROUP STARED at each other for a moment too long. Mims turned to Cali. "It was nice to see you," he said to the empty space. "I had heard there was a ghost here. But to witness it myself was incredible. I doubt I'll see that again in my life."

Cali stepped behind Sella.

Mims pulled the coat more tightly around him, trying to keep it as closed as possible. He looked at Sella with an impossible to read expression. "I can't see her now," he explained. "But I can when I'm in the change."

Lohrna looked at Sella, then to Mims. Sella knew what she was thinking, that this was something they had never considered. An opportunity once a month to truly visit Cali. Sella was impressed that her friend ignored that for now and simply got to the point.

"What are you doing running around as a mouse, Mims?" Lohrna asked, glaring at him. "Did you have anything to do with the stolen Golden Ladle... or with–"

"The Golden Ladle was stolen?" Mims gasped. His tone

seemed genuine. His eyes grew round and he held the coat tighter around himself. "This is a travesty! When? I just saw it on stage!"

Sella rolled her eyes. He was selling it, at least. She crossed her arms. "And Branzo?"

Mims leaned back. "Branzo? Oh, no I didn't kill him," he said, back to his usual relaxed, somewhat pretentious self. He looked at her blankly as if that was that and no further explanation was needed.

Sella waited.

"Listen, I'm not exactly glad he's dead. That would be the basest instinct," Mims said with a raised finger. "But I don't think anyone was particularly sad to see him go. I have an alibi for the evening in question. MAMBOSSA will speak for me."

Sella groaned. "Yes, your cult will, I'm sure," she said.

Beside her, Lohrna flinched.

Sella continued quickly, "You really don't know anything about the ladle? Or Branzo?"

"No, nothing. I stay out of crime. It would be a terrible look for my people if their leader was caught doing something illegal. Especially something like this. Harming people? I could never!"

"Then what *were* you doing sneaking around?" Lohrna asked.

Mims shrugged slightly. He looked down at the ground, to Koukie. There was no anger in his eyes that Sella could see.

She almost pitied him. Almost.

"I... I was ensuring MAMBOSSA's win in the stew competition."

"What?!" Lohrna gasped. She pointed at him accusingly. "You were sabotaging the other contestants?"

Mims's cheeks reddened. He closed his eyes and sighed. "Yes," he admitted quietly. "Nothing dangerous. Just… adding extra salt to everyone's pot."

"Mims! You didn't!"

Sella was rubbing the bridge of her nose, eyes shut tightly. This felt like the stupidest wall she had ever run into. And now her nose was bloody for no good reason.

Cali placed a gentle hand on her arm and Sella shook her head, doing her best to release the tension in her body. She opened her eyes at last. "And you have an alibi for the night Branzo was killed, then?" she asked slowly.

Mims nodded vigorously. "Yes, I do. Please, I know I shouldn't have tampered with the other stews. And I accept responsibility for that. But please, don't let this get out to the public. MAMBOSSA has worked hard for years to build up trust in shifters. This would ruin us. Do whatever you think is best and within the rule of law for me but leave them out of it."

Sella tilted her head back and let out a low groan. She looked up at the dark sky and considered it all. None of it made sense. And yet, it really did. Of course this was how things were shaping up at the last possible moment. "Well," she said at last, "we have to have a redo, right? We can't let everyone have an unfair chance because you salted everyone's pot."

"In my defense, I added it to ours, too," Mims offered, as if that helped. "I just didn't add any to the original…"

Lohrna swatted his hand like he was a child who had

been caught stealing a cookie. "That doesn't make it better and you know it."

"It is clever though," Beejee mumbled quietly.

"It is *not*," Lohrna said bitterly. She turned to Sella. "What're we going to do?"

Sella exhaled, scratched at her temple gently. "Well," she said, "I'm sure the judges will have figured out something here is amiss." She looked at Mims with a harsh glare. "You messed up and you need to make it right. But," she glanced at Lohrna who was looking at the other shifter with a ferocity in her gaze. "I won't tell anyone what you did. To protect MAMBOSSA. You're right. They don't deserve mistreatment because you're a fool."

Mims's body loosened. He smiled, a little chuckle slipped. "Thank you. What a relief!"

"But you go make it right," Lohrna said, driving a finger into his chest. "Go on!"

"How?" he asked, voice higher than Sella had ever heard it. He sounded a little scared. And Sella supposed he should be.

"You messed up. You figure it out," Lohrna said.

"I understand," Mims said sadly. He looked down the alley. "I think I have an idea…"

There was a terrible cascading cracking sound, and the coat fell to the wet stones. Into the darkness, a small brown mouse raced down the alley and toward the hotel.

The group stood there for a moment until Koukie meowed at them loudly. She pressed her head into Sella's leg, then scurried off.

"What'd she say?" Sella asked.

"She says she and the alley cats have the bird next on

their list," Beejee said, the tone of pride filling his voice despite the danger.

"Let's get back," Lohrna said, picking up her coat and dusting it off with her free hand. When that didn't seem to do it, she shook it, then looked it over as if it was going to come alive and bite her. "Eh, it's not cold enough. I think I want to wash this before I wear it again."

Sella's brows rose. She side eyed the coat. "Good idea," she said and led the way out of the alley and back to the festival.

"Another dead end," Lohrna said once they were back among the crowd.

Hazen was up on the chair again, calling out about a redo already in the process of scheduling. A few angry stew cooks were hollering back at him. Some just looked dejected. A group of judges were speaking to MAMBOSSA's table, who were all looking shocked.

Sella shook her head.

"How did he think this was going to turn out?" Cali whispered. She stood on her toes to see above the groups. "I hope he didn't actually add *that* much salt…"

Hazen's voice interrupted just as Sella opened her mouth to speak, "There must be an issue with the salt supply. We are working actively to identify the storages affected!"

"Come on," Sella said, leading the way through the crowd. "I'll do a quick walk around and see if I can find anything not salt related."

"So much for my stew tonight," Cali said. She lowered her body and looked up at Sella. "Scones smelling and murder theories at your place when you're done with your loop?"

Sella glanced at Lohrna. She shrugged. "Cali's going to meet at home for scones and theories. Want to come after the festival?"

Lohrna held her coat at arms length. She grimaced at it. "No," she said, "I think I'll go home myself. And soak this in some vinegar. Maybe pour myself a big glass of red wine… try to get the image of Mims naked out of my mind."

"Mhm," Beejee said. "Suuuure."

Sella toed his back with her boot gently. "Beejee!" she hissed.

Beejee looked up at them with all the casual attitude of a typical house cat. Still, Sella sensed some embarrassment from him. "I meant for everyone to hear that," he said, tail and head held high. "But do soak that in vinegar. It smells like rodent."

"If you're sure… Stay safe," Sella said.

Lohrna laughed, though it sounded forced, as though Sella had just told a bad joke and she was trying, half-heartedly, to be polite. She waved and disappeared into the dark alley.

Sella was just grateful Mims hadn't turned out to be a murderer. Or a ladle thief. And that Lohrna had started to see MAMBOSSA in all its realness.

Finally.

With Cali and Lohrna gone, Beejee and Sella wandered the square together. They overheard parts of conversations. Frustratingly, all were related to the salted soup incident.

They reached the outskirts of the markets when they heard a small, "Sella?"

Both the witch and her familiar turned back to the crowd. Alone, along the edge where the lantern light no longer reached, stood Ipla. She was leaning against a brick building, looking small and lost.

"Ipla?" Sella called back. She approached the woman with quick steps. "Everything alright?"

Ipla shrugged. "All is well, in a sense. But we are worried about the ghosts. With Branzo gone…"

"He's not a ghost, I can promise you that," Sella said. "Only one of those in town."

Ipla smiled. "That's a relief. I think we can only handle the one. I don't have any experiences with ghosts. Is there… a way we can make her more comfortable?"

Sella cocked her head slightly. She studied Ipla's expression but all she got was kindness.

Ipla went on, noticing her hesitation, "Rizan is more, let's say assertive, about the issue. But, I wouldn't mind sharing the space with your ghost. For a while, at least."

Sella curled one arm around her waist. Below her, Beejee purred. She thought about it for a moment. Cali loved quiet spaces. Rain. The sound of the leaves blowing in a breeze. She loved the smell of fresh baked bread, and wyverns, even. "Do you bake?" Sella asked at last.

Ipla shook her head. "But Rizan does."

"Try making bread sometime. And, if you think about it, keep her tea towel out, the one with the embroidered wyvern. And open the shutters when it rains."

Ipla nodded. She pushed off the wall and smiled brightly. "Thank you, I'll try that."

TWENTY-NINE

The Most Likely

SELLA AND CALI sat beside each other on the couch. Beejee slept by the fire, though Sella knew he was only half asleep. He would be waiting for Koukie to get home all night, if that's what it took.

She and the alley cats may have proven themselves formidable, but going after a familiar was a whole different thing. Familiars had magic within them. Enough to do some damage.

Still, Sella had to believe Koukie knew what she was doing and neither she nor the grackle would come to any real harm. Maybe some mild harassment. But no harm.

"So, what do we know about Branzo?" Cali asked. She propped her elbow on the back of the couch. "I think if we figure *him* out, we can figure out a motive. You know, besides, 'he was an incredible jerk'."

Sella considered it. "Well, he was mayor, and liked to hear himself talk."

Cali looked at Sella with an expression that said, 'really?' "So… he was a bit full of himself, and important."

Sella exhaled. "Alright. Yes, I suppose. He was Cirian's cousin. Before he died, I heard him tell Sediri that she needs to 'fix this'... He had a similar marking as the woman at the market." Sella glanced at Cali, but saw no jealousy remaining. She felt herself start to shrug, but breathed out slowly, maintaining her casual posture. "So... I think we can assume he had a similar bad reaction to one of Sediri's potions."

"He's image conscious," Cali said. "It must have been really upsetting for him to wear those long velvets. He looked awfully sweaty most of the time."

Sella nodded. "I'd say he seemed pretty upset."

There was a long pause. In the fireplace, a small crackle burst as embers clung to the deep grooves of wood. The warm light began to dim. "Do you think Sediri did it?" Sella whispered.

Cali leaned in a little. "Branzo was powerful. Influential. Image obsessed. If she thought he was going to bring down her shop because of a bad reaction...? Maybe. I don't think it's, like, premeditated or anything. But maybe they were having a fight and she lost it?"

"But he was struck in the head?"

"You'd be surprised at what a small person can do to a large person. If they get the first strike in. If they're scared enough."

Sella's eyes danced across Cali's face, seeking an answer to a question she was not sure how to speak.

Cali smiled warmly. "My family is all military. Wyvern riders, remember?"

"I remember," Sella said. "I'm just..."

"Trust me, Sella," Cali cut in. "I didn't want that life.

But I know enough about violence to speak to this. I'm not saying it's *likely*. But it's not impossible for someone her size to kill someone his size, even unintentionally. Maybe she was holding a cast iron skillet at the time. We don't know."

"Why would he be outside her door? Why wouldn't she dispose of him in the sea?"

Cali shrugged. "Strong enough to get one good blow in? Maybe even a harder hit than she thought. But not strong enough to carry him all the way to the shore?"

Sella had to admit, that did seem most likely. She leaned forward onto her legs, folding in on herself. "He did hand her a box, too," she said, doing her best to remember the event as it was. Not clouded by his murder. Or her negative feelings about Sediri. She watched the fire dance, casting shadows about the room.

"We can see what's in the box? Go from there? Could be that it's another clue?"

Sella inhaled sharply, she sat up straight. "You could tell her you want the spell," she said, turning to Cali. "And that will get her out of the shop. Then, I can go find the box."

Cali's mouth pulled to one side. She hummed. "I don't know…"

"Of course," Sella said quickly. "I don't want you in any danger."

Cali shook her head. "It's not that," she said slowly. "I just… It's so rare that someone can see me. I'm afraid I've lost the ability to feign sincerity. I don't want to give you away and have *you* in danger."

Sella nearly laughed. She caught it before it escaped her. She hadn't had anyone worried about her, not really, in a long time. "You don't need to worry about me," she said.

"But I do," Cali whispered. Her voice broke, just a little. Enough to shatter Sella. "When... when Isra almost banished me." She paused, her eyes drifting to the rafters above them. "I look back on that. And... I'm frightened for myself. Being nearly banished, you know? But. I'm also frightened for you."

Sella ignited a flame in the palm of her hand. It flickered brightly, illuminating their faces in a gentle glow. "You don't need to worry about me," she said again.

Cali's eyes narrowed, but her expression was playful. She pushed Sella, and her hand was firm. "We get it. You have fire. I can still worry."

"Needlessly," Sella said.

Cali leaned in close, her joy reached her eyes where they crinkled a little at the corners. "If you square up against another witch and... don't make it... will you be a ghost like me?"

"I'll go where you go, Cali," Sella said. Her voice caught in her throat as she spoke. She felt like the words would disappear. She desperately wanted to keep them. "And I won't be in any danger, I promise."

Cali kissed her and the room ignited in warm, little fires.

For the first time since Opora began, Sella was really, truly happy, despite it all.

THIRTY

Bravery Blend

"I THINK I have a way to make it up to the town," Mims said. His head was lowered, hands folded in front of himself sheepishly.

"Out with it, mouse!" Beejee hissed.

Sella looked from Beejee to Lohrna with a furrowed brow.

It was Beejee's turn to lower his gaze, even if it was just a little. He stomped his paw on the table and huffed, as if he had no intention of hurting Lohrna but couldn't be bothered to apologize.

Lohrna, for her part, didn't seem to care. She gestured for Mims to get on with the conversation.

Mims nodded, then went on, "At the hotel, there's a pixie. Apparently, one with an affinity for sweets, and in exchange can help find lost things. It's one of the hotel's selling points"

"Rukus. We're aware. Lives up to the name," Beejee said.

Mims looked down. "Well," he said, "I asked him if he

could help find something lost. I was thinking about the ladle, but he just brought a bunch of old socks."

Beejee waited, far more patient than Sella would have expected.

"He can't find things you know are lost... Apparently," Mims said, exasperation in his tone. "Which, I'll admit, was not advertised."

"Penya advertised the hotel?" Beejee scoffed. "It's the only one in town!"

Mims nodded. "That detail was also left out of the flyers on the way into town. She charges an exorbitant amount." He looked away, then sighed. "But, Rukus came back again, after an offering of more sweet cream, of course."

"Get to the point," Beejee said. Oh good. His usual demeanor was back.

"Rukus found a box," Mims said. "A box in the other witch's shop. He says it has something that Penya's missing but doesn't know is gone. The best part? He says she doesn't know it's gone because another out of towner, a man named Branzo. I'm not saying it's enough to murder someone over, but... If the other witch has it, it must be valuable. It's at least a clue."

Lohrna cast a glance at Sella, then turned back to Mims with hard eyes.

"I'm telling the truth," Mims said. "I want to help. Truly. MAMBOSSA is my life's work. I can't let their reputation suffer because I made a stupid mistake."

"'Mistake'?" Lohrna shifted back in her chair. She crossed her arms. "A mistake is tripping over something. You made a conscious decision. Several, actually."

Sella tried to keep her face still as possible but she

couldn't help but question the intensity of Lohrna's reaction. So the guy salted some soup? It wasn't like he killed someone…

Lohrna was still going, "Finding, or using a pixie to find, whatever you needed to was the least you could do."

Sella watched Mims's expression carefully. Their intensity was about more than the soup contest, but she wasn't sure what. She searched his face for any clue, but, as always, as this investigation had gone so far, there was little to go on.

Lohrna was leaning down to catch Sella's stare. Her arms were still crossed protectively over her chest. "Sella?"

Sella shook her head a little. "It's a lead, definitely," she said at last. Even if it was one they already had, it was helpful of him to confirm that the box was important. That inside was stolen goods. "Thank you, Mims."

"I know I said I don't want to do anything illegal, but… I feel like I still need to atone. I can break into her shop. I should be able to see what's in the box. If you need me to?" Mims offered.

"No," Sella said before Lohrna could interject. "I think I can handle it."

Beejee cast a look at her. His head swiveled like an owl back to Mims, he looked at him like prey. "What kind of box?"

"The pixie described it as black wood with a golden bee inlay on the top. About the size of an arm."

Sella shrugged, imperceptibly, she hoped. She focused back to Mims and Lohrna. "Thank you for the information."

"And you don't tell anyone about… my involvement? With the soup?"

Sella grumbled, mirroring Lohrna's pose as she crossed her own arms over her chest. "No, we won't tell anyone you turned into a mouse to salt a bunch of soup."

Mims breathed a sigh of relief.

"You can go now," Beejee commanded. He sat tall, mighty though small, upon the counter. He moved his head to the door, as if his words weren't enough. "Go on."

Mims stood and his eyes softened. "Thank you."

Once the doors were locked, Lohrna spun in her chair to Sella. "You're not breaking into another witch's shop, are you?"

"To tell you the truth, I had already planned on it. This just solidifies it… I mean, it doesn't exactly sound like I have another choice," Sella said. "You heard him. Something in that box belonged to Penya. Something that Branzo stole and is now in Sediri's possession? You have to admit, it kind of screams 'motive'."

"He could be lying," Lohrna said. "He's a proven liar."

"Could be," Sella said as she put her hands around a metal pot. She felt warmth flow through her and ignite the flame beneath. "But then we'd know it's him."

"So it's either Sediri or Mims?"

"Seems that way, doesn't it?"

"I'll come with you," Beejee said. He pressed his face against the back of her hand. "Just in case your fire isn't enough."

Lohrna stood and made her way to the counter. She looked down at the coffee pot warming in Sella's hands and shook her head slowly. The warm smell of coffee brewing filled the air.

Sella pulled a small jar from behind the counter and

added a spoonful of the red, glittering powder. A sudden burst of spicy cinnamon and a dash of cayenne mixed with the bitter coffee. Just enough to be braver than she ought to be.

"I don't like it," Lohnra whispered at last.

Though if she was talking about the coffee or the plan, or both, Sella wasn't sure.

THIRTY-ONE

The Wandless Menace Strikes Again

CALI WAS GLARING at Sella in the loft above the shop. "Of course the prickled-edge box was important."

Sella figured that was some kind of exasperated swear from across the sea. She made a note to file it away to ask about later, but Cali had already continued her rant.

"I don't want you breaking into the shop and for *once* can't it be *me* looking out for *you?*"

Sella held out a small flame in her hand. "I mean…"

"Put that away!" Cali hissed through her teeth. "Yes, you're a powerful witch. A non-wand-needing-witch. But. I thought we had put this to rest. I'm going. Sella."

"Cali."

The ghost flickered. "Sella."

A long while passed. Both stared at the other with equal heat in their expressions.

Sella broke first. She always did. "Alright, you're too stubborn for me. What do you want?"

"To help!" Cali said with a clap so loud even Koukie's ear twitched.

The orange cat opened one eye by the fire and looked around for her ghost. Not finding her, or not caring too much to interrupt her nap, she closed her eye, yawned, then curled up tighter.

"And how can you help?" Sella asked.

"I can go look for the box."

"She can see you."

"I'm aware. Listen, instead of me distracting her, and you risking yourself to break and enter, how about we switch?"

Sella raised a brow.

Cali leaned in. "You go to Sediri, get her out of the shop. Then, I'll go look for the clues and, if I have the strength, I can even bring the box to you. That way, if she becomes wise to the plan and comes back, I can just–" Cali dissipated from view like a whiff of smoke. She shimmered back, slightly more translucent than before. "See? Easy."

"I don't know…"

"Besides, I trust that you can keep her long enough for me to do my searching."

"You do?"

"Absolutely. She *really* hates you, Sella."

That was not what she was expecting. "Um. Thanks?"

Cali laughed. "Just tell her that her jewelry is ugly. I'm sure she'll keep you busy after that."

Beejee, from across the room, eyes still closed, said, "Cali's got a point. I say we let the ghost go for it."

Sella took in a deep breath through her nose. She rolled her neck. She knew that if both Cali and Beejee had set their minds to something, it would happen. She was tired of fighting it. The only way forward was to do their plan to the safest of her ability. She pinched the back of her neck, then asked, "Where will we ask to meet her?"

Cali's eyes drifted to the rafters. She watched a little flame pass by. "Hazen's? He's got the space… in case you two really need it. And I know he wants to get to the bottom of this too."

Sella scratched the back of her ear.

"I'll go ask him," Beejee said, already heading for the door.

Sella moved to let him out.

He cast a single look at her and she closed the door behind him gently. She leaned her back on the wood and sighed. "I guess that's that," Sella said. Her gaze followed a little flame that passed by above her. "Cali… I feel like I'm drowning. Like everything is piling up on me and it's getting hard to see the surface." It poured out of her. And she wished she could bottle it up again but Cali was already beside her.

"You feel like you're falling into the sea?" The ghost's fingers weaved between Sella's. She looked up at her, her image solid for the moment.

Sella nodded. She closed her eyes slowly, the back of her head rested on the door.

"Then let my light take care of you," Cali whispered.

Sella felt a solid form against her chest.

Cold.

She opened her eyes and saw Cali's body pressed against hers. She let out a breath and her arms wrapped around Cali's waist and shoulders. She held on tightly, and Cali began to fade.

"We got this, Sella," Cali said gently, pulling away at last.

She smiled at the witch and brushed a lock of dark hair from Sella's cheek as she disappeared from view. "No matter what. We're going to be fine."

THE NEXT MORNING, Sella's stomach felt like it was full of rocks. She looked out the round window to the empty street as dawn broke behind the clouds. There was a lingering sense of heaviness in her. And a bit of nausea.

Beejee looked up at her. "It'll be fine," he said, unconvincingly. "Cali can handle herself."

"Sure can!" Cali called from the corner.

Sella turned slowly to see a sheet, plain white with a floral pattern embroidered along the edges staring back at her. Cali had glasses over her eyes as usual and…

Sella felt a dry, coughing laugh, escaping her. "Cali… What is that?"

The ghost stood there as she had many times before. Everything exactly as it always was. A sheet in the shape of a person hovering off the ground. Except this time, dark colored moss rested just above where her mouth would be. It looked like an incredibly fake, though creative, mustache beneath the glasses. "I'm in *disguise!*" Cali's voice said from under the sheet.

"You look ridiculous," Beejee grumbled, clearly not in the mood for any jokes.

A hand raised under the sheet, making her look larger.. "Beejee, you remember my family are all military. I am no stranger to a clandestine campaign."

"Change immediately and get that disgusting quilt moss

out of here. It causes itching if exposed to skin," the familiar ordered.

"Good thing I don't have skin!"

Sella smiled and Cali's laughter broke the quiet morning. Where just a moment ago a sense of dread had settled into her bones, Sella felt an easy lightness of being. She felt joy. Cali, for all she had been through, always seemed to make Sella laugh just when she was sure she couldn't anymore.

The sheet, moss, and glasses lay on a pile in the corner as they locked up.

A witch, and her familiar, turned right at the crossroads. A ghost, and her cat, turned left just as the sirens in front of the hotel began to sing.

The walk to Kepilla was short. Sella felt like her stomach was going to fly out of her, but she kept one foot in front of the other and tried grounding herself in the sounds of her booted heels on the cobblestone street. Click. Click. Click.

Closer to her destination. Closer to a potential murderer.

Click, click.

Closer to a moment she was dreading.

Click.

And she was standing in front of the last place she wanted to be.

Sediri was in her shop, toiling away at a recipe before the doors opened. Sella watched her through the window. She felt like a shark. Worse. Like a sea monster lurking in the depths, looking up at an unsuspecting little fisher boat bobbing in the waves. It all felt wrong.

She took in a deep inhale, trying to find calm among the

anxiety rising in her chest, then knocked on the glass quietly with her knuckles.

Sediri looked up from her work with wide eyes, red hair fell over her shoulder as she rose from her seat behind the counter. She squinted out the window, then Sella watched as she huffed, clearly annoyed by the visitor before opening hours. Sediri hurried to the door, then propped it open a few inches. She looked out the crack with a scowl already etched into her face. "What do you want, you wandless menace?"

Sella retracted as if Sediri had hit her.

Sediri opened the door another inch. "Yes, I know all about your stupid fake stick. I knew from the moment we met at the certification exam. You're not exactly sly, you know."

Sella opened her mouth to speak but just felt like a fish gulping. No words came out, so Beejee spoke for her.

"We want a truce. At least until the end of Opora," he announced. He moved past both of them to wiggle his way into the shop.

Sediri opened the door all the way as she spun on her heel to look at him. "Get out!"

Beejee held his head and tail high. "I will, when you come with us. We want to meet on neutral territory."

Sediri crossed her arms. "And where is that?"

"The tavern," Beejee said. He swiped at the hem of her long black dress. "Come on. We'll discuss our terms. Bring your *grackle*."

Sediri scoffed. "You stray! Just because you can talk now—"

Sella held her hands up. "Bring your familiar, I'll bring mine. Meet at the tavern before opening time."

"We picked the timing generously, since we know you can't afford to miss a sale," Beejee said smugly as he walked, a little quickly, past the other witch.

Sediri clicked her tongue just as the door shut.

The two witches looked at one another through the glass for a moment, then each turned the other way.

THIRTY-TWO

What's in the Box?

"You shouldn't have antagonized her," Sella said. She was pacing behind the counter of Hazen's tavern. She took a sip of the water Hazen had poured her earlier.

Hazen had long retreated to his upstairs apartment so the witches could "have their privacy". But Sella was certain he was just done with magic for a lifetime after everything he had experienced in the past year.

"She's not going to show," Sella said. Worry seeped through her voice and Beejee glared at her in response.

His little gray ear twitched. "I'd know those filthy flapping sounds anywhere," he said and looked at the door. "They're both here."

Sella took another long drink, then set her mug down behind the counter, hiding it away deep. She smoothed her dress with the palms of her sweaty hands.

"She'll be fine, Sella," Beejee said.

Sella nodded, and the two moved from behind the counter and to the large double doors. She took in one final deep breath and opened the door just as Sediri raised her hand to knock.

Sediri stepped back. She hummed and Majla landed on her shoulder. He squawked at Beejee and the cat hissed back.

"Enough," Sella said to the two. She moved aside so Sediri could step through. "We're alone."

"Good," Sediri said as the door shut behind her. She looked up, at the high ceiling, the large pillars, then down to the tables with chairs all stacked atop their surfaces. "It looks different empty," she whispered.

Sella glanced at Sediri. For a moment, just a moment, she saw her. Not as a witch. Or a rival. Just. As she was. A stranger in town with no friends and no one to talk to.

It didn't last long.

"I'm impressed with what he's managed to do in such a… small town," Sediri said as she turned to Sella. "I'm sure this all must feel very grand to Marrans."

Sella bit her lip. "Sediri, can we not insult my home?"

Sediri, with her bird on her shoulder, squared herself. Sella noticed that she had her hand on her wand. That her grip on it tightened.

Sella gestured for the stools at the bar. "Come on, let's sit down. All I want is to talk."

"About how you tried to get our ghost to turn on us," Beejee mumbled.

Sella glared at him. "No, about our truce. There's a lot of moving parts here. You haven't exactly made many friends." She kind of hoped that part stung.

Sediri hoisted herself onto a stool and shook her head slowly. For the second time, and in only a short moment,

Sella saw her vulnerability. She regretted her words. They had come out harshly, as she intended them to. But seeing Sediri's quick pained expression made her want to watch her tone.

The grackle fluttered to the opposite side of the counter, he eyed Beejee. Neither familiar seemed to be sharing any of Sella's hesitance.

"I know I haven't," Sediri said at last. She folded her hands on her lap, her wand nestled between them. She looked down at the wand and watched it as she rolled it between her palms. "It doesn't matter. Friends or no friends, this shop needs to succeed. I'm sorry, Sella. At least, a little…" She looked up at her with sparkling amber eyes. "What kind of truce did you have in mind?"

"I know there's something wrong with one of your recipes," Sella said, in a tone she hoped was kind.

"You want to help me fix it? Why?"

"I don't like the idea of people in town having a negative view of kitchen witches," Sella said. It was true. Partly.

"And in return?"

Sella looked at Beejee. He blinked back at her.

"Give Cali the spell so she can talk," Sella said at last.

"I promised her that spell if she took you down. She made it clear that it wasn't on the table," Sediri said as she straightened. "So, it's off."

"I'll close," Sella said quickly.

Beejee hissed, teeth bared.

"I'll close the shop, if you give her the spell."

Sediri's eyes narrowed. She tapped the counter with her hand, a hollow sound. "Close, then you get the spell," she whispered through the tapping.

"You don't have it!" Beejee yowled. He swatted at Majla who fluttered his wings, talons out in return.

Sella felt like the world around her was collapsing. As if the room had filled with cold water in an instant. "You… don't even have it…do you?"

The doors flew open and Cali stood in the frame with the box in her hand. Her hair and dress were waving wildly about her as if she was surrounded by an ocean storm. "She did it!" Cali pointed to Sediri with a fierceness in her eyes.

The wind stilled, the box fell to the floor, and Cali vanished.

Sella and Sediri looked at each other for a moment.

The scraping of wood, as Sella launched herself from off the bar stool, the clatter of a toppled over chair, filled the room as they raced to the box on the floor.

Sella was faster, but Sediri caught hold of her sleeve. She yanked, hard. Sella stumbled and fell to her knees. Behind her, she heard the scuffle between Beejee and Majla.

She heard hissing and spitting, and squawking.

She heard spells and magic erupt like flickering fires.

Sella was up before Sediri could push her all the way down. She lit a flame in her hand and turned on the other witch quickly.

"You stay put!" Sella shouted, holding the flame aloft, ready to strike.

Sediri paused. She raised her hands and her expression was pleading. "Sella, what's in the box… isn't what it looks like."

From behind the bar, Hazen and Cirian emerged, concern etched into both their faces. They examined the scene before them and Hazen held a large, protective arm out in front of Cirian. "You okay, Sella?" he asked.

"I have this under control," Sella said. She glared at the other witch, then looked to Beejee who had pinned the bird down with both front paws. He was murmuring some kind of spell, one she couldn't quite hear. Flame still in hand, Sella moved to pick up the box and with her other hand. She lifted the lid to look inside.

Sella stared at the pieces of paper, eyes scanning it thoroughly, trying to make sense of it, before she spoke.

It was a drawing, detailed and realistic, a dissection of one of the siren statues outside the hotel. Another paper showed the inner workings, a series of small stone pathways leading to the chest, a seemingly empty chamber. Her brows furrowed, trying to understand what it meant, why Sediri would hide this, why she'd steal it. A small note on the bottom read 'To release the magic bond:' She flipped the page to see the dissection now labeled with different spells at each joint and curve within the statue.

"You... murdered Branzo.... For what? Stolen statue plans?"

"What?" Sediri pulled back, one fist close to her chest. The other tightly gripped her wand. "No, I didn't kill Branzo."

Beejee's claws extended on the other familiar. "You want to get rid of the statues so bad that you killed a man to do it? Really sold yourselves to Kepilla, huh?"

The grackle chirped, wings flapping rapidly.

Hazen took a few steps closer. "Let's all take a deep breath here," he said slowly, his voice was thick with worry. He inched closer to the witches, one hand still held out to stop Cirian from moving closer. "Wand down, flame down," Hazen said. "Come on, now."

Beejee was the first to let go. His claws retracted and he moved to let the other familiar free. He spat at the bird as Majla flew up to a high rafter.

Sella's eyes were still narrowed, watching Sediri carefully. She let the fire in her palm die out, but felt the heat still linger there, ready to ignite again.

Sediri lowered her wand slowly. "I didn't kill him," she said again.

"I heard him tell you to 'fix this' or he'd let everyone know what you did," Sella said. "You'd do anything to please Kepilla. You said it yourself, you *need* the shop to succeed. You found out the statues can't be moved without their plans. They're bonded to the hotel with magic. Admit it, you killed him so your secret would be safe!" Fire burst from Sella's fingertips.

Sediri raised her wand.

"Stop!" Cirian cried from the corner. He rushed past Hazen to get between the two witches.

"Don't defend her," Beejee hissed.

Cirian turned to look at Hazen slowly. He hung his head for a moment, his expression pained. He raised his gaze to Sella. His eyes were hard, but his voice shook. "She didn't kill Branzo… I did."

The fire in Sella's hand dimmed.

"Cirian…" Hazen said sadly. He moved to stand beside him, placing a hand on Cirian's shoulder.

Cirian blinked away a tear that had begun to gather in his eye. He squeezed Hazen's hand and then moved toward Sella with shoulders slumped.

Sella stepped back as he did. She had never seen him anything less than joyful, even in the darkest of circumstances. To see his posture change so quickly felt like a crime of nature. She couldn't believe him. He had to be lying. "Why?" she asked, her voice unrecognizable to her.

Cirian pushed back another tear. "It was an accident. But one I still own. I am responsible, no matter the intention. You can take me away."

Sella couldn't move. Her feet felt frozen to the floor, cold and unmovable. The chill raced up and into her scalp.

Cirian only held out his hands to her. "Do you… need to shackle me?"

It was Beejee who spoke the words Sella could not. His voice was loud and clear, "How'd you *accidentally* kill Branzo?"

Cirian looked weak, pale, and sick. He shook his head. "I should have said something right away, but I panicked… Branzo was my cousin. He could be a terrible person sometimes, but I loved him. We were close, once…" He looked from Beejee, to Sella. "It doesn't matter now. I found him outside of the new witch's shop late at night. He…" Cirian took in a long breath. "He was fighting with one of the new shifters in town. A small man. I intervened."

Hazen's eyes pleaded with Sella silently, as if begging her to stop more terrible words falling from Cirian's lips.

Sella bit her tongue and stayed quiet. She couldn't stop him, no matter how much she wanted to. No matter how much she wanted this to be some ridiculous dream. But, she wasn't sure he wanted to stop. Cirian needed to speak his truth, that much she could see.

"When I stopped him, the other man ran away. I'm glad

he did… he shouldn't be a part of this," Cirian went on. "Branzo said he knew that the shifters were behind the missing ladle. I didn't even know he knew this one was a fake, to be honest." He wrung his hands, but kept them outstretched as if waiting for Sella to bind him. She didn't make a move and he continued. "He was going to go after them. All of them. And turn the festival into a frenzy to drive them out of town. Or… worse. I told him he couldn't and… I shoved him. He pushed me back. He must have slipped, or didn't realize how hard he hit me. He stumbled and hit the cobblestone. I tried to grab him when he went down but… I wasn't fast enough. I didn't think the fall killed him at first… but. I couldn't let him hurt the society. He'd lock them all away if he could."

Sella looked down at the floor. It all seemed impossible. Cirian. Of everyone in town? It didn't make any sense. "The one hit..?"

Sediri lowered her wand. "He was already weak," she whispered.

The group turned to her. She looked at each of them with a solemn gaze. "One of my potions," she said, this time louder. "It caused a bad reaction. Like one I've never seen before. Marks on his body… that was something I've experienced. But the fever? He was losing his balance, decreased appetite. I hadn't seen anything like that before. He told me if I didn't cure him, he'd tell everyone my shop was dealing curses." She turned to Cirian with what looked like kindness in her eyes.

Sella couldn't be sure. She had never seen this look on Sediri before.

"We both killed him," Sediri said. Tears pooled in her

yellow eyes and she sank to the floor. Her familiar fluttered to her, pressing his head against her cheek. "And… I stole the ladle, Sella."

Sella's jaw tightened. "What?"

Sediri brushed away tears with the back of her hand. "I stole the ladle. But I knew I couldn't get it out of the town on my own. Not when you'd be able to hear the magic. So… I had Branzo help me steal the plans to hide it in the statues. I figured… since they make sound, you wouldn't be able to hear the ladle over it." She closed her eyes. "Kepilla doesn't want the siren statues. Not really. I lied so I could take them, and the ladle, with me. You were right, Sella. I am desperate for the money. But I'm not a killer. And neither is…"

Just then, the doors burst open. Lohrna blew into the room like a storm. She held her hands overhead. "We know where the ladle is!" she cried triumphantly. "Thank the tides for our ghost! She travels fast!" When no one said anything, she stopped in her tracks, frowning. "What did I miss?"

THIRTY-THREE

What Nature Does Best

"I wish Benka was here," Lohrna said with a heavy sigh. She was slumped on the table, wild curls bouncing with each small bang of her head as she gently lifted it and let it fall with each word. "Never thought I'd say that. But I do."

Sella set three mugs at the table. Purple in front of Lohrna, yellow for Cali, who sat with a sheet over her head, and a blue mug for herself. She sank into the chair then rubbed Lohrna's back gently until her friend rose up.

"What are we going to do? Who really killed Branzo? Sediri for the bad potion? Cirian for hitting him? Kepillia for *providing* the bad potion? Ugh. Does it even matter?" Lohrna asked each question in rapid succession. At last, she turned her head to the side, cheek still adhered to the table top. "And what about the ladle?"

Across the table, Cali leaned in to smell the steam.

Mists of spicy cinnamon, and rich honey swirled through the air.

Sella took a long sip. She waited for the clarity to kick in.

She had added it, along with just a hint of clove, at the very end.

She held the mug close to her chest and thought, but her mind was swirling like the steam in front of her. Unable to hold it in place, unable to make sense of any of it. "I don't know what to do about any of it, honestly."

Lohrna rose, pulled her mug to her. She breathed in deeply, then gestured to Cali. "What do you think?"

Cali shrugged under the sheet. She tilted her head and said, "I'm not sure it's right but... maybe... let it all go?"

Sella's brows rose. She turned to Lohrna but couldn't quite say it.

Cali went on, "I mean. Take Branzo. He was kind of killed by a few factors, I think. One completely accidental. One the negligence on the company's part for supplying a bad product, don't you think? And one while trying to defend Lohrna. And the ladle? I don't agree with her methods but... she had no other option. She's indebted to the company and... I mean, will anyone even know it's a fake?"

"She can't get away with it," Beejee interjected from his place on the counter.

Cali turned to him. "I understand. She's kind of the worst."

Lohrna looked on as if hearing every word. She waited while Cali continued. "How about we sneakily switch the two? Replace the fake with the original, but Sediri can take the fake? She can sell it to whoever she was going to before. You know? People who buy stolen goods? It's not like I'd feel all that bad about it if they're buying things that aren't theirs anyway. And... maybe we say we concluded our investigation on Branzo. Say he slipped on the stones and hit his head. It's partly true."

Sella rubbed the bridge of her nose. She cast a sideways glance to Lohrna. "She says we let it go. Replace the fake ladle with the original and let Sediri sell it like it's the real one. And say Branzo slipped."

"Well, he kind of did," Lohrna said. "Cirian had the first push but it was Branzo who pushed back and slipped."

"So we're just going to let them out of jail then?" Beejee asked. "Have I lost my mind here?"

Sella tapped her mug gently, listening to the *ting ting ting* of her fingertips on the ceramic. It echoed the gentle patter of rain on the window. "I don't like Sediri getting away with it. But. At the same time… What would locking her away really do? She's not a danger to anyone. I think she's learned her lesson."

Beejee looked like he just smelled something foul. His nose crinkled, teeth exposed as his lips pulled back. "Learned her lesson?"

Lohrna slurped her own tea, breaking the uneasy feeling in the air. She set her mug down with a hollow clank. "Well, she needs to do something really nice for you in return then," she said at last. "Really nice."

Sella stared into the dark tea in her cup. Her reflections gazed back at her through the heavy steam. "Yeah, maybe. Maybe it is what it is this time. I don't think Cirian should be locked away for this. He's a good person, and he acted in defense of a shifter. I'm sure we could confirm the story with the one who Branzo was picking on…"

"Tazel did mention to us to be very wary of Branzo," Lohrna said. She pushed her mug to Sella for a refill.

Sella rose to get the pot and filled Lohrna's cup, then topped off her own. "Oh?" she prompted.

Lohrna took a sip and nodded. "He seemed nervous, but I figured that was just his nature. But I'm guessing he was the one who Branzo had tried to shake down."

"Hmm," Sella sighed. She looked down at her mug. "Listen, I don't know if I want Marra being looked into for a high value stolen item. Penya gets to keep her statues. MAMBOSSA keeps their reputation."

Lohrna sank in her chair. "I'm not sure I agree on every part. But I do understand. And, I really think, at least with Cirian, it's hard to say that keeping him locked away would really be justice."

Beejee jumped onto Sella's lap. He popped his head up over the table. "I'm with Lohrna, for once."

"Don't agree but won't argue?" Cali prompted.

Beejee meowed, a fake, silly sound. "If anyone asks me, I'm pretending I lost the ability to speak," he said.

Cali laughed, a light and happy sound despite the subject matter. "You're a good one, Beejee. You'd want another witch to do the same for Sella, if they could."

Beejee only growled in return.

"How about this," Sella offered, leaning forward in her seat until it creaked beneath her weight. "Sediri can sell the fake, but she has to split the profits with Tallam. After all, he was the one who crafted a look-a-like so good it fooled basically everyone."

Lohrna and Beejee both tilted their heads to the side, considering it.

"I'd feel better about that, in that case," Lohrna said at last.

Beejee nodded. "Better."

Since when had Beejee developed such a strong moral compass? Sella was certain if the positions were reversed, he'd be willing to sell a fake ladle to any rich criminal. She decided to press him on the matter later. For now, she said, "Alright. If we're all good with it, I say we let them out of jail before anyone starts to question where they are."

"Yeah, we wouldn't want any rumors about *those two* starting," Cali said, sarcasm dripping in her tone.

THE LATE AFTERNOON air was crisp and still. Above the market, lanterns burned brightly under an overcast sky. Sella and Lohrna stood next to each other at the edge of the crowd that had gathered to see the winner of the Golden Ladle. It had come down, Sella overheard, to three: a Marran, an out of towner, and a Tollintal human woman who had held her own during each event, much to the surprise of everyone. Except Cali.

"Don't mess with human women. We're stronger than you'd think," she had said.

Sella's eyes glanced over the crowd, from the tops of heads to the bottoms of boots. She was looking for Sediri, her grackle, or even the little mouse form of Mims. Having everyone in town meet here for the final ceremony was step one to getting the ladle out of the statue unseen. The rest of the plan was a little more chaotic.

Hazen stood on the stage with the three final contestants. He was speaking something she couldn't quite hear. She focused in on his eyes. They were filled with dread. He, too, was squirming about, looking to be sure the plan went off quickly and without notice.

Sella heard the flutter of wings. She glanced up. The grackle chirped, the sign that the real ladle had been acquired. She stood on her toes to make eye contact with Hazen. She waved one hand from the back of the crowd, then sank back down quickly.

"It's time?" Lohrna whispered.

"Wait a few moments," Sella whispered back.

Hazen carried on as if nothing had happened. He held the fake golden spoon in one hand, saying something about the best winner, the honor of the town…

At her feet, Beejee swatted at her skirt. He gestured with one paw to the alley where Sediri and Mims lingered in the shadows.

Sella nodded at them, Sediri lifted her hand to show the shine of real magic infused gold.

"Okay, now," Sella said.

"Here we go!" Lohrna said. Suddenly, she threw herself into the closest person near her and screamed so loud Sella swore it was genuine fear.

The person she hit turned and shoved her before realizing she was in distress. The woman moved to grab her, shouting, "Sorry! Are you alright?"

Lohrna only continued to screech. Her eyes were wide as she pointed down to the cobblestone road.

Beejee ran through the crowd, hissing and spitting, swiping at every ankle he could. Behind him, Koukie and the alley cats, a dozen or more, came barreling through the crowd, chasing a squeaking and scratching mouse Mims.

Overhead, Majla swooped and clawed at horns and hair.

All around was chaos. People jumped, ran into each other. Lifted skirts, and scrambled to the outskirts of the square as they tried to avoid the sudden small animal chase.

Sediri snuck around the crowd and behind the wooden platform.

Hazen and the contestants ducked as Majla swooped and the cats dashed loudly across the stage.

Sella watched closely as Hazen's hand came down low and Sediri quickly swapped the ladles. In her other hand, she held her wand up and chanted an incantation, casting a haze of fog about the crowd.

The other witch hurried off as quickly as she had come.

The cats and Mims scurried off with the grackle flying in chase overhead.

The crowd was still in an uproar as Hazen stood back up, tall and proud, a genuine smile on his face. He held the ladle, the real one, up high. "Calm down, calm down," his voice boomed through the square. "It's only a little bit of nature doing what nature does. No need to be alarmed!"

The crowd settled, mostly, and turned their attention back to the stage.

Hazen went on, but Sella was distracted. Beside her, Aadel squeezed in beside her and held her arm gently. "We ought to do something about these alley cats," she said with a wry grin.

Sella smiled, glancing down at her. "It's the cabbits I'm more concerned about," she said.

Aadel nodded and hummed a bit. "Yes, and the pixies every new moon, eh?"

Lohrna pushed through the crowd and between her mom and Sella. She put an arm around each of them. She pulled them close and laughed lightly, as if she had just told a good joke that only she found funny.

Sella side eyed her friend. She was about to ask a question when Hazen's voice boomed again.

"We are at the end of the Opora, and what a journey it has been!" His voice ran out loud and clear throughout the crowd. "I am pleased to announce this year's winner of the Golden Ladle is…" He paused, dramatically.

Sella sighed, but Lohrna was shuffling her feet with her arm around her, making her sway alongside her. Her excitement, as usual, was contagious.

Sella smiled.

Their plan had worked. And though she wasn't where she wanted to be, and there was still much work to be done, she felt the tension in her jaw relax.

Things were going to be alright.

"From the far north, we have our winner!" Hazen called. He presented the ladle to the small man in the middle. The other two final contestants clapped, though a bit less enthusiastically as the crowd erupted in applause.

Sella missed the name of the winner, but she didn't really care. A part of her was a little disappointed it wasn't the human, even more so than the Marran. She put an arm around Lohrna who rested her head on her shoulder in turn.

"We did it," Lohrna said with a long sigh. "We made it to the end of the festival." She let go of her mom and Sella and turned to the both of them. "I think tonight I won't take the suppressant potion," she said, her voice almost lost in the sound of the crowd both celebrating and mourning. Her expression was soft and kind.

"Whatever makes you happy, my daughter," Aadel said. She brushed Lohrna's cheek with her thumb, squeezing a little at the end. "I think MAMBOSSA has helped the reputation, even if their rules are odd."

Lohrna nodded. Her eyes shifted to Sella. "Maybe I can see Cali tonight. I won't be able to talk to her, but for once, she'll be able to talk to me."

Sella's arms and legs tingled. She rubbed one arm with her hand to warm her skin. It wasn't much. In fact, it was so little, it ached. But it was something. Something she could do for Cali and Lohrna. But then, she snapped her fingers. "Wait. What if I gave you the potion that helped Beejee talk?" she said. "I'm not saying it would work. But maybe then you could talk… as you are on full moons?"

Lohrna nearly jumped, she clapped her hands. "Sella, you genius!"

"That could work?" Aadel held Sella's wrist gently.

"In theory?" Sella said. "Are you up for the possibility of a third *incident?*" She was half joking, but Lohrna didn't seem to care.

"Yes, yes, yes!"

THIRTY-FOUR

More Cake

LOHRNA DIDN'T EVEN LOOK TWICE at the bowl that Sella placed before her. She simply gave Beejee a wink, then ate the mixture quickly, leaving not a single crumb behind. Her long gray snout finally free from the bowl, she looked up at Beejee and a pink tongue licked her lips clean.

Lohrna, in this form, made the room above the shop feel incredibly small. Sella had pushed aside the table and chairs to the edge of the room by the wardrobe to make enough space for Lohrna's massive form. She wished she could have done this outside, but Beejee had insisted they do it here, away from the rain. And, Sella suspected, where they would have an arsenal of potions at the ready in case something went wrong.

Beejee waited on the foot of Sella's bed, far away from them. "Just in case she explodes," he had said.

In fairness, whenever Sella made a potion with Lohrna too near, it often turned out wrong. At least, when they were kids. Sella figured it was because her more risky potions were done in her presence, rather than her friend having any real direct relationship to the magic. Sella liked to experiment with remedies, but it was always Lohrna who moved her forward into truly exciting new territory. Like this evening, she readily accepted the potions Sella made with far too much trust.

Still, Sella watched Lohrna carefully, her arms crossed, waiting for any kind of reaction.

Lohrna was, if standing on all fours, a few heads taller than Sella. Silver and dark gray fur covered her body. Long, sharp ears stuck up toward the roof, alert and twitching at any sound. Sharp white teeth peaked out from her top jaw, making her wolf head all the more intimidating.

Sella had seen her like this before and she wasn't frightened. And when Lohrna looked at her, her eyes were still very much her friend's. Kind, hopeful, wide with wonder.

"It tastes terrible," Lohrna said with a small burp. She crossed her front paws daintily. "Like, genuinely terrible."

"Tides, it worked," Beejee gasped.

Sella felt pride in her chest bubble up. She could cry. "Lohrna! We hear you!" She approached her friend and placed a hand on her forehead, losing her fingers in the thick, soft fur. "We can hear you," she said again, a faint whisper. She felt her head hit Lohrna's. She breathed in deeply. She was exhausted from the magic but wanted more than anything to stay awake all night. She sighed and pushed off her friend, taking a few steps back.

"And to think I could've been doing this for a year!" Lohrna smiled, exposing the long slit of her mouthful of dagger teeth. She looked around the room, her eyes finally settling on the wooden island counter where Cali sat, feet swaying slightly as she waited. "Cal! Oh, you're shorter than I thought—"

"You can see me!" Cali cried. She leapt from the counter and flung herself onto Lohrna's face, holding the giant wolf head with both arms. She squished her own face against Lohrna's forehead, nuzzling her with a huge smile.

Sella could have laughed. Lohrna did always look just a few inches higher than Cali's face actually was.

"I can! And you're so beautiful, for a human," Lohrna teased.

"A dead human," Cail giggled through her words. She pulled back, her smile still broad but tears welled in her eyes. She still held Lohrna's face in her hands. She shook her hands in the thick fur. "You can hear me!"

Lohrna nodded. Her large eyes moved to Beejee. "Do you have any grievances like our buddy over there did?" she asked Cali.

Beejee hissed. But Sella only laughed. The first thing Beejee had said when he was able to speak to everyone was a long list of grievances and annoyances that had been building up. Even now, she suspected his list had grown, and he always told people what he thought.

Cali shook her head, waves of auburn hair fell over her shoulders. "None at all. I am just happy to talk with you at last."

Lohrna rested her head on her paws, her long neck stretched out in the small space carefully. She blinked slowly. "I have some questions for you," she said. "Things I've been dying to know for the past year."

"'Dying', nice," Cali said with a genuine laugh. She sat on the floor in front of Lohrna, looking so small by comparison. She didn't seem unnerved or in the least bit uncomfortable by Lohrna's size, form, or threatening appearance. She rested her chin on her knees and reached a hand out to pat Lohrna's wet nose. "I'll answer anything as long as you answer mine!"

"Deal!"

Sella stumbled a little on her feet. The magic usage from making the potion was starting to hit her hard. She felt drained. She was certain she would pass out in a moment, or drift away on a current of joy. Perhaps both. She closed her eyes and curled up on the foot of the bed beside Beejee.

She fell asleep to the sound of Lohrna and Cali talking excitedly in hushed tones, her familiar's pur, and the steady trickle of rain on the window.

IT WAS STILL night when Sella awoke. Lohrna was lying, belly up, on the floor in her wolf form. Her head was thrown back and the tip of her pink tongue stuck out from her jaws. Both cats had curled up on her neck, snuggling into her. Sella yawned silently and stretched her arms up over her head.

Her eyes moved about the room slowly. Cali was nowhere to be seen, but that didn't necessarily mean she wasn't there. She didn't want to call out to her, though. She didn't want to do anything to disturb the adorable fluffy scene before her.

Instead, she rolled her neck and shoulders a few times, then crept slowly out of bed and across the hardwood floor, careful to avoid any of the floorboards she knew were prone to creaking under her weight. She slipped on her boots and headed downstairs.

She knew she had to check in with Seaglass before the town woke up. She wasn't sure what she was going to say. She supposed she could start with how the Niminé's words would have, as usual, been helpful had she actually listened properly. The Golden Ladle had a magic sound that, for all her power, she hadn't bothered to listen for. And the statues hid it well.

It was really the only place they could have been hidden.

It would've saved her a lot of time.

Or, she thought, she could ask if they were doing the right thing by letting Cirian and Sediri go. If it was any different than when she took Isra in. And if so, how? But she knew she was solidified in her place to keep the two of them from jail. Seaglass wouldn't be able to change that.

Perhaps she'd tell them that she was able to help Cali talk after all, even if it was only to one person during the full moon. Or she'd ask again how to open the rose spell she had been given years ago.

Yes, she thought. She'd go with that.

THE SALT BREEZE drifting from the ocean waves made Sella's brow itch. It was overcast still, but along the horizon of the sea, she could see the light of the full moon, slowly setting. She rubbed her forehead with the back of her hand and squinted at the house, all alone in the dark.

The lanterns were still a light inside. From the windows, they cast a warm glow over the lavender flowers.

The bees were all asleep.

Sella took a deep breath in, and the magic surrounding the house quieted, allowing her inside.

Sella slipped in through the front door and was greeted by the smell of sugar and vanilla coming from the kitchen.

"I'm making a cake," Seaglass' voice called.

Sella carefully approached the table at the center of the room and sat patiently. She knew she had to keep her mind quiet, but it was racing, trying to remember where she knew the smell. What the occasion had been…

Seaglass waddled into the room, empty handed. "You're having trouble remembering. That means you're tired."

Sella blinked a few times. "I am," she said. "But I don't think that's the issue."

"You came here to ask me if you're doing the right thing," Seaglass prompted. "The right thing changes as the sand on the shore is never really the same. Time. Place. The hearts of those involved. All change. Don't you think so?"

Sella sighed. More riddle talk. She cut to it, "I actually wanted to ask you about the rose spell you gave me. I still am worried about how to open it."

"Worry is only your mind trying to predict the future," Seaglass said. "The future is a flame. It flickers and spreads in directions you cannot foresee. I would not waste your time on worry. Shall we enjoy a slice of cake? It's ready." Seaglass did not wait for a response. They made their way back into the kitchen where Sella heard them rummaging about in cabinets.

"I think I can't stay," Sella called. She lifted herself from her seat. Her hand found its way into the pocket of her dress where the spell paper was still folded into the shape of an intricate rose. "I'm sorry, Seaglass."

Seaglass' form appeared in the doorway. They stared with their intense, pupiless eyes, arms raised with yellow oven mitts, laughably oversized for their small hands. "Do not apologize for doing what you think is right, Sella. So long as no one is hurt."

Sella sighed. It would hurt her if she made a cake for someone and they left before she could serve it. But, she supposed, that was the thing about hurt. Different people hurt for different reasons. Who was she to tell a deep sea legendary creature how to feel?

"More for me," Seaglass mumbled and walked back into the kitchen. It shocked Sella as uncharacteristically funny.

Sella wondered if this was the side of the Niminé that her mother knew.

She shook the thought from her mind and walked out the door, and down to the rocky edge of the sea.

Sella removed her boots and made her way down into the waves. The cold, rhythmic water hit her calves, causing shivers every time the water swelled. She listened, but could hear nothing but their sound, like a steady heartbeat. She fished the spell from her pocket and turned it over in the dull light of the early morning.

It was impossible to open on her own.

She let it slip from her fingers and fall into the water.

The spell drifted on the surface for a moment. She watched it go out, then push back to her on the small crest of a wave before it began to slowly sink. The water illuminated briefly, a bright red of fire under the surface.

Carefully, Sella scooped the paper from the water. She lit a flame in the palm of one hand and examined the spell with the other. It had unfolded itself, and she read the inscription aloud. "For the Repair of Broken Things…" She looked up at the sky.

Of course.

She'd go into the woods for the wand later.

For now, she was ready to go home.

THIRTY-FIVE

The Gift

SELLA SAW three figures lingering outside her shop. She was surprised to see people already gathered before dawn and opening, until she got closer. Aadel, Hazen, and Cirian stood by her door.

Aadel was shamelessly peeking in through the glass of the bay window when she approached them.

Sella raised a brow. "We're not open yet," she said. She hoped her tone conveyed that it was a joke, but the three of them startled. She bit her lip. She was too tired to sound funny, she supposed.

"Good morning," she said, trying to smooth things over. She wasn't really sure what else could be said out in the street. No one was awake yet, but she knew it probably wouldn't be the case for long. She snapped her fingers and the door unlocked. "Come in," she said. "I'll make us a pot."

Beejee sprung up from behind the counter. He stood at attention looking at the group with narrowed eyes. "Are you starting a club?" he asked.

Sella waved her hand at him and he moved to the other end of the counter so she could make a large pot of coffee. "Never mind him," she said as she busied herself prepping the water and starting a small fire beneath the metal kettle. "Why are all three of you here, though?"

"It looks suspicious," Beejee said. He trotted away to the little pillow on the bay window. His nose smudged the glass as he looked outside into the fog, keeping watch.

"Oh, Beejee," Aadel said quietly. "Always so concerned. We old folks are known for being up at the first sign of dawn. Never you worry."

The three took their seats at the counter, almost in unison. A club might be exactly what they needed.

"Lohrna with you?" Aadel asked. "And make the coffee as strong as you can."

Sella nodded. "She can speak now during the full moon, too," she said quietly. Her bones ached as she reached down below the counter to pull coffee grounds and a few potions in glass jars.

"Ah," Aadel patted Sella's hand gently, quieting her work for a moment. "Leave it to our little Sella to find a way."

Hazen sighed, then turned to Sella. "We wanted to thank you, officially," he said. "Cirian and I are indebted to you. More than we can repay, we know." He cocked his head to the door. "The other witch is too."

"It is overwhelming," Cirian said. His tone was so solemn that she stopped working at the sound. "Sella, I truly don't know how we can ever repay what you've done for me. I haven't known kindness like this since…"

Hazen placed a heavy hand on Cirian's shoulder.

Sella pushed three cups of hot, dark coffee in front of

them. She had filled it with acceptance and hope. A combination of cozy clove and the slightest hint of spiced honey.

She sipped her own cup, then leaned on the counter. "I didn't do much," she said honestly. She wanted to add that, as usual, she seemed to simply blunder her way through. That this time was no different and it was merely luck, and Cali and Lohrna's hard work that saved the day. Instead, she said, "It just all feels like the right thing to do. I know you were just trying to protect Lohrna and the others. I'm sorry it ended this way."

Cirian held his mug with both hands. He gazed into his own reflection past the steam. "Me too. I can't know what would have happened if we hadn't fought. I think about it every waking moment… If only I acted better."

"You did what you thought was right," Hazen said.

"You did what was right," Aadel corrected after a long drink. "You stood up for my daughter. She has it hard enough here without someone in power threatening her just because she's…" Aadel glanced at Sella and the witch felt a sting in her throat. Aadel went on, "Anyway, it's no fortunate thing that the potions the new shop sells have bad reactions. But it also is simply not your fault."

"That I know of," Cirian said. "Sediri and I are both to blame. Or just one of us. We'll never know."

Hazen squeezed Cirian's shoulder. He looked at him with warmth in his eyes. "You have any scones, Sella?" he asked at last.

Though every muscle in her body didn't want to move, she nodded. "I do, upstairs. Pumpkin, if that's alright?"

"Anything extra?"

Sella felt her jaw loosen. "Safety," she said.

"Bring the tray down," Hazen said. It sounded like an order, in the kind way only he could muster.

Sella opened the door to the loft slowly, careful to not make a sound. It was still predawn, and Lohrna was still in her furry form, asleep on the floor. Beside her, Cali shimmered into view.

The ghost waved and pointed excitedly at Lohrna.

Sella gave her a quick wink before quickly tiptoeing to the kitchen to retrieve the tray of pumpkin scones. She pointed down and then held up three fingers.

Cali nodded. She pointed to the sheet crumbled at the bottom of Sella's bed.

Sella grabbed the tray and the sheet, and headed back downstairs.

She set the tray down at the counter and gestured for them to take a few. "Lohrna's still asleep," she told Aadel. She shook out the sheet and placed it over Cali's head at the last stool.

The outline of Cali was clear beneath it. The wrinkles in the fabric turned to the group. She held up one hand beneath it to signify 'Hi'.

Sella smiled gently.

"Hi, Cali," Hazen said. He took in a deep breath, steadying himself as he usually did in her presence. "It's good to see you again."

"You too," Cali said. "I miss our talks."

"She says she misses you," Sella said as she placed a coffee cup in front of Cali too so she could feel included.

"Ooo," Cali said, leaning down to smell the steam. "Honey?"

Sella tipped her head at Cali.

The group sat for what felt like a long while just drinking coffee and eating scones. Savoring the time together in silence. Opora had been so… loud. Busy. Wild. It was nice, Sella thought, to just spend a quiet moment together just being.

At last, Cirian broke the stillness. "I promise to make every day count. You've given me a gift. I'll use it well."

"Oh would you quit being so somber?" Beejee called from across the shop. "Your whole charm is that you're frivolous and ridiculous. Hazen's the glum one."

Sella smacked her forehead. "Beejee!"

"It's true. I said what I said." He jumped off the pillow and made his way back to the counter. He cast a glance at Cirian. "If you want to do something good, leave a generous tip for today's coffee and scones."

Cirian and Hazen both laughed and the tension fled the room.

"That, I can do!" Cirian said.

"And keep looking out for the ones most don't," Beejee added.

Cirian nodded. "I can do that, too."

Beejee sat and looked up at a little flame passing by. "Did we ever find out what that odd human's issue was?"

Sella leaned across the counter again.

"The one who would never answer a question?" Aadel asked. Of course she knew who he was talking about. Aadel knew everything in town. Opora did nothing to stop her gathering of knowledge.

Hazen and Cirian both shrugged.

"I never did find out his name," Aadel said. "He was

odd, though. I had him pegged as our culprit for both crimes. I wonder if he's still in the hotel being cheap."

"No human slander, now," Cali said.

"I never thought I'd see Opora," Aadel said over the rim of her mug. "And now I'm glad it's over. Too many odd characters."

"Yeah," Beejee said. "As opposed to you lot."

THIRTY-SIX

The Letter

THE FESTIVAL WAS FINALLY OVER, but the steady stream of customers persisted the following day. Folks needing remedies for the night before, sea sickness cures, and calming blends, all came and went throughout the day as the town cleared out. Business, despite the rainy day, was good.

Sediri had promised to close her shop, start packing up as soon as the ladle was replaced, and it seemed she kept her word.

When the sky grew dark, Sella turned the sign to 'Closed', and locked the door. She waved her hand and the fires overhead stilled, the quiet music, and ambient sound ceased. From the corner, Cali shimmered into view. She smiled brightly. "Good news," she said.

Sella gestured for her to join her on a stool at the counter. "Do tell."

"Well," Cali said, hoisting herself on the counter instead of the stool, "I managed to haunt the renters out. I'm pretty sure. That, or they felt bad eventually after your talk with them. They announced, very loudly, that they'll be moving to one of the neighboring units once the festival clears out."

Sella felt her face relax. "That's wonderful," she said. "I'm glad, Cali. Really."

"But," Cali said with her hand raised. "I was thinking maybe it's time to let the place go anyway."

"Oh?"

Cali folded over, resting her chin in her hand. "Yeah. You know, I've been living alone since I moved out of my family's home… and that was… a long time ago. I think it'll be nice to have some company. And I miss Koukie, you know?"

Sella raised a brow. "Is that so?"

Cali tapped her fingers on her cheek, she looked up at the ceiling. "Yep."

Sella smiled, her cheeks grew red. "Well, I have the space for you. And Koukie lives with me."

Cali's green eyes drifted to Sella's lazily. "How fortuitous."

"And, you know, I've always wanted to live in a haunted house."

Cali pushed herself closer. She looked down at Sella with eyes half closed.

A small rap at the door broke their thoughts. They turned to the bay window and squinted out into the fog to see Sediri, Majla, and Lohrna, cast in shadow.

"I'm haunting them next," Cali grumbled under her breath.

Sella squeezed Cali's hand quickly, then went to let them in.

"Look who I found lurking," Lohrna said once the door

opened. She led the way inside, with the other witch and her familiar close behind.

Once Sella shut and locked the door behind them, Lohrna went on, "Let's go upstairs. And get the sheet. Sorry, but I won't be the only one here who can't see Cal." Lohrna, as if she owned the place, was already halfway up the steps as she continued with some grumbling that Sella couldn't quite hear.

Sella and Sediri both cast Cali a look as they passed her on the counter.

"Well," Cali said, hopping off, "This time I want the sheet with the holes cut out."

"You cut holes in my sheets?" Sella asked as they made their way up behind Sediri.

"Yeah, you never use those ones! I found them in the depths of your wardrobe. Very musty smelling. The blue ones?"

Sella rubbed her eyes. They made it to the tops of the steps. Lohrna had already let herself, and Sediri, in. "What if those were sentimental?" Sella teased.

Cali gasped, her hand flew over her mouth. "Were they?"

"No," Sella said with a chuckle. "But, I feel like *I* finally got *you*."

Cali nudged past Sella. Her shoulder check was semi-solid, and Sella stumbled just a bit. She rubbed her arm dramatically, then shut the door behind them.

The four sat around the table. Sella had placed a tray of leftover scones, warmed with magic, at the table. Each had a mug of herbal tea in front of them. The steam rose, obscuring their faces gently as the smell of fresh, wet earth and cut grass filled the room.

Cali sat with the blue sheet over her head. The eyes were cut out in large holes so she could see, but the glasses were still placed over them so she looked more solid. She turned to Beejee at her right, then looked at Sediri across the table. "Well? What were you doing 'lingering'?"

Sediri looked down at her mug. Her hands were in her lap. She took a deep breath of silver steam. "Calm?" she asked Sella.

Sella nodded. She sipped her own mug carefully, watching Sediri closely over the rim.

Sediri sighed again. "I wanted to thank you. You didn't have to… You didn't have to do anything you did. I wanted to make it up to you." She looked up at last, hands moving to the tabletop. "I'm going to Tollintal to be with my partner. Finally. You remember him?"

Sella nodded, but her memory of him was fuzzy. She only remembered he was human and that Sediri had been devastated when he had to go back home.

"I've had it with Orakan. The ways they treat witches here. The Wyldes who think they're better than humans. The ones who give us a bad name. All of it," Sediri said. "But, even with half the sale of the ladle, it will be more than enough to get me there and start fresh. I plan to open up my own shop once I'm there. One away from the Kepilla brand." She paused and turned to Cali. "I hear Tollintal is more accepting of witches."

Cali nodded. "They are."

Sediri continued, "I wanted to give you the rest of the money. And offer you partnership in my business there."

Sella retracted. She held her mug close.

"Sella has a shop already," Lohrna said.

"Yeah!" Beejee agreed.

Sediri put her hands up in surrender. "I understand. It's not really that I'd want you to stay there long term. No offense."

Beejee narrowed his eyes.

"I just. It's not easy to admit, but I'd like some help getting started. Recipes that work and don't make people accidentally sick." She gestured to Sella. "Getting on with locals." She looked to Cali.

"I can decorate," Lohrna grumbled, offended she hadn't received the same offer, no doubt.

"Of course," Sediri said quickly. "And... in exchange, you'd own part of the shop."

"I—" Sella started.

"Don't answer now," Sediri cut in. "Please. Just. Think about it."

"You don't need to tell her twice," Cali said, playfully under her breath.

Sella cast a glance at the ghost. "She can hear you," she said.

Lohrna raised a brow. "What'd she say?"

"That I don't need to be told twice to think on something," Sella mumbled. She crossed her arms across her chest.

Lohrna laughed. She swatted Sella's arm playfully. "That's true. Remember how long it took you to help Cali out?"

Sella's head hit the table.

"Oh, we love you!" Lohrna said.

"We do," Cali whispered.

Sella's face burned. "I'll think about it," she said loudly.

I love you too, she wanted to say.

"YOU'RE NOT REALLY CONSIDERING this are you?" Beejee asked. "Moving to Tollintal?"

The two were walking back from Cali's old place, a small box in Sella's arms with the last of Cali's things. An embroidered Wyvern tea towel. A small glimmering purple crystal. A blue rock. A silver locket and an already dead plant that Cali insisted could come back as a ghost just like she did.

"It wouldn't be forever. Not even a few moons…" Sella shrugged.

They paused at the two statues of the sires outside of Penya's hotel. It felt empty now, even though Sella knew that the steady stream of seafarers coming into the small port still took up lodging there. Since the festival, the town did feel incredibly small. Boring, even.

Sella reached down and scratched behind his ear and he leaned into her affection with a pur. "Besides, you've always wanted to travel across the sea."

"True."

The sirens began to sing as a salty sea breeze blew. They moved on, down the glossy cobblestone street toward their home.

"And maybe it would be good for Cali?" Sella said. "They're more open to witches there. Maybe someone could help me find the spell to help her talk to others?"

"So you *are* considering it?"

She nodded. "Yes, I guess I am."

They stopped outside the shop door when they each noticed a letter wedged into the crack just above the handle.

Sella's expression shifted. She set the box down as she felt her hands suddenly warm.

Strange. She never got messages.

She plucked the letter from the door and examined it. On the fold, it was sealed with a burgundy wax seal. A sea monster was etched into the wax. Unmistakably Kepilla's logo. Sella grumbled to herself and opened it quickly.

"What's it say?" Beejee asked.

Sella read the letter quickly, then her hand fell to her side. She looked up at the gray sky with a sigh. "They got Sediri's resignation. They want me to go to Tollintal and try to open up one of *their* shops to compete with hers. They invited us to meet with them to discuss terms"

"Did they give you a plus one?" Cali asked, her head suddenly through the door.

Sella laughed lightly. She looked down at the letter again and shook her head. She flicked her wrist and the door unlocked.

Inside, Sella nodded her head and a light music began to play throughout the store. She set the box down on the counter and stared into it. The last few things Cali owned, now making a home here.

She looked around them as Cali's hand slipped into hers. Glittering trinkets, potions and teas in glass jars, reflected the warm glow of little fires floating by. Her mother's shop. Sometimes, even with her own things here, it didn't feel any more 'hers' than running a store owned by a large company.

This was home. But not entirely.

"We'll go, if you want to," Sella said at last.

Cali's fingers squeezed. "Maybe."

"But to help Sediri get her start," Sella said. "I don't want anything to do with Kepilla."

"I'd never imagine you would."

"I can't believe they thought you would. The *audacity* of these witches," Beejee said as he sauntered up the stairs.

Sella turned the sign to 'Open' just as rain began to fall.

Practical Potions
busy bee blend

INGREDIENTS:

1. your favorite mug
2. 1-2 tsp honey
3. tiny dash of cayenne
4. dash cinnamon

HOW TO MAKE:

(If possible) add cayenne and cinnamon to
coffee grounds prior to brewing… you can
also add these with the honey
pour coffee into your favorite mug
and wait to cool slightly
add honey
stir well while imagining yourself at your
most productive and collaborative
add splash of cream if desired

Practical Potions
confidence blend

INGREDIENTS:

1. a mug that makes you smile
2. dash of cinnamon
3. 1 tsp ground ginger

HOW TO MAKE:

pour coffee into a mug that brings a
genuine smile to your beautiful face
add ground ginger and stir well
add dash of cinnamon and breathe in
the steam
with each breath, sit (or stand) taller
shoulders back, chest out, you got this

Practical Potions lucky day blend

INGREDIENTS:

1. a cup you've rarely used
2. 2-3 tsp cinnamon
3. 1 tsp ground cloves
4. 1 tsp ground nutmeg
5. pinch of salt

HOW TO MAKE:

(If possible) add cloves, nutmeg, and cinnamon to coffee grounds prior to brewing... you can also add these later

pour coffee into your mug

add pinch of salt

stir clockwise and repeat these affirmations:

I am lucky

I am worthy

At least three good things will happen to me today

Practical Potions
calm blend

INGREDIENTS:

1. espresso shot
2. 1 cup milk or milk alternative
3. 2 tbs lavender syrup
4. drizzle of honey

HOW TO MAKE:

warm a cup of milk or milk alternative in
your coziest mug
add lavender syrup
use a frother wand if you have one
prepare espresso shot and add to milk
drizzle a bit of honey on top while taking
four deep belly breaths
anything you're worried about can wait
right now, you are safe and cozy

Certified! About the Kitchen Witch

Sella is tired of being a failure.

She has a lovely, cozy shop—an heirloom from her mother—, a snarky feline familiar, and one, single friend to call her own. It should be enough. But Sella's magical abilities left a stain on her hometown, and even years away didn't repair her reputation. The life of a kitchen witch is rough when everyone thinks Sella's magical blends of coffee and tea will leave them with boils instead of the intended "motivation" or "self-compassion."

But when a murder shakes the town and Sella's best friend becomes suspect one, failure is a luxury they can't afford. Luckily, the murdered woman—a confident ghost with a fiery determination for justice—is ready to help... and she's more than Sella ever bargained for. With her friends, her familiar, and a bit of magic, Sella is ready to prove herself once and for all.

Although, perhaps she should brew a strong cup of "courage" first.

Just in case.

The End...

For now.

Practical Potions will open a sister store across
the sea for more
fantastical mysteries and cozy adventures
in Book Three.

Acknowledgments

It's been a year since I wrote the first book in this series, my debut novel. And that year has been full of beautiful humans that I have to thank for this one's creation.

Thank you to all my friends, both IRL (as they say) and online. I feel grateful everyday that I met so many amazing readers, writers, and friends through social media and the online community. Even if we've never officially met, I consider you all true friends. Your support has meant the world to me and made me keep pushing forward when I started to think that this book might never get done.

Thank you to my group of friends who have stuck with me through all my awkwardness and growth. Sometimes, I can't believe my extraordinary luck at meeting you. Getting lost on the way to class and deciding to go to a random write-in are coincidences that make me think I may just be the luckiest person in the world.

Thank you to my huge, wonderful family who championed me through this process and kept believing me when I definitely thought myself a fraud. You are all my safety net. Without you, I would never be able to take the leap.
And to my supportive husband, delightfully fun kids, and two ridiculously cute cats– You are the best reason for missing deadlines. Never stop distracting me. But it'd be super cool if you could respect bedtime going forward.

And thank you, reader, for coming along with me on this adventure.

What's Sella putting in your cup today?

A special thank you to the people who made the audiobook of Practical Potions and Premeditated Murder possible. Without you, the book would not have come to life for so many readers. There are not enough ways to show you how much your support has meant to me. But this is a start.

Thank you to Leslie, your light shines brightly and I am thrilled to be part of a family with someone like you. Your humor and wit are unmatched.

Thank you to Jenn, I cannot wait for you to join our family soon! Your tireless work to help others is amazing.

Thank you to Goldbachs, you have welcomed me warmly and I am so grateful.

Thank you to John, those D&D days were my favorites. I can't wait to have another Ghibli fest and I'm lucky to call you my friend.

Thank you to Savanah, you're basically my daughter's favorite person (and you're one of mine, too). You have one of the kindest hearts I've ever met.

Thank you to Michael, I am always thrilled to hear your thoughts on books. You are one of my first and greatest supporters. I cannot thank you enough for helping PP&PM get out there.

Thank you to my Yiayia, who is the voice in my head asking me if I'm "still writing."

Thank you to my Thea Mina who inspired me to do this and to my incredible cousin Katrina who was my social media champion.

Thank you to my parents, my mom, my dad, and stepmom. That you all knew me as a teenager and young adult but still believed in me really speaks to your poor judgment. But this time, you were right. The audiobook rocks.

About the Author

Wren Jones lives in the Sonoran Desert with her family and two cats. Like most writers, she has been a storyteller for a long time. She is known for doing "the most" at the oddest times. Like deciding to pursue a writing career (finally) while raising two humans and working full time in a public school. She writes what she'd want to read: Stories where things turn out alright in the end.